COLORADO SILVER, COLORADO GOLD

By Terry Irene Blain

CLOSER TO THE TRUTH

He took a step forward, causing her to take a step back. "Mrs. Peterson was right, you know. I'm not the type of person you should talk to."

"Really, Mr. Westmoreland." She sounded indignant. "I'm a grown woman. I'm capable of deciding with whom to talk."

He liked the way her back went up when challenged. He took another small step. Her retreat brought her shoulders up against the high side of a wagon. He wanted to hear her say his name. "Well, if you're going to talk to me, call me Wes."

She looked puzzled. "Wes Westmoreland? Surely Wes isn't your first name?"

"No, but I've always been called Wes." He didn't want to discuss why. He moved closer again, her skirts brushing his boots. "What should I call *you*?" He wanted her to say her first name, wanted to hear clearly what he'd only half-heard Mrs. Peterson call her. Wanted a name for his thoughts, something warmer, more real than Miss Lawson. "What's your *name*, sweetheart?"

COLORADO SILVER, COLORADO GOLD

By Terry Irene Blain

Boroughs
Publishing Group

www.BOROUGHSPUBLISHINGGROUP.com

COLORADO SILVER, COLORADO GOLD
Copyright © 2015 Terry Irene Blain

ISBN 978-1-942886-08-2

To all sisters, who give each other support and love.

For Ann and Robyn.

CONTENTS

Chapter One

St. Louis, Missouri, 1889

Whistle shrieking, the train jerked to a stop, the sudden lurch throwing Julie Lawson forward. The black silk of her skirt slipped on the hard wooden seat and only the firm bracing of her feet kept her from slipping to the floor. She glanced down at the small valise that hadn't been out of arm's reach since she fled Philadelphia.

Julie shifted back in her seat, hearing the echo of her grandmother's favorite phrase, *your impulses will get you into trouble one day, Juliette Marie, you mark my words.* Gran had certainly been right.

She let out a shallow sigh. The widow's weeds she'd hurriedly dug out of the trunk in the attic required a corset so severely laced a shallow sigh was all she could manage.

The train whistle gave a short toot. "St. Louis! St. Louis! Thirty-minute stop in St. Louis!" came the sing-song voice of the conductor.

She glanced at the watch pinned to her bodice. Enough time for her to walk down the platform and back. As she stood, the hat and heavy veil wobbled. Using her reflection in the dusty window as a mirror, she readjusted the long hat pins. The hat more secure, she peered through the glass.

The platform bustled with activity. Fellow passengers came and went, dodging scattered trunks and carpet bags. The harried-looking conductor strode by, a piece of paper in his hand and a pencil tucked behind his ear. A small boy in corduroy knickers trailed a large, hairy dog, the boy clutching a piece of twine attached to the dog's collar.

A telegraph office stood at the platform's west end near the panting engine. Standing in front of a row of round-topped steamer trunks, a man waited quietly beside the office. His coat and trousers were the color of bitter chocolate. A perfect match to his wide-brimmed Stetson and western boots. A pair of saddle bags hung over one shoulder.

Leaving her coat draped across the seat, she lowered the black lace veil, and drew on her black kid gloves. Picking up the small valise, she left the railroad car.

She walked along the platform, the warm summer air smelling of coal smoke and dust. As she neared the west end of the platform, she noticed the man she'd seen from the window. A growing commotion behind her caused her to turn. All down the platform, people scrambled and yelled, their shouts mingled with a dog's deep bark. A flash of tabby fur streaked past her skirt. The dog bumped her knees as he gallumped past.

Off balance, she stumbled backward. And into a solid, warm male body. Strong arms wrapped around her. Her flailing bag struck him, bringing a muffled exclamation. With a thud they came to rest against a steamer trunk. Turned sideways, she half-sat, half-lay over his long legs. She fought to regain her balance, thwarted by the slick silk of her skirts.

"Hold still, lady," he muttered as he hitched her more securely over his lap. "I don't want to drop you."

Throwing her arms around his neck, the bag she still held thumped into his back. Another exclamation, this one not so muttered, sounded in her ear.

With one arm about her shoulders, the other stretched across her lap grasping her hip, he kept her from sliding to the ground. For a few seconds neither of them moved. She started to breathe again inhaling a faint scent of leather, tobacco, and shaving soap.

The masculine scents made her instantly aware of the intimacy of their position with her draped across his lap, the surrounding warmth of his arms and body. She loosened her grip around his neck and brought the bag back over his shoulder where it plopped to the ground. Unable to get her breath, she blamed the too-tight corset. "I... I beg your pardon," she managed to get out.

Her hat dipped so far forward it practically sat on her nose. The pins pulled hurtfully at her hair. Without thinking, she reached to fix it and flipped back the veil. She glanced up and got a good look at her rescuer.

His hat gone, his gold-blond hair curled slightly where it lay too long about his ears and collar. His muted green eyes widened in surprise. His gaze flicked from her face, to her hair, and back to her face. Julie's stomach dropped like a stone. She jerked the veil back into place.

Without the obscuring veil, she looked even younger than her twenty-one years, her hair a pale, but unmistakable, blond. Not the gray-haired widow he'd obviously expected. "I do beg your pardon," she repeated. "I'm so sorry."

A grin tugged up one corner of his mouth, white teeth flashing under his blond mustache. "I'm not," he replied.

Her heart jumped into her throat, reminding her of her scandalous position on his lap. She squared her shoulders, stiffening in his grasp. She swallowed her heart back to its proper place. "Please, sir," she said in her best touch-me-not voice.

His fabulous smile faded. "Yes, ma'am. Sorry." Carefully, he loosened his grip, allowing her to slide from his lap. Once she'd regained her feet, he stood. For some reason she still couldn't catch her breath. Drat the corset for making her so breathless and light-headed.

After a second, he stooped to pick up his hat. Her gaze followed his movement and she spotted her valise tangled with his saddle bags. "Oh," she gasped.

He shot her a quick glance then extracted the small bag from the snarl of leather.

She twisted her hands together, resisting the impulse to grab for her bag.

"May I carry your bag?" the blond man asked as if to make amends. He gestured with the bag toward where passengers were re-boarding. His face showed a carefully neutral expression. But his green eyes reminded her of the waters of the Chesapeake in a storm. She didn't want to imagine what thoughts those eyes might hide.

"No," she stammered, "no, thank you." She couldn't even get a simple sentence out. When he handed her the valise, her hand brushed his strong, tanned one. Even through her glove, she imagined the warmth of his touch. "Thank you," she was able to murmur as she turned.

She concentrated on walking with as much dignity as possible as she returned down the platform. He had to be watching, for she felt his gaze between her shoulder blades as she fought to keep her steps at a sedate pace. At last she regained the haven of the railroad car. Relief washed through her.

She took her seat but couldn't resist looking out the window. He still stood in front of the telegraph office, hat in hand, looking down the platform toward her railroad car. After a moment, he slapped the hat against his thigh before resettling it on his head.

"Al-l-l aaaa-board!" shouted the conductor. The train whistle echoed with a toooo-too-toot! A loud clanking was followed by a sudden forward jerk. The whistle shrilled again. A series of short tugs became smooth forward movement. Through the window the train depot and platform began to slide away.

Don't look. Don't look. Her head remained straight forward, but in spite of her admonishments her gaze crept toward the window as the telegraph office scrolled by.

Saddle bags resting near his booted feet, he scanned the train. His gaze seemed to penetrate the dusty window and her veil with no problem. His eyes held hers for a split second, making her breath catch. He briefly touched the brim of his hat and nodded as his figure slid past.

* * *

Wes ducked his head against the soot and sparks that swirled after the caboose. After the flurry died away, he raised his head to look down the tracks again. He absently rubbed his shoulder wondering if tomorrow he'd find a bruise where the widow's small carpet bag had struck him.

He slapped the soot from his coat and turned to look toward the telegraph office. The operator shook his head. He returned to the steamer trunks clustered at the end of the platform. He leaned his butt against a rounded top and crossed his ankles.

Again he looked west, watching the receding caboose grow smaller. That was some widow. Under that obscuring veil her hair had been a striking silvery blond.

Of course, someone that young and pretty could be a widow, but something about her nagged at him. He closed his eyes and let his mind see her again. The widow's weeds she wore were old fashioned. And there'd been a faint odor of camphor from the black silk. But if she'd been widowed suddenly, it wouldn't be too surprising if she wore make-shift mourning.

What else didn't ring true? Her eyes. There'd been no pain, no sorrow in her eyes. They'd been as clear and beautiful and innocent as the blue sky they resembled. He remembered the feel of her in his arms, half-lying across his lap. Remembered her eyes wide, her lips parted as she tried to get her breath.

His eyes popped open and he took off his hat to run his hand through his hair. Why in hell spend all this time trying to figure out what was wrong with a widow lady he'd never see again?

With a sigh, he resettled his Stetson, acknowledging he was suspicious because that was his business. Suspicion kept him alert and kept him alive, made him good at his job. His hand touched his coat pocket as though he could feel through the fabric the brown leather case with the shiny metal badge that defined his life.

"Mr. Westmoreland?" The telegraph operator's voice jerked Wes from his reverie. The telegram from San Francisco you've been waitin' for is here."

Wes crossed to the telegraph window and took the piece of paper the operator held in his direction. He heard his boss's sharp, hard voice as he read:

Congrats Rayburn job. Proceed Denver, instructions wait.
Ultimate destination, Durango, Colorado. Use own name.
Dan Challenge, Wells Fargo

Wes folded the note and put it in his pocket.

"Too bad that there telegram didn't come a few minutes earlier." The operator chuckled.

"Why's that?" Wes asked.

"That there's the Denver train," the operator said with unconcealed glee. He nodded where the widow's train was nothing but a faint puff of smoke on the horizon.

"Figures," Wes said with a sigh. Over the last ten years, he'd learned patience. But the telegraph operator's amusement rankled. Keeping his voice neutral he asked, "When's the next train and where do I get a ticket?"

"Next train same time tomorrow, goes to Denver and then on to San Francisco. Tickets just inside to the left." He chuckled again. "Yessirre, too bad that there telegram didn't get here sooner."

Nodding a thanks he did not feel, Wes slung his saddle bags over his shoulder and started down the platform. He must be more tired than he thought to allow the telegraph operator's attitude to put him out of sorts. Or maybe, he was more than just a little disappointed he wasn't on that there train with the flaxen-haired widow.

After purchasing a ticket for Denver, he got a room in the hotel across the street. What was the chance, Wes wondered as he lay on the narrow, hard bed, that he'd run into the widow in Denver? And what might have happened if that blasted telegram had come an hour earlier?

* * *

Julie Lawson peered through the window as the train clattered over the wooden bridge spanning the Rio Los Anamis and headed south into Durango. By concentrating on the breathtaking scenery of the rugged mountain canyons and the swift river, so different from

Philadelphia or the endless plains west of St. Louis, she'd pushed the thoughts of what brought her here to the back of her mind.

The sign on the Denver and Rio Grande train depot proudly announced Durango, Colorado. Julie brushed her hand across the royal-blue skirt of her serge traveling suit, tugged at the black lapels and cuffs of the matching jacket. She took a deep breath, thankful to be in her own pliable corset. She'd hidden the widow's weeds at the bottom of her trunk and changed into her own clothes during the layover in Denver.

Following a balding merchant to the exit, she descended the train steps. She shaded her eyes against the harsh noon sun, searching the people milling about on the platform. Had Uncle Frank received the telegram she sent from Denver?

"Julie! Julie!"

Her name echoed over the noisy doings of the busy depot. She turned to see Uncle Frank striding toward her. He looked just as she remembered him. His Lawson family fair hair largely hidden under a bowler hat. With his white dress shirt, dark suit and tie he looked like any Philadelphia businessman.

"Welcome to Durango," he said as he opened his arms. Julie threw herself into his embrace. She'd reached her destination. She was safe. Her knees shook at the relief.

Uncle Frank must have felt her tremble. "Here now," he said, holding her away from him to look into her face. "Are you all right?"

"Yes, just tired. It's been a long trip," she reassured him. Just being with family made her feel better, feel more secure. She could do this. "Sorry I didn't give you more warning, but you always said I could visit anytime."

They headed toward the baggage area for her trunk. "Guess I gave in to one of my impulses as Gran would have said. With Papa in Europe and Cory in the country, the house was just too lonely." Pretend this was just an ordinary visit. Forget the outrage and anger that propelled her to action. Forget the panic that followed in her dash from Philadelphia.

Uncle Frank retrieved her trunk and paid a man to load her baggage into his buggy.

"How is Aunt Marie?" She asked as Uncle Frank drove the buggy through the traffic of wagons, riders, and other buggies on Main Street.

Uncle Frank cleared his throat. "Actually, she's in San Francisco, taking care of Grace."

"Is Grace sick?" she asked in surprise. Her cousin Grace lived in San Francisco with her husband and small daughter.

"No, it's just that Grace needs extra help now that, ah, she's, ah..." Uncle Frank looked uncomfortable.

Julie smiled. "You're going to be a grandfather again. When?"

"Not for six more months, but Grace was feeling poorly, and Marie was worried about her."

"I understand her worry." More than Uncle Frank knew.

Apparently the conversation reminded Uncle Frank of Cory's delicate condition as he asked, "How is your sister?"

"Cory's doing fine this time. The baby is due in two more months. I wrote you that she and Mark are taking extra precautions this time. So to make sure she isn't upset, two weeks ago he sent her to the country with a nurse."

After two previous miscarriages Mark wasn't taking any chances and had ordered quiet with no responsibilities for Cory's mental as well as physical health. Nothing could be allowed to jeopardize this pregnancy. Julie looked at the carpet bag, resting in its usual spot beside her feet. Just two more months to keep herself and the contents of the bag hidden. For Cory.

Shaking off the uneasy thoughts, she glanced around. Here in the Rocky Mountains the summer sun shone harsh through air that was somehow less substantial than in Philadelphia. The stark light gave a clear, sharp focus to the town and the landscape. She took a deep breath. Away from the train station and the main street the breeze carried a faint scent of pine from the western mountains.

As Uncle Frank turned east off Main Street, she caught a glimpse of a blond man in a dark brown hat. Her breath lodged in her throat. Then he turned and she saw he was clean shaven. Silly, she thought as she exhaled. How could it be him? She blinked away the memory of sea-green eyes and a devastating smile.

* * *

Three days after Julie Lawson arrived in Durango, the Denver and Rio Grande brought another visitor. As the train came in, Wes studied the lay of the land. Standing on the gently swaying platform between two cars, he had a widespread view. He spotted the smelters. Trailing dark plumes of smoke from a half-dozen stacks, the two smelters sat southwest of the city like dark giants against the mountainside.

The wire waiting for him at the Wells Fargo office in Denver had been brief.

Proceed Durango. Possible sabotage or subversion at smelters.
Production down. Determine problem and notify.
No contact available Durango. Wire Denver office for assistance if
needed.
Dan Challenge
Wells Fargo

No contact available? That was odd. And why was the head of Wells Fargo's investigation department interested in trouble at the Durango smelters? He knew Wells Fargo transported the vast amounts of gold, silver, copper, and other mineral wealth that poured from the smelters, but something didn't add up.

The train rolled into the Durango station. As the whistle blew to announce their arrival, Wes slid his hand inside his jacket to check the short barreled .32 nestled under his left arm. He hitched his saddle bags more squarely over his shoulder, reseated his hat, and stepped from the platform as the train pulled to a stop.

His first order of business was obtaining information. And there was only one place where a stranger could sit and talk, and find out what was going on without drawing attention to himself. At the end of the platform, he stopped a teamster loading boxes into the back of a wagon. "Which way to the nearest saloon?" he asked.

Chapter Two

"Head north on Main," the teamster directed. "You can't miss 'em. There's a whole row of saloons, take your pick."

Wes started north, strolling past various retail establishments offering items from dry goods and gents' furnishings to stationery. He passed the Hotel Stratler, its four stories crowned by a clock tower. Directly across the street was a large empty lot. Several wagons and buggies parked haphazardly, and there were even a few Indian ponies waiting patiently as two Indians had set up a blanket offering trade goods.

Halfway down the next block, he fell in behind three ladies as they exited a mercantile. When they reached the corner Wes noticed the ladies abruptly turned right and minced their way to the east side of Main Street, where they turned and headed north again. Idly pondering their behavior, Wes dodged a lumber wagon as he crossed the street. Once past the First National Bank on the corner, he stopped and grinned.

The teamster hadn't been joking. The whole block north of the bank was a solid row of saloons. While a number of men went about their business, no ladies ventured on this side of the street.

Wes assessed each saloon as he passed until he came to the corner. He retraced his steps to stop before Kate's Double Eagle. A nice, middle-rank place where men came to relax and talk, as well as to drink and gamble. He pushed through the batwing doors, stepping from sunlight to the dim interior. He paused for his eyes to adjust.

With a deep breath he took in the smell common to all saloons. The mingled scents of whiskey, stale tobacco smoke, overheated male bodies, cheap perfume, and carbolic soap. The old, familiar pungency stuck in the back of his throat. All the smells of home, he thought sourly.

A skinny bartender gave him a brief glance, then continued to swipe lazily at the bar. Two men deep in conversation stood at the far end of the bar. A few scattered patrons, mostly miners and a few suited businessmen sat at the tables. From the depth of the long, narrow room a player piano pumped tinny music.

Wes dropped his saddle bags at his feet and reached in his pocket for a coin which he dropped on the bar with a faint ting. "Whiskey."

A door opened from the back of the saloon and Wes heard the sharp, quick click of a woman's high-heeled shoes. A dark-haired woman in a red dress stopped to exchange a few friendly words with the men at the table. She patted one of them on the shoulder, and then headed in his direction.

She came to a stop a few feet from him, her hand resting on the bar. "Howdy, mister," she said, her tone professionally friendly.

He turned to answer, and the words of reply caught in his throat as he recognized Kate Valdez.

Her brows pulled together in a frown as she looked at him. "Wes?" she asked. Then with more confidence, "Wes Westmoreland, it is you! Look at you, all grown up." She opened her arms to give him a hug.

"Hiya, Kate." He returned the hug. Once over the shock, he was truly glad to see Kate. He still counted her as a friend. And he didn't have many. Ten years hadn't made a difference in the way she looked. Though she had to be six or seven years older than his twenty-six, her glossy black hair held no hint of gray. Only a few wrinkles decorated the corners of her eyes.

Kate settled them at a table, calling for the bartender to bring Wes another drink and a sandwich. He set his saddlebags and hat on one of the spare chairs. "So," she said, "what do you think of my place?"

"Kate's Double Eagle. I'm impressed." Wes leaned back in his chair. Gathering information was his job, but this was first time he'd set out to get it from a friend. "How long have you been in Durango?" He took a bite of the sandwich, wondering how much he'd get her to tell him.

"Came here in '85. I made a packet following the gold strikes. A good dealer could make a lot of money in those towns." Kate picked up a deck of cards, cut, shuffled, and fanned them across the table. "Once I had a stake, I came here." She sat back and smiled. "This is a long way from the Red Garter and San Francisco. Looks like we both managed to escape."

Escape. She had the right word. He understood what Kate hadn't said outright. Not only did she own this place, but she only dealt cards these days. His father, Sam, had managed the Red Garter, a saloon with rooms for working girls on the second floor. Wes had grown up there. The women working there had treated him with either affection or indifference, as their nature dictated. The only women he'd known as a child, he'd never thought any the worse of them for the way they made their living.

"Looks like we did," he agreed.

"You still working for Wells Fargo? I remember how you used to run messages for them around San Francisco. You were talking about getting a job as a guard when I left."

Damn, she would remember that. Wells Fargo employed a handful of boys to deliver messages around San Francisco. The company had supplied the horses and had paid twenty-five cents a message, the first money he'd ever had. Since he was here under his own name, and Kate recognized him, Wes told the truth as far as it went.

"I got the job as guard." He remembered how proud he'd been. Sixteen years old and full of himself, riding shotgun to guard the distinctive Wells Fargo green box. "I'd been a guard about six months when we got held up. The box had a five-thousand-dollar bank transfer no one was supposed to know about. There was some question afterward about whether the outlaws had inside information. Who'd believe a saloon kid would have passed up a chance for some quick money? Nobody had any evidence, but that didn't keep Wells Fargo from firing me."

That was the version of events the company gave out. Actually, he'd been so damn mad about being robbed he'd taken out after the bandits on foot, while the driver went on into the next town to report the robbery. The three outlaws hadn't gone far, too anxious to examine what they'd stole. Wes' first shot winged one of them and they scrambled for their horses leaving the box. The robbers had loosed a couple of rounds in his direction as they took off.

The posse from town had found him limping down the road, the green box slung over his shoulder. Wes absently rubbed the scar just above his left knee where the wild shot nicked him.

"Too bad," Kate commiserated. They both knew too well that who you were and where you grew up, counted against you.

"Yeah, too bad. So, what's going on in Durango?" he asked turning the conversation away from himself.

Kate related how her army customers were still laughing about some idiot, fresh out from the east, had seen one of the local Utes riding down the street and ran screaming to Ft. Lewis to call out the cavalry. She told about the plans for the Fourth of July celebration next week, including a parade, town dance, and fireworks.

Eventually she hit on the topic that interested him. The owners of the two local smelters were in a stew over a series of accidents and misadventures. "The owner of the Mineral King claims it's more than just accidents. And just last week the Rio d'Oro's bookkeeper up and took off back east after his wife died, leaving the books a mess."

"Don't suppose either one's looking for a man-of-all-works to help out do you? I need a job."

Kate pushed the deck of cards in front of him. "Cut and deal."

Amused, he picked up the cards, cut, shuffled, and did the same slick fan Kate had done. He cut the cards once more, then dealt a hand for each of them, face down on the table.

With a flick, Kate turned her cards over. Two pair, jacks, and sevens. Reaching across the table she flipped over the cards he'd dealt himself. Three tens. She smiled. "You can have a job here; I could always use another dealer."

"No, thanks. Sam taught me how to cheat at cards, but I never had the love of the game he did." Cards were the only thing his father had loved.

Kate gasped. "Wes Westmoreland! Your father never cheated at cards."

"No," he agreed. "Sam didn't have to, he was that good. But any decent gambler knows how to cheat so he can spot anyone else trying. I'm not as good as Sam. Besides, I've had enough of saloons." He shuffled the cards together and put the deck back in front of Kate.

She sighed. "No harm in asking."

The bat-wing doors creaked and Wes turned to see a man in a black suit enter the saloon. His purposeful footsteps echoed as he came to a halt behind Kate's chair. He rested both hands on her shoulders with casual possessiveness. "Hey, Kate," he said, staring over the top of her dark head at Wes. "This a new friend of yours?"

"Hello yourself, Tom." Kate reached up and laid one of her hands over his. "This is an old friend."

The man s intense gaze moderated and he extended his hand. "Sheriff Tom Rickman," he introduced himself as Wes shook his hand.

As the sheriff took the seat across from him, Kate completed the formal introductions. Wes guessed Sheriff Rickman to be in his late thirties. His frame, close to Wes, almost six feet in height, carried maybe thirty pounds more weight, putting him near the two hundred mark. His dark hair and mustache were course and straight with a few streaks of gray. A southern accent marked his speech. He also wore a Colt Peacemaker, one of the few men Wes had seen armed in town.

"Tom's just the man for you see," Kate told Wes. She patted Rickman's knee. "He's a friend of Landham Kennedy who owns the Mineral King smelter. Wes is looking for a job," she explained to the sheriff.

* * *

Julie sat primly at the desk in Uncle Frank's outer office as she sorted through the numerous books and ledgers before her. Light streamed through the dusty window behind her. In the near distance the Rio d'Oro's heavy machinery provided a low, steady thump-thump as the smelter turned out refined minerals. Julie ignored the dust and noise, just as she'd ignored the rattle of the streetcars and the heat when she did her charity work in the office at the Bradley Center in Philadelphia.

Thank goodness she'd talked Uncle Frank into letting her help out. Three days of sitting around the empty Lawson house with only Clare, the day girl, for company gave Julie too much time to think and worry. To fret about all the things that could go wrong with her plan. Too much time for Gran's warning about the cost of impulsive acts to ring through her thoughts.

When Uncle Frank told her about his bookkeeper leaving, she'd reminded him how good she'd always been with account books and numbers, and how she'd helped in the office at the Bradley shelter along with Cory. She'd convinced him to let her see what she could do with the mess that the departed bookkeeper had left. He'd agreed, partly because he knew she had worked in Philadelphia, but mostly, she suspected, to give her something to do.

The office door opened. A man, about Uncle Frank's age entered and stopped abruptly. Behind him she glimpsed a second man standing, hat in hand.

The man in the suit scowled and his mouth tightened before he grudgingly removed his hat. She recognizing the signs of a man who thought all women belonged at home. He didn't bother to hide his distaste in his voice as he said, "I'm Landham Kennedy. I want to see Frank Lawson."

As Julie stood, Uncle Frank opened his office door. Seeing Mr. Kennedy he extended his hand in greeting as he said, "Landham." Mr. Kennedy moved forward to take her uncle's hand, revealing his companion.

Him! Julie barely managed to smother a gasp. There he stood, wearing a tan corduroy jacket and denim pants, turning his Stetson in his hand. The filtered sunlight turned his blond hair and mustache gold. She stared, mentally ticking off the remembered broad shoulders, lean hips, his booted feet planted slightly apart. How could he possibly be more handsome than she remembered?

She realized she'd been holding her breath and started to breathe again. For a split second she was puzzled that he showed no sign of recognition. But of course! She'd been disguised in her widow's weeds. Belatedly, the word disguise rang in her brain causing a flutter of panic. Her first reaction to him should have been fear of recognition. Whatever she had felt, it certainly hadn't been fear. With a start, she realized that Uncle Frank was introducing her to Mr. Kennedy.

After acknowledging her with a brief nod, Kennedy turned back to Uncle Frank. "This is my new man, Westmoreland." Kennedy indicated the blond man with a jerk of his thumb then continued, "It's time you and I did something about our troubles. I want to discuss a plan with you." Kennedy moved toward Frank's open office door. "Wait here," he ordered Westmoreland.

"Now, Landham," Frank replied in a placating voice as he followed Kennedy into the office. The door closed behind them.

With just the two of them alone in the office, her heartbeat sped up. The fear of discovery formed a hard knot in her stomach. Hoping she hid her unease she extended her hand and said as formally as possible, "How do you do, Mr. Westmoreland?'

Wes blinked and looked at the outstretched hand she offered him. He couldn't remember a woman ever offering to shake hands with him. He didn't actually shake her hand, just closed his fingers around hers for a few brief seconds before letting go. "Howdy, Miss Lawson," he said with a nod, making sure nothing but casual politeness sounded in his voice. Even if he hadn't recognized her, the way his gut clenched when he touched her, skin to skin, confirmed her identity. By damn, this pretty Miss Lawson was his St. Louis widow.

From his position behind Kennedy, he'd seen her before she'd seen him. He hadn't missed the slight widening of her eyes or her sharp intake of breath when she first noticed him. She'd recognized him, all right. What the hell was going on? Why was she now Miss

Lawson without widow's weeds? Lawson'd introduced her to Kennedy as his niece, but did she have any connection with the smelter's troubles?

He gave himself a mental shake. He'd better quit thinking about the woman and start concentrating on his job. He'd made that mistake once before. And he sure as hell didn't intend to make it again. He'd just have to ignore the way her silvery hair glistened in the sunlight from the window behind her.

"You expect them to be long?' he asked, nodding toward the closed door of Lawson s office.

"I really can't say. Why don't you sit down?" She gestured him toward a chair across from the desk.

He sat, draping his hat over one knee. He gave a pointed look at the desk, making sure she noticed, before asking, "Looks like a lot of work there. You work for Mr. Lawson long?"

To his surprise, she gave a laugh. "No, not long. Mr. Lawson is my uncle. I'm here in Durango for a visit. I thought I'd see if I could help out with the books. Uncle Frank's bookkeeper s went back east and left them in a mess."

Her answer, so open and detailed to his probing question threw him. In spite of the difference in dress, the certainty she was the widow he'd held in St. Louis burned in his belly. Today his widow dressed in a white cotton shirtwaist and a deep green skirt. The simple outfit would make most women look dowdy, but it looked damn attractive on her. She'd twisted her silvery hair into an elaborate knot with short, wispy tendrils springing free to frame her face.

Cursing his wandering mind, he forced his thoughts back to the collection of information. "Lucky for your uncle you're here to help out." Could Lawson be doing a little skimming? Looking at a company's books was always a place to start when a business had trouble.

She gave him a mischievous half-smile. "We'll see how much help I'll be. Today's my first day in the office."

Again, she answered direct and to the point. Damn, what was going on? The way she'd reacted when she recognized him half-convinced him she didn't have much experience with lying. The uncertainty made him even more suspicious.

"Have you been in Durango long?" she asked.

"Not long." Years of experience kept any sign of tension from showing. Would she now try to get information from him?

"Did you come in on the railroad? The scenery was unbelievable, the gorges, the river, the mountains. I've never seen anything like it."

Nice question. He agreed he'd come into town on the railroad. But in getting an answer from him she'd indirectly told him this was her first time in the west. If, that is, she told the truth about never having seen scenery like the rough, beautiful country between here and Denver.

"Looks like you have your work cut out for you. What happened to the bookkeeper?" he asked just to see what she'd say. She gave him the same story he'd heard from Kate.

"…so he went back east."

"Works like that sometimes. Civilization is only skin deep a lot of places out here. The west can still be tough. Some people can't last." Damn if he wasn't making a speech. Why was that?

"Why, Mr. Westmoreland, you're quite a philosopher." At her smile, a dimple made a brief appearance in her cheek. Before he could think of something to say that would make her display the dimple again, the door to Lawson's office opened, and Kennedy came out. Wes rose.

"Think about what I said, Frank," Kennedy said. "We have to take action."

"I'll think about it," Lawson agreed.

Kennedy gave Lawson a curt nod. "Come on, Westmoreland," he said as he put on his hat and headed out the door.

Wes looked at his departing boss then back at Miss Lawson as she stood behind the desk. Temptation prompted him to hold out his hand. "Glad to have met you, Miss."

She hesitated then she placed her hand in his. Just as before, his gut tightened at the warm contact. After a long moment, he allowed her hand to slip from his. With a brief look into those bluer-than-blue eyes, he nodded, then putting on his hat he turned and followed Kennedy.

Julie stared at the open doorway, the flutter in her stomach fading. Her right hand still tingled with the memory of how his fingertips stroked the sensitive center of her palm as she withdrew her hand from his. Her left hand had wrapped protectively around her right, and they rested against the center of her chest as though to calm her heart.

"Are you all right?" Uncle Frank asked.

She quickly dropped her hands, feeling like a fool. "Oh, yes." But added inanely, "He's very handsome." As if Uncle Frank couldn't have guessed. With a sigh she sat down.

"Surely there are handsome men in Philadelphia?" Uncle Frank's chuckle exuded sympathy, reminding her he'd raised a daughter. He hitched a hip onto the desk. "A pretty girl like you ought to know how to handle handsome men."

Yes, there are many handsome men in Philadelphia. She'd handled, as Uncle Frank put it, those Philadelphia men with ease. But an inner voice cautioned that Mr. Westmoreland did not look like a man who could be easily handled. Wanting to change the subject, she asked, "What did Mr. Kennedy want?"

Uncle Frank sighed. "Landham thinks there's something behind the rash of accidents we've been suffering."

"Accidents?"

"The last two months both the Rio d'Oro," he gestured around the office, "and Kennedy's Mineral King smelter have been plagued with accidents. Machine breakdowns, things like that. Thank goodness no one's been hurt. Landham's trying to convince me it's more than just bad luck. I'm not so sure myself, although it would seem the problems are worse than normal."

"Oh," Uncle Frank didn't seem overly worried, but then again, nothing much flustered Uncle Frank.

Uncle Frank indicated the books and ledgers spread over the desk. "Kennedy sees this as one of the symptoms of a conspiracy. I hardly believe Howard's preoccupation with his wife's illness was the result of some conspiracy. Landham's overreacting," Uncle Frank said with a shake of his head. "What did Mr. Westmoreland have to say?"

"Nothing at all, we mostly talked about the scenery. What does he do for Mr. Kennedy? Is Mr. Westmoreland an engineer of some kind?"

Uncle Frank gave a short laugh. "Not likely. Landham called him a man-of-all-works. He just hired him to keep an eye out around the Mineral King, to spot trouble before it happens, that type of thing. I don't know exactly what Landham thinks Westmoreland can accomplish.

"Man-of-all-works," Uncle Frank said with a snort as he stood. "A few years ago, a man like Westmoreland would have been called a hired gun."

Chapter Three

Julie exited the grocery, a basket with a dozen eggs in one hand. Saturday morning shopping was in full swing, the street lively with carts and buggies, foot traffic on the boardwalk. As she looped the basket over one arm, she cast a discreet glance across the wide, dusty main street.

Unbelievable. No wonder Clare, the day girl, had warned her to stay on the east side of Main Street. The entire west side consisted of saloons. Her gaze swept the block, taking in the bold signs with outlandish names, the lettered windows proclaiming whiskey, beer, billiards, cards, faro, and other games of chance.

Her scrutiny reached the middle of the block. Her gaze locked on a figure in a corduroy jacket and denim pants as he left a saloon, the funny, half-doors swinging behind him. With a quick glance right and left, he dashed into the traffic, his long, quick strides moving him through the wagons and carts. What kind of a man came out of a saloon midmorning? Uncle Frank's character assessment of Mr. Westmoreland may have been correct.

Trying not to jar the eggs, she struggled with her parasol, but the sticky catch refused to cooperate. She should have brought a better one, but she hadn't been thinking of such details when she packed. First anger, then fear and desperation, had occupied her thoughts while she grabbed the first things that came to hand and stuffed them in the trunk.

She worked at the catch. At least this one with its multicolored ribbon trim matched her rose walking dress. She glanced up to see Mr. Westmoreland had gained her side of the street. With a dazzling smile, he headed straight toward her. A frisson, somewhere between apprehension and excitement, shivered in her stomach.

"Morning, Miss Lawson." He nodded, fingers at his hat brim.

"Good morning." At least her voice worked. The rest of her seemed frozen into immobility.

"Allow me." He took the parasol from her hand. With no trouble he opened the recalcitrant thing, took the basket from her arm and returned the open parasol. "There now. Which way are you headed?"

Propriety and decorum probably had something to say about allowing a near stranger to escort you, but he looked so expectant she didn't have the heart to refuse. And even though he had come from the saloon, he didn't smell as though he'd been drinking. Anyway, this was the main street of Durango.

"Thank you. This way," she said and gestured south. As they started down the sidewalk, he positioned himself between her and the street. At the corner, he placed his free hand under her elbow as she stepped down from the boardwalk. Regardless of what Uncle Frank had said, someone had obviously taught Mr. Westmoreland his manners.

"I appreciate your assistance, but surely a man-of-all-works such as yourself has more important jobs than carrying groceries?"

"Not at the moment. Mr. Kennedy does give his workers time away from the job."

He deftly guided her through the wheeled traffic and helped her step up on the boardwalk of the next block. He tested the limits of proper behavior when he didn't release her elbow once they gained the walkway. The fluttery sensation intensified and she fleetingly wondered if she should shrug off his hand.

"Tell me," he interrupted her thoughts, "are those eggs for dinner?"

Puzzled, she allowed him to draw her to a stop. "No."

"Good. You aren't in any hurry then. Perhaps you'd allow me to buy you a sarsaparilla?" The store they stopped in front of said Tiffany's Drugs in gold letters on the wide window. He gestured inside. Easily visible from the walk, a soda fountain stretched the length of the building.

He must have sensed her hesitation, as he said, "We have been properly introduced, you know. Although that's not as important out here as I suspect it would be in Philadelphia."

She hesitated. Not out of a sense of propriety which had never been her strong point. Her inner voice echoed its warning about western men not being as easily handled as Philadelphia boys. For all his charming manners, there was no mistaking Mr. Westmoreland as anything but a man.

He held the door open for her.

It was only a soda. "Yes, thank you." She lowered her parasol and entered.

Inside, he hung his hat on the rack by the door. With another dazzling smile he gestured toward a table. When she turned, he placed his hand in the small of her back. Solid and warm, his touch made her breath catch. Odd how she'd been perfectly capable of walking and thinking at the same time until he touched her. Conscious of his touch, she let him guide her to one of the wrought iron tables. He placed the egg basket on the floor and held the chair for her. Going to the counter, he ordered two sarsaparillas from the young man in the white apron.

"How are you coming with the books?" he asked as he placed the glasses on the table and took his seat.

She made a face. "I've finally located and organized all of the relevant papers. Monday I'll get into the numbers themselves." She took a sip.

"Better you than me," he said swirling soda around in the glass. He looked up, and must have seen her baffled expression. He explained, "I'm not too good with numbers. I'm better with cards."

Before she could think of an appropriate response, he asked, "How come you know ledgers and numbers? Seems a pretty girl like you would be more likely to know about dresses and dances."

Nice that he thought her pretty, but not at the expense of thinking that was her only virtue. "Perhaps I know about ledgers and numbers the way you know about parasols," she said with asperity. "Experience."

He looked blank for a second. Then the corners of his eyes crinkled, telling her he was amused rather than annoyed by the implication of his experience with parasols and women. "I stand corrected." He took a drink of sarsaparilla. "I really would like to know how you come by your knowledge," he said with a smile.

Oh, dear. A man with a smile that sincere was dangerous. The combination of dancing sea-green eyes and white teeth half-hidden by his soft looking blond mustache made him irresistible. "I work in the office at the Bradley Center in Philadelphia."

"Bradley Center? Some kind of charity?"

"Not really a charity, more of an institute. We provide various types of community services to workers who live nearby. We hold classes on domestic skills such as proper diet and hygiene, classes in English for the foreign born, female health-care classes. I worked in the office there, helping with correspondence, scheduling the classes. Cory felt those kinds of jobs were fitting for me."

"Cory?"

"My sister, Cordelia." At the mention of her sister's name, the worry immediately flooded back. Oh, Cory, she silently prayed, please be all right. Let me have done the right thing. Then catching her companion's gaze, she quickly pushed the concern for her sister from her mind.

Her worry must have shown on her face for he said, "You close, you and your sister?"

"My mother died when I was six and Cory twelve." At their mother's death their laughing, happy Papa had become sad and quiet, leaving the two girls to draw closer together. "Papa only remarried this spring, so it was Cory who did all the mother things for me. Taught me to cook and sew, how to keep house.

"Our mother s family had helped found the Bradley Center, so of course Cory and I volunteer there." She must stop talking about Cory or surely something would show in her voice. She stopped to take a sip of her soda. "This is good."

She looked across the table to see him draining the last of his sarsaparilla, while her glass was still almost full. She must have been staring, because he looked up, quirking an eyebrow.

"What?" he asked.

What kind of a man comes out of a saloon before noon and then so obviously enjoys a sarsaparilla? "It just seems odd, somehow, to see a grown man enjoy a soda."

He shrugged and looked sheepish. "Guess I never got enough when I was a kid. Still seems like a treat."

Even with the death of her mother, her childhood gave her overwhelmingly good memories. She never had to do without anything she needed and she'd had most things she wanted. From her work at the Bradley Center she knew not all people were as fortunate. Whether he meant to or not, Mr. Westmoreland had just told her that his childhood was probably closer to those of the grubby, hungry children who lived and played in the streets neighboring the center than it had been to her own childhood.

She considered asking about his childhood, but his comment had been casual, obviously not a ploy for sympathy. To keep him talking, she asked, "How is your work for Mr. Kennedy coming."

Mr. Westmoreland leaned back in his chair, looking comfortable and relaxed. One hand idly played with the empty sarsaparilla glass. As his long fingers with blunt clean nails turned the glass in place, she remembered the heat of that strong hand guiding her across the floor. She pulled her attention back to his words.

"I've worked in a smelter before, back in California, so I've been familiarizing myself with Kennedy's operation."

He talked of stamps, vanning, amalgams, and other terms she didn't understand. She'd only seen the office of the Rio d'Oro, which sat some distance from the smelter itself because of the noise and dust. But she didn't interrupt him with questions. Just sipping sarsaparilla and listening to his voice gave her pleasure. Behind her, the door of the drug store opened and several people come in.

Mr. Westmoreland paused in his explanations. "Do you know the lady in the green hat? She finds us interesting."

Julie glanced over her shoulder to see a large, firmly-corseted woman scrutinizing them. "That's Mrs. Peterson, the editor of the town newspaper. Uncle Frank says not much escapes her notice or her pen."

"Does she know you?" His dark blond eyebrows pulled together in a frown over eyes suddenly devoid of expression.

"Well, yes. That is, we met when she came to pay a welcome call the day after I arrived. Why?"

He didn't answer, but continued to frown, evidently deep in thought.

She turned again to see Mrs. Peterson excuse herself from her companions and walk straight toward the table where she and Mr. Westmoreland sat.

"Julie, my dear, how are you?" she said as if they were long lost friends. She spoiled the effect by looking past Julie. "Who's your friend, dear?"

Turning back to Mr. Westmorland the introductions died in her throat at his transformation. The well-mannered man who'd escorted her from the grocery was gone. The flashing smile she'd admired might have never touched the cold, hard face that stared at Mrs. Peterson. After a hesitation just short of rudeness, he stood to acknowledge Mrs. Peterson presence. Baffled by the change, Julie made the introductions.

"Oh, yes," Mrs. Peterson said, "You're Mr. Kennedy's new... man."

"That's right." Even his voice sounded hard now. A feeling of unease and dread began to displace her bafflement.

Fortunately, one of Mrs. Peterson s friends called her name. The older lady gave Julie a parting look. "Well, dear, nice to have seen you again. I do so worry about you, what with your aunt Marie in San Francisco, and only your uncle to supervise your, ah, acquaintances." She shot a parting glance at Mr. Westmoreland. "Take care, dear," she admonished and went to join her friends, leaving Julie to stare after her.

"Let's get out of here."

Mr. Westmoreland's voice jerked her back. She barely had time to react as he picked up her basket and parasol and grabbed the back of her chair. He muttered to himself under his breath as without touching her, he escorted her out the door and onto the boardwalk.

Upset by his sudden change in character, she gladly took the basket and parasol he handed her. He touched the brim of his hat, nodded, turned on his heels and strode down the walk. The man striding toward saloon row looked, not the gentleman he'd first appeared, but now seemed the perfect example of what Uncle Frank had called him. A hired gun.

Standing in the bright summer sunlight, Julie shivered, and wondered why she suddenly felt like crying.

* * *

Boot heels thumping, Wes marched across the boardwalk and pushed into Kate's Double Eagle, leaving the doors swishing behind him. Talk about being stupid. Who the hell did he think he was? He tossed his hat on the bar. Without being asked, Jake the bartender poured a shot of whiskey and set it beside his hat.

"Thanks." He tossed the shot down in one swift gulp. The spirits burned down his throat, washing away the lingering sweetness of the sarsaparilla. This is who he was. Whiskey, harsh and scorching his stomach, not soft, fizzing sarsaparilla

With a slow exhalation of breath, he sat the shot glass on the bar and ran his hand over his face. Jake looked at him, eyebrows and the whiskey bottled raised. Wes shook his head, so Jake turned his attention to customers at the other end of the bar. Close to noon, the room was more than three-quarters full. Men drank, talked, and played cards and faro.

Wes turned around and leaned back, resting his elbows on the bar to look out the front windows. Only this time he saw nothing to send him hurrying out, as he'd done before when he'd seen Miss Lawson come out of the grocery. Another deep breath helped dissipate the anger. After ten years on the job, he should be able to keep his mind on his work. He'd even taken her switch of the conversation away from herself as common politeness.

There he'd been, sitting with a lady, drinking soda and showing off a little with his knowledge of smelting when Mrs. Peterson had given him the fish-eye, reminding him he was Kennedy's hired man. Not only did he forget he was supposed to be on the job, but he'd actually forgotten who he was. A saloon kid. Sure as hell not the type to be with young, pretty Miss Lawson.

"Wes?" A deep voice interrupted his thoughts. Wes turned to find Jake at his elbow.

"Can you cover the bar for a few minutes while I set out the free lunch?"

"Sure." Wes served one or two customers while he watched Jake carry cheese, crackers, pickles, and hard-boiled eggs from the kitchen and set them at the end of the bar. The last trip out of the kitchen, Kate followed on Jake's heels.

"Just what do you think you're doing?" she asked in mock exasperation, hands on her hips.

He gave her his innocent who-me smile. "Just tending bar. Look," he said, when she started to protest. "You won't let me pay rent for the room you gave me in back. It's no effort for me to help out a little. I like to pay my own way."

Kate still frowned.

He gave her the who-me smile again, and she laughed. "You were always too good-looking for your own good. Go on, now. Here's Jake." She gave Wes a push out from behind the bar.

"How's your job with Kennedy coming," she asked while Wes returned to the customer side of the bar.

"Not too bad."

Kate nodded to the doorway. "Well, here he comes. Somehow I think it's a good thing you aren't still behind the bar. Kennedy isn't the type to appreciate his employee working for someone else."

Wes looked to see Kennedy, followed by Sheriff Rickman entering the Double Eagle.

Kennedy stopped in front of Wes. "What are you doing here?" his voice belligerent.

Already in a sour mood, Wes bit back a sarcastic reply. "Lunch," he answered. He gestured toward the spread on the end of the bar.

Sheriff Rickman moved to stand next to Kate, slipping his arm around her waist. Kennedy acknowledged neither Rickman nor Kate.

He frowned at Wes. "I'm paying you to look out for trouble, not hang around saloons."

With effort, Wes kept his irritation out of his voice. "I was at the Mineral King last night at the shift change," he said, in case anyone had seen him wandering around and mentioned it to Kennedy. "I was there again this morning at the change of shift when they shut down to scrape the amalgamation tables. I'll go back after I eat."

Kennedy answered with a non-committal grunt. "I expect value for my money." With that parting remark, he turned to sit at a nearby table.

"Bring us a couple of beers, will you?" Sheriff Rickman asked Kate. He gave her a smile and a quick hug and went to sit with Kennedy.

"How do you put up with the way he treats you?" Kate asked Wes as she drew two glasses of beer.

"He's paying my wages, just like he says."

"That's no reason for him to treat you like an errant schoolboy in front of other people. Never did understand how he and Tom get along so well together."

He shook his head. "Don't worry, Kate. I can put up with him." He'd put up with a lot worse. Knowing he didn't have to work for Kennedy any longer than necessary helped. He knew himself to be a hundred times better off than those men who actually depended on Kennedy for their pay. Anyone who worked at the Mineral King learned soon enough that when Kennedy said jump the employee was expected to ask how high on the way up.

"You finding any trouble? The kind of suspicious accident Kennedy thinks is happening?" She sat the beers on a tray.

"Not yet. These accidents have been about a week or ten days apart." Neither of the smelters have had any problems since he started. "I've only been on the job a couple of days. Give me time."

"I think it's Kennedy who may not give you too much time." Kate picked up the tray and went to serve her customers.

At the end of the bar, he picked up a handful of crackers, a hunk of cheese and a hard-boiled egg. On his way through the kitchen he stuffed an apple in his pocket then grabbed a cup of coffee.

Balancing the coffee and his lunch, he let himself out the back door of the Double Eagle. He flopped down on the back step. The summer sun was bright, but not too warm for comfort especially when the other choice was the smoky, noisy saloon under Kennedy's disapproving stare.

From his seat, he looked out west. Across the railroad tracks, across the shacks in poverty flats, and across the river beyond to where the Rockies thrust their sharp edges skyward as if challenging the clear sky. The view was a lot better than the cramped, filthy alley afforded from the back step of the Red Garter where he grew up. The free lunch at the Double Eagle was better, too.

As he munched the cheese and crackers, he thought back over his conversation with Miss Lawson. She certainly seemed without duplicity. In fact, the word that came to mind when he tried to sum up all his impressions surprised him. She was nice. He shook his head. But then again, what the hell did he know about nice?

Much to his disgust he found himself remembering how her hair looked pure silver in the sunlight. How her dark pink dress fit her a lot better than either the widow's weeds or the shirtwaist he'd seen her in before. Although a little on the slender side, the walking dress revealed she had curves in all the right places. He'd let himself be sucked right into those clear blue eyes, watching her pink mouth as she sipped. With a curse, he shifted his position.

Damn, he should just stay away from her. Not that he'd have much choice after Mrs. Peterson got through with her warning. He'd be lucky if Miss Lawson didn't cross the street when she saw him coming.

Yeah, he'd just stay away from her. Right. He hurled the apple core out to land on the trash heap. Only one thing wrong with that idea. He pulled out his tobacco pouch. Sooner or later his investigation would take him to the Rio d'Oro. And a chance to look into those bluer-than-blue eyes again. He groaned, and cursed himself as he heard the combination of dread and anticipation in his voice.

* * *

Landham Kennedy sat back in his chair scowling at Tom Rickman, as the sheriff smiled across the room at Kate. "Can't you stay away from that whore?"

Tom turned back, the smile fading and set his beer on the table. "I told you, she's not a whore," he said tiredly. "That's past."

Kennedy snorted.

"Come on, Land. Lots of things are past. Who should know better than you and me?"

Kennedy's face went hard and cold. "Don't ever, ever mention that," he said between clenched teeth.

Tom fidgeted in his seat. "Sure. Sure."

After a moment, Kennedy relaxed. "Just remember." He took a sip of beer. "Just remember who we are now."

The back door of the saloon opened and Westmoreland entered. He stopped to say a few words to Kate, and with a nod in Kennedy's direction, he strode out through the bat-wing doors onto Main Street.

Tom watched him go, eyes narrowed. "I don't trust him"

"You don't trust him because he's a friend of Kate's and too damn good-looking."

"Not that. I think he's sharper than he seems."

"I'll grant you he's tough," Kennedy said, signaling the bartender for another beer. "But that's all. Grew up in a whore house, you said."

"Saloon," Tom corrected.

Kennedy waved his comment away. "Saloon, whore house, what's the difference, places like that are both. Besides you told me he helped pull a robbery but got caught. That's not too smart." He leaned forward. "Smart men don't get caught."

Chapter Four

Julie stood in front of her aunt's chevalier mirror, holding the ball gown against her. She turned this way and that, imagining how the gown with its bodice and underskirt of pale peach and an overskirt a deep peach, would look now that she and Clare had finished the alterations.

"Miss Julie!" Clare called up the stairs. "The irons are hot."

"Coming!" With the gown draped over one arm, she went down the stairs and headed toward the kitchen.

During her days in Durango the sunny kitchen at the back of the Lawson house had become a familiar and comfortable place. She went around the large, oak worktable to the cast iron stove, where two flat irons waited, the ironing board ready nearby.

"Are you sure this gown won't be too formal for an outdoor dance?" she asked.

Clare tsk-tsked as she worked the pump at the sink. "'Course it won't. I told you, Mrs. Lawson wore it last year to the Fourth of July dance, and it was the easiest one of your aunt's dresses to alter. Don't worry. You'll be fine."

Of course the dress would be appropriate, even Uncle Frank had said so. Why should she be so worried about her appearance at a dance where there would be no one for her to impress? Memories of stormy-green eyes and a smile half-hidden by a blond mustache jumped into her mind.

With a sniff of disgust, she picked up an iron. Why should she worry about him, after the way he'd left her standing on the sidewalk four days ago? Thank goodness Uncle Frank had dismissed Mrs. Peterson's 'word in his ear.' The whole encounter had been a tempest in a teapot. Hadn't she dismissed the whole incident from her mind?

"Tell me more about what will happen today," she asked as she started to press the seams she and Clare had taken in.

Clare did the breakfast dishes while she talked. "Why, Fourth of July is just about the biggest holiday around Durango, what with the parade, and the picnic, and the dance, and all. 'Course you know about the parade, what with Mr. Frank on the committee again this year."

She placed the first iron back on the stove and took up the second. "He certainly left in a rush this morning." She worked the iron around the hem where it had been let down.

A loud series of pops came from the yard. Clare shrieked and dropped a dish with a splash. Julie jumped, almost burning herself with the iron. The popping stopped, followed by boyish laughter.

Of course, firecrackers, she realized with a smile.

"Gracious," Clare exclaimed hands pressed to her ears. After a few seconds of silence, she pushed aside the curtain and peered through the window. "I see you, John Thomas Malone!" she shouted. "You get home right now or I'll be a-telling the sheriff on you!"

"Clare's a fraidy-cat, Clare's a fraidy-cat." The singsong chant faded with the sound of running feet.

Clare let the curtain drop. "Dratted boy, he knows there's no fireworks in the city limits. I hope Mrs. Malone paddles his britches good."

"Perhaps he's a young admirer," Julie suggested.

Clare harrumphed as she went back to the dishes. "He's a little brat. He did it a-purpose. I was helping Mrs. Malone can peaches last fall when a thunderstorm came up without warning, like they do out here. Well, any loud noise, especially thunder, just scares me silly." Clare gave a shudder. "Just can't abide thunder."

"How ever do you get through today?" Julie asked.

"Oh, it's not too bad. Like I said, sheriff says no fireworks in the city. Why, last year he arrested two cowboys who were shooting their six-shooter off, right there on Main Street."

Clare must have noticed her look of astonishment. "Now, don't go worrying, Miss Julie. Durango's all civilized nowadays."

Durango may be civilized, as Clare put it, but it certainly wasn't Philadelphia. Durango seemed more alive, young, more... she didn't know what. She shook her head, traded irons and went back to listening to Clare.

"Just like I was telling you, first there'll be the parade this morning, then everyone goes over to the picnic grounds for the afternoon. Then patriotic speeches and the volunteer fire department will play the miners in baseball. The dance starts at eight." Clare wiped her hands on a towel. "How you coming with that dress?"

She switched irons again. "I'll be finished in a minute. Then we can get started on the food."

An hour later as Julie wiped the table, and Clare put the lunch in the icebox, hoof beats sounded in the backyard.

Clare peered between the lace curtains. "It's my brother, Ryan."

Before Julie could respond, a knock sounded at the screen door and a male voice called "Clare?"

"Come in," Clare answered, hurrying toward the door.

The door opened to reveal a tall man in an army uniform. He took off his cavalry hat uncovering dark, curly hair. "Are you ready? We have…" His voice trailed away as he caught sight of Julie.

Clare took her brother's arm, smiling up at him in obvious admiration. Her brother glanced down and smiled back. The expression of sibling affection caused Julie a pang, reminding her how she and Cory exchanged such smiles.

Clare introduced them, saying Ryan was a lieutenant stationed at the nearby Fort Lewis and telling him Julie was here for a visit.

Slightly embarrassed by the lieutenant's admiring gaze, a gaze she'd seen too often, Julie acknowledged the introduction and offered him a cup of coffee. To her relief, he refused.

"Thanks, but I think Sis is almost ready. Right?" He smiled at Clare.

"Just let me get rid of this apron and get my hat and gloves." Clare untied her apron and headed for her room. "Back in a minute."

"Are you enjoying your visit, Miss Lawson?" Lieutenant Sullivan inquired.

"Yes. Durango is quite pretty." With practiced social skill, she answered the questions of how was her trip out, how she liked the city, how long she'd stay.

Clare appeared, a summer straw hat trimmed with daisies perched on her own dark curls. "Ryan and I are going to wander around town, see the parade and all. Maybe we'll see you and Mr. Frank at the picnic."

"I'm sure we'll run into each other later in the day," Lieutenant Sullivan said with a hopeful smile. "But in case we don't, I'll take the liberty of asking you to save me a dance tonight."

"Of course." She closed the screen door after the Sullivans left. Perhaps Lieutenant Sullivan was just what she needed. He seemed a perfectly nice man. She should be quite taken with him. But the thought of dancing with him didn't do funny things to her heartbeat. However if Mr. Westmoreland were to ask for a dance....

* * *

"Oh, Uncle Frank!" Julie exclaimed, as she and Uncle Frank stood on the boardwalk in front of the Stratler Hotel. "It's beautiful." The scene before her was completely different from any dance she'd ever attended. And completely charming. No ballroom could ever compare with the open air dance floor in front of her.

"The whole town comes out," Uncle Frank explained, "and there's not a building big enough to hold us all."

Filling the center of the empty lot across from the Stratler Hotel, wide wooden planks had been nailed together to make a dance floor. Music floated on the air as dancers swirled. Hundreds of Chinese lanterns hung from heavy strings over and around the dance floor, candles flickering inside the colored paper lanterns like captive fireflies. Overhead the purple velvet sky still concealed all but a few stars.

At the other end of the dance floor, a raised platform held the regimental band from Fort Lewis that had headed this afternoon's parade. The addition of a few violins transformed them into the post orchestra for the evening.

"May I have this dance?" Uncle Frank offered his arm to lead her to the dance floor.

As she and Uncle Frank danced, she breathed in the evening's unique scent. The cool, pine-scented air drifted in from the mountains to overlay the hot, dusty, sunny summer-day smell. From the dancing crowd, spatters of perfume, bay rum, and tobacco smoke added to the potpourri.

"I'm glad you're here," Uncle Frank said. "Keeps me from missing Marie so much."

The words brought a tightness to her throat. The best thing about family was how they loved and cared for each other. To hide her reaction, she kissed Uncle Frank on the cheek. She tried to keep her tone light. "You're my favorite uncle."

Frank smiled. "I'm your only uncle."

Maybe someday she could tell Uncle Frank just how much comfort his presence gave her. She regretted not being able to tell him her real reason for being in Durango.

She must believe her actions would buy the necessary time for Cory. Concentrate on the here and now. The parade, the picnic, the things that made her visit seem so ordinary, just as she wished her visit to appear. Keep the illusion of her being in Durango as just a visit to relatives. With renewed determination she decided to throw herself whole-heartedly into the evening's festivities.

The song ended and Uncle Frank walked her back toward the hotel end of the dance area.

A few minutes later, as she danced with one of Uncle Frank's friends, her gaze swept over the crowd. Not that she was looking for anyone specifically of course. She noted Mrs. Peterson and a few of Aunt Marie's friends. She saw Clare and her brother the lieutenant. Recognized Mr. Kennedy and the sheriff. Then next to the bandstand, her gaze locked on the figure of Mr. Westmoreland.

Even though the dim and flickering light half-hid his features, she recognized him. As she'd first seen him in St. Louis, he wore a suit the color of bitter chocolate with a white shirt and string tie. He stood talking to a dark-haired woman in a somber black dress. She must have said something to amuse him, for he laughed and shook his head. The contrast of his easy camaraderie with the woman created a bitter lump in Julie's throat, making her feel young and uninteresting.

Over the next hour or so, she caught glimpses of him every so often as Uncle Frank or one of his friends danced her around the floor. She briefly considered asking Uncle Frank who the woman was, but decided to leave well enough alone. Then, as she stood fanning herself, she just happened to glance toward the bandstand.

What she saw answered her unasked questions. Still laughing together, a match flared in the woman's hand, and taking her hand in his, he brought the match to light the cigarette clamped in his white teeth. Julie's heart sank and she felt incredibly naïve. The dark-haired woman obviously knew him well, and she obviously was no lady.

* * *

Wes leaned against the side of the bandstand while the orchestra played a reel with military precision. Durango sure knew how to throw a birthday party. Since sunrise the whole town had been aflutter with flags and bunting. So many people took part in the parade he'd been amazed anyone was left to watch.

"See, I told you," Kate said. "The entire population of Durango is here. The crowd by the hotel may politely ignore us, but they know how much we pay into the city coffers."

"Just like in Frisco? I remember Sam slipping money to the deputy who just happened to stop by the Red Garter, and all the other saloons, every Saturday night."

"Durango's more upfront. We pay taxes, saloon licenses and then we get 'fined' ten dollars a month for each girl. The saloons pull in the cowboys and miners who spend money in the rest of the town, too. So on occasions like this we take care not to offend each other."

While men circulated around the dance floor, he'd noticed a definite segregation. Kate, in her respectable, black business dress, and the other women of saloon row stayed to the bandstand. Along the sides of the dance floor the shop girls and maids held court, dressed in their Sunday best. Directly across from the hotel was strictly upper class, women in true evening gowns and white gloves mingled with army officers, smelter engineers and managers, bankers, and others of society.

"See you later," Kate said. Wes looked around and saw Sheriff Rickman heading toward the bandstand. Kate drifted away and in a few moments the sheriff joined her.

Wes rolled another cigarette. But after a few drags he ground it out with his boot. He rotated his shoulders, feeling the tension in his muscles. After the incident at Kennedy's smelter this afternoon, things were starting to happen. He flexed his hand, the white bandage still tight over his palm.

The accident at the smelter had to be the reason for the knot between his shoulder blades. Couldn't be Miss Lawson who he'd noticed as soon as he'd arrived. He'd seen her on her uncle's arm. Her fair hair gleamed like silver in the pale light, her skin appeared like rich cream. Damn, but she reminded him of peaches soft, sweet, warm.

He'd been a saloon kid, a boy other boys were not allowed to play with. He remembered as a kid standing in the hot, dirty alley behind the saloon, skeptical of trading a bucket of beer for an unfamiliar fruit. He remembered the first taste of the peach, the sweet, sticky juice running down his chin. He hadn't known something so delicious had existed.

He watched her circle the dance floor with her uncle. Just like the fruit, she tantalized him. Way too good for the likes of him. He couldn't help watching as she danced with her uncle a few times, and then with several older gentlemen, obviously friends of Lawson's. When the band struck up a waltz, she took the floor with a dark-headed army lieutenant.

"What are you frowning at?" Kate asked, appearing at his side.

"Nothing." He made an effort to look unconcerned. Seconds later the young lieutenant danced by with Miss Lawson in his arms.

Why should he care? Ladies probably liked dancing with tall, dark army lieutenants. His frown came back double strength.

"Is it the pretty girl in the peach-colored gown you're not scowling at?" Kate asked. She didn't wait for an answer. "You can dance better than half the men here, certainly better than that yellow-leg cavalry officer. What the hell are you waiting for Westmoreland? Ask her to dance."

Hell, he might as well take the chance; find out if Mrs. Peterson's warning had scared Miss Lawson off for good. Besides, he should be trying to find out what she'd been doing in widow's weeds in St. Louis. With a conscious effort he unclenched his jaw, rotated his shoulders, and edged his way through the crowd heading toward the hotel side of the dance floor.

The waltz ended and the officer took Miss Lawson back to a group of women. Luckily, she immediately headed for the punch table. Wes moved to intercept her. She hesitated a split second when she saw him, but she kept coming.

"May I get you a glass of punch, Miss Lawson?" He sounded only casually interested, but his throat felt dry and his palms damp. She gave him a speculative look. Not surprising, considering how he'd left her on the boardwalk. Finally she nodded, not speaking.

Pleased she hadn't retreated he carefully ladled a cup of punch. He purposefully turned the handle toward her so she wouldn't have to touch him. She took the cup, still not saying a word.

"You aren't thinking of pouring that over my head are you? I probably deserve it for the way I acted last time." He gave her a half smile.

She looked at the punch in her hands, and then with a sideways look, said, "I considered it. But right now I'm thirsty, so I guess you're safe."

Relief she'd finally spoken had him relaxing. Then she added, "For the moment."

She looked so smug at her retort, he laughed, which drew a smile and a flash of dimple from her.

"I'll be on my guard." He took the empty punch cup, returning it to the table. The band struck up another waltz. "Miss Lawson." He gave a slight bow. "Would you honor me with this dance?"

He watched her face in the candlelight, seeing first pleasure and then doubt. Afraid if he gave her a chance she'd talk herself into saying no, he took her hand, giving her a faint tug. He suppressed a sigh of relief as she willingly followed him toward the dance floor. Her right hand settled in his left, her other hand held her skirts, as he placed his free hand at the side of her waist. Not wanting to press his luck, he allowed enough distance between them for her skirts to barely brush his boots.

They danced in silence for a few moments. Just as he'd suspected from watching her all evening, she danced well. Enjoying the effortless way she floated, he twirled her through a few quick turns. To keep her balance she gripped his hand harder and he winced.

"Oh," she exclaimed, immediately relaxing her grip. "What happened to your hand?"

"Nothing."

She gave him that skeptical look all women seemed to know when they don't like your answer.

"Just a deep scratch, but it hurts a little," he confessed.

She stroked her thumb along the back of his hand. He wondered if she knew how soothing the gesture felt.

"Is that why you haven't danced tonight?" she asked.

Ah, so she'd been watching him just as much as he'd been watching her. "You've danced a lot," he couldn't help commenting.

"Not with anyone who dances as well as you," she said with a smile as she followed him through a complex maneuver. One fine strand of silver hair had come undone and caressed the back of her neck. Her blue eyes smiled at him. Under his hand, the pale peach silk of her dress felt warm and sleek.

He wanted more. He fought the urge to tug her close, to feel her body move against his in the rhythm of the dance. Cautious, he drew her closer. She stiffened, but allowed him to slide his hand from her side to the small of her back, but she kept the few inches of air between them.

The music ended. He offered his arm and walked her toward the punch table. He couldn't dance with her again without causing comment. But he didn't want to let her go. Walking briskly without giving her a chance to stop, he skirted the punch table and within a few yards entered the maze of parked buggies and wagons. She withdrew her hand as he turned toward her.

"Mr. Westmoreland, this is improper." She sounded extremely formal.

He relaxed slightly. If he thought he'd frightened her, he would take her back to the dance floor. He smiled at her. "So why did you dance with me?"

"Because you asked."

But both of them knew she could have said no. He took a step closer, causing her to take a step backward. "Mrs. Peterson was right, you know. I'm not the type of person you should talk to."

"Really, Mr. Westmoreland." Now she sounded indignant. "I'm a grown woman. I'm capable of deciding with whom to talk."

He liked the way her back went up when challenged. He took another small step closer. Her retreat brought her shoulders up against the high side of a wagon. He wanted to hear her say his name. "Well, if you're going to talk to me, call me Wes."

She looked puzzled. "Wes Westmoreland? Surely Wes isn't your first name?"

"No, but I've always been called Wes." He didn't want to discuss why. He moved closer, her skirts brushing his boots. "What should I call you?" He wanted her to say her first name, wanted to hear clearly what he'd only half-heard Mrs. Peterson call her. Wanted a name for his thoughts, something warmer, more real than Miss Lawson.

He rested his hands on the wagon side just above her shoulders. Even in the dim light he saw the pulse in her throat beat. Close enough to feel her warmth, hear her slightly accelerated breathing. Her tongue nervously crept out to moisten her lower lip and his gut tightened. Did she taste as sweet as he suspected? Feeling his own blood pulse, his voice hardly more than a whisper, he asked, "What's your name, sweetheart?"

Chapter Five

Her knees strangely weak, Julie leaned gratefully against the high side of the wagon. Her heart raced and she couldn't seem to catch her breath. On impulse she had allowed him to lead her past the punch table. With his nearness he'd stolen her ability to think clearly.

Why was she being so jittery? They were still only yards away from the dance floor, she still heard the orchestra, the buzz of conversation.

But how could she think when he was so close? Every breath she took carried the scent of soap, tobacco, and his warm, musky indefinable male scent. The dim light cast his face into planes and angles. Would the mustache be stiff and scratchy or soft and silky? The thought of finding out made her breath catch.

"Tell me your name, sweetheart," he repeated. His mouth moved closer to hers, his low voice a velvet caress that sent shivers across her shoulders.

"Julie," she managed to whisper. "Juliette Marie."

"Julie," he repeated as if he liked the sound of her name in his mouth. He bent his head. Her heart raced with anticipation and dread. She wondered wildly if she was afraid his kiss would be just like others—or more afraid it wouldn't.

He touched his lips to hers. At the soft caress of his mouth, her eyes fluttered closed. His gentleness left her without resistance, the liquid heat of his kiss seeped through her body to lodge in the most unusual places. How could the warmth of his lips and the silkiness of his mustache make her breasts tingle? He lifted his head and she realized the soulful sigh she heard was her own.

"Peaches," he whispered under his breath. He bent his head kissing her again and the world squeaked and tilted.

"Damn," he said, putting his hands on her shoulders to steady her. Only then did she realize the wagon she leaned against had moved.

The low murmur of a mother soothing a cranky child came from inside the wagon. Holding her hand, Wes took a couple of steps backward tugging her after him. He looked over his shoulder toward the deeper shadows away from the dance floor. Slowly he turned back to her. In the dim light, his face looked harsh, predatory. The muscles in his jaw clenched. Apprehension shivered up her back. His hand tightened around hers. With a steady force he pulled her closer, his expression hard and intense.

Fear shot through her. "No," she gasped, her voice thin. He stopped. Silence hung heavy between them. After a moment, the muscle in his jaw flexed and the fierceness she'd seen in his face faded. He relaxed his stance and let go of her hand.

She fought to keep the panic from her voice. "Good night, Mr. Westmoreland." She turned to walk back to the dance floor.

"Wait." He moved to her side. "If you show up alone, someone might wonder where you've been. I'll take you back to the punch table so people will think we've just finished dancing." As he spoke, he put his hand under her elbow. He was right, so she allowed him to guide her.

Once again, he dipped a cup of punch. "Thank you for the dance, Miss Lawson." Then under his breath added, "Smile."

She manufactured a polite smile.

He gave a slight bow, then turned and walked toward the bandstand.

She put the untasted punch back on the table. Silly for her hand to shake now, when the danger was gone. When the danger was once more standing by the dark-headed woman next to the bandstand.

* * *

Julie turned over for what seemed the twentieth time. Would she ever get to sleep? She sat up, drawing her legs up under her lawn nightgown. She couldn't even blame her restlessness on sleeping in a strange room as her cousin Grace's cozy upstairs room at the back of the house had been hers ever since she'd arrived.

With a sigh, she watched the moonlight play across the floor as the breeze moved the curtains at the open window. What could she have been thinking of, letting Wes lead her away from the dance floor? Would she ever learn to resist her impulses? Back in Philadelphia she'd always resisted such suggestions to take a breath of fresh air. She shouldn't have gone, should have fought his charm, his allure. The dangerous appeal of him.

Perhaps that was the problem. Wes hadn't asked; he just kept on walking. Once again she sighed, she'd let her impulses lead her into a predicament.

The predicament wasn't so much the kiss. After all, she'd been kissed before. But his kiss had shaken her, made her shiver. She touched her tongue to her upper lip, remembering the silky caress of his mustache, the soft pressure of his mouth. Suddenly warm, she sat up and leaned against the headboard. When he'd attempted to draw her into the deep darkness, she'd recognized the way a man looks at a woman he wants. His intense gaze made her aware she was a woman, female to his male. With a groan, she kicked off the sheet.

He was a man, not a boy. That made him different from the males she knew in Philadelphia. The difference was more than a simple matter of years. His body, hard and lean, had moved easily to the music. His face was unlined except for a few crinkles at the corners of his eyes. But his eyes seemed so much older, as if his soul were somehow older than his body. She trembled, remembering again how he had looked at her when they stood between the wagons.

She tried to imagine one of her old beaux looking at her with the same intensity. She shuddered at the thought. If one of them had looked at her like that, she would have been repulsed. To her chagrin, Wes's look hadn't inspired revulsion, but a different kind of panic. Not fear exactly, but as if she were standing at the entrance to a dark, dangerous cavern where the candlelight revealed a golden treasure, tempting her to enter.

She lay down, pulling the sheet up over her. She wouldn't look, she wouldn't enter, she couldn't have anything more to do with

Mr. Wes Westmoreland. She couldn't afford to have people talking about her. She recalled Mrs. Peterson's interested glance when he left Julie at the punch table. Her stay in Durango had a purpose. The health of Cory and her unborn baby was the goal, not involvement with some man. A man who could be gone from Durango perhaps even before she was.

She'd think about tomorrow, Friday. She had to be ready to go to the smelter with Uncle Frank. She had to get up early and fix breakfast, since Clare had gone with her brother to Fort Lewis to visit until Sunday. Planning breakfast, she rolled over and snuggled into the bed. The next thing she knew, it was morning.

Julie dressed and hurried to the kitchen. By the time Uncle Frank entered she had pancakes and coffee ready. "Good morning," she said, as she poured coffee into the cups on the table.

Uncle Frank draped his suit coat over the back of the chair. "Mm, sure smells good". He ate two stacks of pancakes, finishing the second while she finished her first stack.

"Time for another cup of coffee before you hitch up the buggy?" She stood up. "I'll be ready to go out to the Rio d'Oro as soon as I get these dishes done.

Uncle Frank took his watch from his vest pocket and snapped open the cover. He nodded. "We have time." He closed the cover and returned the watch to his pocket. "I've got a new employee coming at ten this morning."

She dipped hot water from the stove boiler to the dish pan. "Who's coming?" she asked absently.

"Mr. Westmoreland."

She almost dropped a plate. Not Wes! Gathering her wits she asked, "I thought he worked for Mr. Kennedy."

Frank nodded and took another sip of coffee. "He did until last night. You left the dance with Clare and Lieutenant Sullivan before the excitement started."

"What happened?" She continued to wash dishes, hoping to appear only politely interested.

"Kennedy and Westmoreland got into an argument, Kennedy waving his arms and yelling at Westmoreland." Uncle Frank took another drink of coffee. He grinned when he put the cup down, "Sure wish I'd been close enough to hear whatever Westmoreland said to Kennedy. Made ol' Landham turn redder than a turkey gobbler."

Uncle Frank leaned back in his chair. "Seems night before last there was another accident at the Mineral King during the night shift. Westmoreland had warned Kennedy about some faulty equipment, but Kennedy paid him no mind. Westmoreland was talking to the night manager when one of the stamps broke a shoe, just liked Westmoreland warned. Luckily, no one was hurt badly."

Though she didn't understand Uncle Frank's explanation of the accident, she remembered the white bandage around Wes's hand. She picked up the towel to dry the plates. "But why did you hire him?" Why now, when she'd decided not to think about him. How could she forget the feel of his lips on hers if she saw him every day?

Uncle Frank rubbed the back of his neck and exhaled. "Guess I'm beginning to worry Landham might be right. Maybe there have been too many accidents to be just bad luck. Westmoreland seems to have a nose for trouble. Can't imagine why Landham didn't listen to him.

"Just before you got here we lost a stamper, so the Rio d'Oro had to turn away three days of work. We couldn't process what we'd already contracted to do until we repaired the stamper." He shrugged. "We can't take too much bad luck. Figure it can't hurt to give Westmoreland a chance to look around."

"Is there anything I can do?" She remembered how worried Papa had been during a bank crisis a few years ago. Even if all she did was lend a sympathetic ear. Just listening to Papa talk about his troubles had seemed to help.

Frank stood. "You're already helping with the books, that's more than plenty." He shrugged into his suit jacket. "I'll have the buggy ready in a couple of minutes."

On the buggy ride to the smelter, she worried about what she would say to Wes. If nothing else, he certainly kept her from worrying if what she had done would protect Cory. At least this was Friday. If she avoided him today, she'd have two days of peace before she had to face him again.

After all, a man like that probably had kissed lots of women. Probably by Monday he'd have forgotten about her.

* * *

At ten-thirty Wes followed Frank Lawson out of his office, not knowing if he was relieved or disappointed that Julie hadn't been in the outer office when he arrived. The company books and ledgers still sat open on the desk, but she was nowhere in sight.

He shook his head. Concentrate on business. He followed Lawson out of the office. In the smelter entry they donned one of several long dusters hanging on a row of pegs in the entry. He concentrated his attention on the job as Lawson showed him around the Rio d'Oro.

Even at first glance, Wes saw the difference between the smelters. Here at the Rio d'Oro, the equipment looked well maintained, and the men either waved or nodded as Lawson walked Wes through the smelter. A hell of a lot different from the sideways glances Kennedy got from his workers on the one occasion when Wes had seen him in the working area of his operation.

Back at office, still minus Julie, the two men took off the long dusters they'd donned as protection against the grime during their tour of the Rio d'Oro.

"What do you think?" Frank asked. He took a seat behind his desk, waving Wes into an adjacent chair.

"Nice operation. Now that you've shown me the layout, I'd like to nose around on my own."

Lawson nodded. "I've told the engineers and shift managers you'd be poking around, but they're not authorized to make any changes on your say-so. That will have to come from me."

"Fine. I don't like to keep a regular schedule, makes it harder for anyone to figure out when I might be around. I'll make rounds tomorrow and Sunday, too."

"Keep me posted."

Wes rose. Lawson followed suit to walk Wes through the outer office. Still no Julie.

"Your niece..." the words spoken without conscious intent. Damn. He searched for some way to finish the sentence. "She enjoyed the dance last night?"

"Yes. She came in with me today. Can't imagine where she got to." Lawson looked around vaguely, as if he expected her to appear. He shrugged. "Well, good luck." With a nod, Lawson headed back into his office.

Wes left the office building. He walked around the grounds, getting the geography of the smelter buildings set in his mind. Too bad the task only took part of his attention, because the rest of his concentration kept returning to Julie. Frank hadn't known where she was, and though Wes didn't either, he could guess why she hadn't been in the office. She was avoiding him.

The thought both pleased and irritated him. He hadn't looked forward to seeing her this morning, so he should be pleased she wasn't around. Every time he thought about last night he wanted to kick himself. Why had he gone out of his way to put himself in a difficult situation? Stupid to have danced with her, even more stupid to have kissed her, knowing he would eventually would want to work for Lawson.

He knew better than to get involved with someone connected with an investigation. He learned that lesson in Tucson seven years ago. His involvement with a woman had cost his partner a bullet in the arm. If a saloon girl, someone from his own background had fooled him, how easy would it be for a nice girl to fool him? But then again, why would a nice girl need to fool anyone?

Why did he feel so restless and frustrated because Julie avoided him? So what if he'd kissed her and she hadn't resisted. When he'd walked her back to the punch table she'd been calm and collected. He'd been stunned by the sudden jolt of desire, the urge to pull her deeper into the shadows, not to stop with just a kiss. She wouldn't have been so cool if she had read his mind.

He kicked a dirt clod, sending it on a lopsided roll. Hell, a girl as pretty as that must have been kissed before. All the men in Philadelphia couldn't be blind or dead. Could she really be as wholesome and naïve as she appeared? But if so, why had she been disguised in St. Louis? The contradiction nagged at a corner of his mind as he continued to walk and look and listen.

Wes waited until the night shift manager arrived before calling it a day. By then the relentless thump of the crushers, coupled with his lack of sleep the night before, had his head pounding.

"Night, Mr. Westmoreland," the night shift manager called to him as Wes mounted up to ride back to town.

Back in his room at the rear of the Double Eagle, he lay on his bed, listening to the music and laughter. The sounds reminded him of last night, of dancing with Julie, of kissing her. He cursed his memory and his body's reaction. He shifted his position, rolling over.

To distract himself, he turned his thoughts to his job, and his mammoth argument with Kennedy. The smelter accident made an argument easy. All he had to do was say I told you so. He smiled in the darkness, remembering the disbelief and outrage on Kennedy's face when he hadn't meekly subsided. It had been a real pleasure goading the arrogant bastard into an argument. As Kennedy's voice rose, Wes had been surprised to hear hints of a southern accent. He turned those southern sounds over in his mind. He'd had heard a lot of accents growing up in a saloon, from the customers to the girls themselves.

Kennedy's angry shouts reminded Wes of Rita. A Georgia cracker was what Sam had called Rita. For certain, Rita's southern accent differed from Sam's. No matter how angry or how much Sam drank, Wes never heard his father's accent or manner of speech change from its aristocratic southern lilt.

When Kennedy started shouting, Sheriff Rickman had been quick to try and quiet him down.

Wes warned himself not to jump to any conclusions just because he didn't like Kennedy himself. The fight accomplished Wes's goal. Kennedy had fired him and Lawson had hired him.

Now Wes had a chance to check out Lawson's smelter. This brought his thoughts back to Julie. He rolled over again and puffed out a breath. He suspected the image that would disturb his dreams tonight would be the same as last night. The image of a pale blonde in a peach dress.

* * *

Julie nudged the kitchen door open with her hip, her hands full with a laundry basket. For a moment she turned her face up to the warm Monday morning sun then crossed the yard toward the clothesline.

She enjoyed the rhythm, the physical actions of stooping, picking up shirts and clothes pegs, straightening, hanging the shirt on the line, then stooping for another garment. The clean, damp scent of the laundry filled her nostrils and the growing line of fluttering laundry gave evidence of her effort.

The basket empty, she straightened and sighed. Anything to help fill up the time and keep her thoughts away from the small valise, safely hidden in the bottom of her trunk. By hiding herself and the contents of the bag she could keep Cory safe. While she swore her heart was in her throat during her whole flight west, she now realized her frantic trip had been the easy part.

The inaction, just waiting, was the hardest thing she'd ever done. Much harder than she had anticipated.

She picked up the laundry basket and headed back to the kitchen. Two weeks gone, only six or so more weeks to wait and pray for the news that Cory's baby was safely born.

She entered the kitchen and set the basket aside. She and Clare maneuvered the laundry tub out the back door, dumped the water on the grass next to the garden, and set about fixing lunch.

"You still plan on going out to the smelter with Mr. Frank this afternoon?" Clare asked.

"Yes, he said he'd come back here after lunch. His meeting is supposed to be over by then."

Clare sniffed. "Probably was over before lunch, but he was afraid to come back here. Knew he'd only get the end of the soup and bread and butter on laundry day. Good excuse to have lunch with his friends at the hotel dining room."

She laughed. "You could be right."

A few minutes later Clare donned her hat and gloves and with a basket over her arm, set off to do the some shopping.

Julie washed and rinsed the bowls, spoons, and soup pot, and then hurried upstairs to change so to be ready to go to the smelter. By now she felt silly, the way she'd avoided Wes on Friday. She'd overreacted, like a scared school girl.

A few moments later she heard a horse in the yard, the creak of saddle leather as the rider dismounted. Assuming Uncle Frank had arrived she took off her apron and draped it over the back of a chair. From the corner of her eyes she saw a man's figure appear on the back porch, but he didn't come in.

"Miss Julie?" a low, mellow voice called.

Wes Westmoreland stood on the other side of the screen. Why did her heart insist on leaping when she saw him? She gripped the back of the chair.

"Miss Julie," he repeated.

"Yes?" Thank goodness her voice didn't betray her fluttering pulse.

"Your uncle sent me. He said he couldn't get away and for me to take you out to the Rio d'Oro. If you still want to go."

Did she want to go? He'd offered an excuse. She could easily say she was too busy or too tired. Anything but the truth, which was she was too scared. The thought made her straighten her back and raise her chin, remembering Cory quoting their grandmother saying the only way to overcome fear is to confront it.

She crossed the kitchen and opened the door. "Won't you come in, Mr. Westmoreland?"

"Thanks." He entered the kitchen taking off his hat. He glanced around the kitchen, giving her the oddest impression that with one look those stormy-sea green eyes had memorized the room. Shaking off the feeling, she summoned up her manners. "Please sit down. Would you like a cup of coffee?"

He cast her a sharp glance, as if she'd suggested something questionable. After a moment's hesitation he said, "Coffee would be fine," and pulled out one of the kitchen chairs to take a seat.

She poured him a cup and placed it on the table. "Cream, sugar?"

Again he looked surprised for a second before he shook his head. "This is fine."

"I'll just dry these dishes." She picked up the towel. As she dried the plates, she glanced at him out of the corner of her eye. Wes sat quietly, sipping the coffee. He took a deep breath, and then with eyes half-closed, let out a slight sound that sounded suspiciously like a sigh.

Puzzled, she looked around, finding nothing to cause his reaction. Just an empty kitchen. She put the second dry plate on top of the first before another surreptitious glance in his direction. He sat back in the chair, his long legs stretched out under the table. His denim pants and corduroy jacket seemed to hang just a little looser than fashionable. The angles and planes of his face, his lean, lithe look took on a new meaning.

"Are you hungry?" she asked not thinking. "May I get you something to eat?" she corrected politely.

This time he did look startled. He put down the cup. "Look," he started, but his stomach growled loudly. A flush rose around his ears.

She smiled. Suddenly the dangerous man became no more frightening than a tousle-headed school boy. And a woman knew how to deal with a hungry man. She was capable of dealing with him now, instead of just reacting to his exciting and disturbing presence.

"Yes, I guess you are hungry." She repressed her smile. Without giving him a chance to speak, she briskly took a loaf of bread from the breadbox and cut two slices. She took slices of roast beef from yesterday's roast, added a dab of mustard, and placed the sandwich on a plate.

Without thinking too deeply on how much she enjoyed fussing over him, she set the sandwich in front of a bemused-looking Wes Westmoreland, saying, "See if this will do for now."

Chapter Six

Wes eyed the generous sandwich in front of him. His mumbled thanks sounded embarrassed. What the hell. He was hungry. He picked up the sandwich, discovering he needed both hands. The fresh bread, tender beef, and tangy mustard tasted better than good. Sure beat the cheese and crackers of a free lunch.

"This is really good," he said after a couple of bites.

"It's just a sandwich," she demurred, but looked pleased as she refilled his coffee cup.

Wes glanced around the kitchen again while he chewed. This was probably how respectable people lived. He wondered why he didn't feel out of place. He cast a discreet glance at Julie while she put away the bread and meat, her skirt swaying as she moved. Somehow she managed to look efficient and graceful at the same time.

Maybe this was the way she treated her uncle, and just naturally did the same for him. Hell, she'd probably do the same for a stray dog. But he couldn't stop the funny feelings she'd started when she asked him to sit down and offered him coffee. When was the last time someone went to the effort to make something specifically for him? Who noticed when his cup needed refilling and poured seconds without being asked?

He finished the sandwich, and she took the empty plate. He drained the last of his coffee and started to get up, thinking he'd better get them on their way to the Rio d'Oro.

Just as he pushed away from the table, Julie set a bowl of water and a tin box on the table. "Let me see your hand."

"What?" Before he realized what she planned, she'd taken his hand and started to unwrap the soiled, untidy bandage. He tried to tug his hand from hers.

"Oh, stop," she scolded, pulling his hand back. "This won't hurt." She continued to undo the bandage, her brow furrowed in concentration.

Short of jerking his hand from her grasp and stomping out the door, he didn't know what to do. Might as well admit it, she had him buffaloed, leaving him feeling like a misbehaving school boy.

Only with her this close, her soft hands holding his, he didn't feel much like a boy. With her attention on his hand, he indulged himself and stared at her hair.

Always before she'd worn a hat or the light had been bad. But in the bright daylight of the kitchen, her hair reminded him of molten silver. She'd pinned it into an elaborate silken knot, but fine wisps escaped at her temples and down the back of her neck. Would it be warm if he were to reach out and touch? If he pulled out the pins, would it tumble down her back to her waist? Or even farther?

"Oh, my."

Her exclamation pulled him from his reverie. She stared at the jagged scab that bisected his palm. Embarrassed, he started to stand.

She caught his hand, forcing him to remain seated. "This needs cleaning." She opened the tin box and extracted a wad of cotton wool, a clean bandage roll, and a bottle of disinfectant.

Holding his hand over the bowl, she washed away the dried blood with a swab of the cotton wool. The sight of her small white teeth caught her bottom lip in concentration, and the gentleness with which she bathed his hand made his chest tight. He wanted to reassure her somehow, but his tongue seemed stuck to the roof of his mouth. He wanted to hold her, to comfort her, as if she were the one who was hurting.

Water splashed in the bowl. "Drat. I got your sleeve wet," she said. "Take off your coat so I can finish this."

Her command hit him like a bucket of cold water. How in hell could he take off his coat without letting her see his gun? Nestled under his left arm, the .32 was so much a part of him he usually didn't notice. Now the revolver seemed to scorch his side, reminding him of his job. Reminding him she was a lady and he was a saloon kid who made his living by pretense and deceit.

"Forget it." He stood, the chair scraping across the floor. His voice sounded hard, angry, but he forced himself not to care.

A look of shock crossed her face. "But your hand!"

"It's fine." He grabbed the bandage roll from beside the tin box. "I'll go hitch up the buggy." He seized his hat and jammed it on his head. Swift steps took him outside. He heard the screen door bang after him.

But no matter how fast he walked, or how he cursed the bandage he wound around his hand he couldn't get away from the knowledge that drove him from the kitchen. In spite of the differences between them he burned with the knowledge.

The knowledge he wanted her.

She must have been watching out of the window, for as soon as he pulled the buggy to a stop she came down the back steps. She'd donned a straw hat with trailing ribbons and carried a pair of gloves. He alighted from the buggy and waited for her. She appeared cool and collected, as if he'd never been rude to her twice now. Apparently good breeding and good manners allowed a lady to ignore the lack of breeding and bad manners of a less than respectable man.

Wordlessly, he held out his hand to help her into the buggy. Without meeting his gaze, she allowed him to take her elbow to help her into the buggy. She kept her eyes straight ahead, her hands folded in her lap, as he walked around and climbed aboard and took up the rein. He called giddy up to the horse. The buggy rolled out to the street and turned toward the smelter.

He drove south along Boulevard, past the scattered homes of Durango's moneyed people. When he crossed G Street, she turned toward him. "Why are we still on the Boulevard? Uncle Frank usually turns west on G street, and then goes down Main."

"We can take G all the way." He didn't look in her direction, hoping the answer would satisfy her.

She shot a glance at him. He could practically see her thinking, and damned if she didn't figure it out. "Are you avoiding Main Street?"

He didn't answer. He pulled the horse to a stop at the next corner, waiting for another buggy to cross in front of them.

"Well?" Her pique at being ignored obvious in her tone.

"Well, what?" he snapped back.

"Are you avoiding Main Street?"

He turned and glared at her. How could she be smart enough to figure out what he was doing, but not see the why of it?

"So what if I am?" He called to the horse, and took them forward again. After a moment he exhaled deeply. "Look, I'm doing you a favor."

"A favor?"

"I may work for your uncle," he said with exasperated patience, "but it won't do your reputation any good to be seen with me any more than you have to. No point in going down Main Street for the whole town to see." He glanced over to see the astonished look on her face.

"But, it's too late," she blurted out. Her fingers went too her lips, like closing the barn door after the horse got out.

"What do you mean by too late?"

"I mean it's too late," she said as if explaining to a simpleton. "Any number of people saw us at the drug store drinking sarsaparilla, and the whole town saw us at the dance."

"That's my point." He purposely used the same talking to a simpleton tone she had. "People have seen us together. But since I work for Frank, they'll pass it off. Besides, we only danced together one time." He remembered how gracefully she'd moved to the music, how sweet she'd tasted when he'd kissed her. Something must have shown on his face, for she suddenly blushed and looked away.

Julie looked straight ahead as the heat of her flush fade. His Stetson shaded his eyes, and he seemed totally absorbed in driving the buggy. But his green eyes had stared at her mouth, compelling her to remember the soft brush of his mustache, the warmth of his lips on hers. Much better for him to suspect she'd been embarrassed by the reminder of propriety.

They completed the rest of the drive in silence. The buggy reached the edge of town, rattled across the bridge and headed up the hill toward the smelter. Even from here she heard the low, steady thump of the stamps in the air. Air that carried the acrid smell of refining, a bitter, dry metallic taste that lingered on the tongue.

As always, the immense size of the smelter amazed her. The many levels had been built right into the side of the mountain, so gravity moved the ore down from level to level as it was processed.

At the top of the long, winding drive, Wes pulled the buggy to a stop next to the office. He got out, came around, offering his hand to help her. She'd carried her gloves to give her hands something to do, and now the warm, rough strength of his hand stirred a strange feeling in the pit of her stomach. No wonder Gran had insisted a lady should always wear gloves. This man scrambled her thoughts with his touch.

With a polite thank you, she headed for the office. She set out the books, taking satisfaction in her neat columns of figures. She'd found no major errors, just the kind of mistakes that come from sloppy or poor work. Her guess was that the books would prove exactly as Uncle Frank had said money down a little, but the smelter in good shape financially. She began to add the column, but soon her pencil faltered. She remembered the way Wes had stomped out of the kitchen, his exasperation about being seen together, the way he'd reminded her of their kiss without saying a word. Were all men this complex?

Well, it didn't matter. She picked up the pencil. She had worked with men at the Bradley Center for years and never became involved or interested in anyone of them. Perhaps that was her problem. Maybe Wes intrigued her because he obviously lived his life independent and free.

Since fleeing Philadelphia she felt as if her own life was in limbo. Being on her own in Durango made her realize that up to now she'd been living the life that Papa and Cory and others had expected of her. Even here, her life revolved around protecting her pregnant sister by guarding the information hidden in the carpet bag. While she would do the same thing again, the whole episode was making her wonder and think about what she wanted from her life.

She had to keep her attention where it belonged. She definitely had too much else to be concerned with to spend her time worrying or thinking about a man.

She mentally crossed another day off the calendar of waiting for word of the baby. One day at a time. Each day closer to success.

* * *

At four o'clock Thursday morning, Wes tied his horse to the hitching rail outside the Rio d'Oro office. The full moon hung low in the southern sky, casting enough light to make the ride from town easy. A good time for him to poke around unnoticed. The night shift workers would be beginning to think about going home in a couple of hours when dawn and the day shift would arrive.

He checked the handle of the office door. Locked, as it should be. He walked a few paces and checked the door of the chemist laboratory next door. This door, too, was locked. Nothing suspicious here. This near the end of the shift, the chemist had likely gone down to check the final assay of the smelting process.

Once he knew the office area was secure, Wes walked around the corner and looked down the hillside. From this angle, the smelter looked like a hodge-podge of buildings, all stuck together as they straggled down the slope. An assortment of roof ridges marked the various areas within, punctuated here and there by vents and chimneys. Each ridge sported a series of large water barrels to guard the shingle roof against sparks from the furnace. The barrels gave the whole night-shadowed smelter a crenellated look, like a series of medieval castle walls.

His gaze drifted beyond the smelter to where the river lay like a silver-gray ribbon. Beyond that, the town of Durango showed as clumps of thick darkness. A few points of light shone here and there, early risers or those late to bed. Perhaps one of those lights marked a saloon where a little boy was just going to bed. He'd been fourteen and running messages for Wells Fargo before he ever saw the sun come up. How could a man long for an ordinary life if he never had one?

With a snort of disgust at his odd thoughts, he turned, intending to walk down through the smelter. He'd check with the chemist and the foreman about the night's work. But as he turned, something not quite right caught his eye. He studied the shingled roofs.

There. One of the fire barrels. A dark line streaked away from the bottom of the barrel. He swore and hurried inside the smelter.

Two minutes later, he made his way along the roof ridge, cursing his boots' tendency to slip on the shingles. He reached the barrel and confirmed what he'd guessed. Instead of being full, only five inches of water remained. Carefully crouching, he put his hand to the small gouge near the bottom. Water still seeped from the barrel, leaving the trail he'd spied from above.

Moving with care to avoid the risk of a fall, he checked the other four barrels on this section. Each barrel bore the same gouge near the bottom. All but the last few inches of water had run out.

* * *

Early morning sun shone through office windows, where Frank Lawson leaned against the front of his desk, arms folded, legs crossed at the ankles. Only the rapid, dark puffs of smoke from his cigar betrayed any agitation.

Wes paced back and forth in the confined area as he continued. "I'd guess he used a railroad spike. All it would take would be a couple of blows with a hammer. Hell, he could have used dynamite and nobody would have heard anything over the noise of the stamps." He turned. "He didn't have to worry about someone hearing anything, only about being seen. Since the moon came up after twelve, it probably happened earlier."

"Sit down," Lawson said in exasperation. "You did well to find the problem."

Wes ran his hand through his hair. He stopped pacing and flopped into the armchair next to the desk. "But I should have prevented it."

"How? By standing guard twenty-four hours a day? I'll be happy to settle for the fact you discovered it and took care of it. You posted a fire watch. Arranged to have the barrels fixed." Lawson looked thoughtful. "We've had a lot of trouble with vandals in Durango this summer. Week before you got here they stole the clapper out of the bell in the Methodist church, and before that they altered the time on the clock on the Stratler hotel.

"At least Julie isn't here to be upset by all this." Lawson glanced at him, adding, "Clare wasn't feeling well, so Julie stayed with her."

He pulled his watch from his vest pocket. "Think I'll go visit Kennedy at the Mineral King. He should be there by now."

Wes nodded. Lawson had taken the news calmly, listened, and was already planning. The smelter owner's reaction reminded him of his real boss, Dan Challenge. Both men possessed an outward calm that hid a fierce determination. His respect for Lawson increased. He suspected many people underestimated the mild-looking Frank Lawson. He'd better not make the same mistake himself.

After a thorough check of all areas of the smelter, he returned to the office. He hung the duster on a peg, and walked outside. Leaning against the hitching rail, he squinted at the sun, now practically overhead. He pulled his tobacco pouch from his pocket and started to build a smoke.

Lawson rode up just as he finished his cigarette. With the stiff movement of a man who usually traveled by buggy, Lawson dismounted. Wes took the reins and tied them to the rail.

"Well?' Wes asked.

Lawson took off his bowler hat and wiped the hat band and his forehead with his handkerchief. "Let's go into the chemist's office. There's a pump there and I could use a drink of water."

He followed Lawson inside suspecting Lawson's indirect comment meant bad news. After both men drank a tin cup of water, Lawson leaned against a windowsill. Wes leaned against the work counter opposite.

"You aren't going to like this," Lawson said.

"Tell me something I don't already know."

"The fire barrels at Landham's mill were vandalized last night just like ours."

"Damn."

"Exactly." Lawson took another drink. "Kennedy says since both smelters were vandalized and since no harm was done, it was probably the kids who stole the clapper and altered the clock."

"So there's no way to prove if this was some kid's prank, or an attempt to set you up for another accident." He put the cup back on the hook by the sink. "But why only those four barrels? Why not all of them? Doesn't make sense unless something interrupted him. It's a pretty chancy way to try and damage the Rio d'Oro unless he also planned to start a fire. If that was his plan, what kept him from doing it?" Double damn. He was no closer to finding an answer and fixing the problem. He rubbed the back of his neck.

"Don't look so glum," Lawson interrupted Wes's thoughts. "You did your job. Nothing happened that couldn't be fixed." He sighed and returned his cup to its hook by the pump. "Go back to town and get some rest."

The men walked outside, Wes heading for the hitching rail and his horse.

"Wes," Lawson called.

He turned to find Lawson studying him with a serious expression, as if trying to see something more than just his employee.

"Don't play up this incident, should Julie ask you about it. She worries too much sometimes."

Ah, that explained the look. Lawson had been considering him not just an employee, but as a man in regards to Julie. "I'll tell her to ask you."

Lawson nodded, apparently satisfied.

Wes swung into the saddle. "If you need me before tomorrow, send a message."

* * *

Julie closed the office door behind her. She unpinned her hat and put it, along with her gloves and reticule in the bottom drawer of the desk. The books sat where she'd left them Monday afternoon, untouched during yesterday's excitement. Of all the days to miss! She'd heard everything secondhand during supper. Uncle Frank had glossed over the trouble, referring to it as vandalism, not sabotage. But she wasn't a fool. According to the rumors she'd heard at the grocery store, the question of why the barrels had been attacked remained unresolved.

Midmorning, the sound of hoof beats drew her attention from the column of figures. She stood to glance out the dirty window in time to see Wes dismount. Her heart did the same silly double-flutter it always seemed to do at his appearance. He wore what she now thought of as his work clothes, denim pants, tan corduroy coat. He still wore a bandage around his hand.

If Uncle Frank wouldn't talk, she could get information from Wes. After all, he'd found the leaking barrels. Before she could change her mind, or listen to her inner voice reminding her of her plan to have nothing to do with him, she swept out of the office.

The bright sun caused her to shade her eyes with her hand. "Good morning, Mr. Westmoreland," she called.

Wes dismounted. Tying the reins to the hitching rail gave him a moment to compose himself before he touched the brim of his hat. "Morning, Miss Julie." Every time he saw her, she got more beautiful. Maybe the plain, dark-green skirt and shirtwaist made her look too slim, but he didn't mind.

"I understand there was some trouble here yesterday."

"You should ask your uncle about that."

Even frowning, she looked good to him. "Uncle Frank told you not to say anything," she accused. The answer must have shown on his face.

She muttered "men" under her breath as if it was a curse.

He hoped she asked the question to the world in general, because he sure as hell didn't know the answer to that. Apparently, she saw that thought on his face too, for she looked at him like he was a simpleton. After a moment she gave a ladylike sniff. "Oh, come inside, it's too hot to stand out here," she said, and turned back to the office.

Thinking himself a fool, he followed. Sure as shooting she wasn't ready to quit asking questions, and he had no answers to give her. Her annoying habit of being able to read his face didn't help much either. But he couldn't bring himself to pass up the chance of her company.

The office seemed overcast after the bright sun. "Frank says you have the books up to date," he commented, hoping to get her on a new subject.

She took a seat behind the desk and waved him to the chair. "I also know enough to understand them. While the Rio d'Oro is in satisfactory financial shape, she can't afford too many accidents."

Wes nodded in agreement, keeping his expression bland. "Miss Julie, you'll still have to get any information about yesterday from your uncle."

Chapter Seven

Julie eyed Wes, his casual pose contrasted with the vexation inside her. He leaned back in the chair with his hat resting on his knee, his mustache almost camouflaging a faint smile. Though he'd been nothing less than polite in the last few minutes, she knew she would get no additional information from him. Uncle Frank, at any rate, would be pleased with Wes's behavior.

At least he seemed willing to talk to her today. Maybe, she thought dryly, because there was no one to see them. She gestured to the books. "Am I right, the key to whether or not a smelter makes money is in the assay? That's where you decide how much to charge the owner of the ore, right?"

Wes nodded. "The assay tells you how much gold or silver or whatever will smelt out of a ton of ore."

"I thought you just picked up nuggets of gold from the ground."

Wes laughed, white teeth flashing. "That's placer gold."

He suddenly looked younger, more carefree than Julie remembered. She felt her own lips smile in return, wanting to keep the unexpected cheer on his face.

He continued, "You can still find loose nuggets in some places in California. Now most gold comes from mining, and that means you have to separate the gold from the rock it's in." He hesitated a moment, as if debating with himself while he rotated the Stetson resting on his knee. "If you want to come next door to the chemist's, I could show you a little more about smelting. If you have time," he added.

She looked down at the books and ledgers stacked on the desk. As she'd worked on the books, she'd become interested in what exactly went on in the Rio d'Oro smelter. Here was a perfect opportunity to learn more.

"Lead the way, Mr. Westmoreland." She crossed toward the door he held open for her. Be honest. Even if she'd had no interest in smelting, she'd choose the company of this intriguing man over the dry, old books. Perhaps sharing time with him wasn't the wisest choice. Her tendency to act impulsively had gotten her into more than one scrape as a child, but those same impulses had given her some wonderful childhood adventures whose memories she still treasured. With a smile, she followed Wes next door

"The chemist won't mind if I show you his office," he said. He opened the door to the chemist's office and she went inside.

The air had the ubiquitous smelter scent of dust, but overlaid here with strong chemical smells. A table filled the center of the room and a workbench ran around two walls. Both held a clutter of instruments and flasks. She recognized scales, mortars and pestles but the rest was a mystery. Most surprising was the pump and sink, and what appeared to be a small oven of some sort. In one corner stood a desk littered with papers.

Wes hung his hat on the back of the chair by the desk and rummaged through the papers. He unearthed an open box.

"This is what the ore looks like." He pointed to a black and white rock. "This is silver ore, the black's the silver. This yellow-looking rock is pyrite and has gold. And this," he handed her a glittering bluish-gray rock, "is galena."

She turned the sample over in her hand. "But it doesn't look like anything."

"It contains both silver and gold. They're so mixed in with the rock you can't see the individual minerals. Smelting separates the minerals from the tailing. Tailings are the part you don't want, what's left over," he added.

"The trick," he continued, "is to find out what minerals are in the ore. The ore from each mine is different. The chemist has to figure out which mineral and how much the ore contains. Then he decides which chemicals are needed in the soup to separate the gold or silver from the rock." He gestured to the rows of flasks on the workbench. "Because the chemist makes up a new soup for each load of ore, he's usually called the witch-doctor by the workers."

"What's the soup?" Perhaps he wasn't so different from other men she'd known. She certainly recognized the signs of a man showing off his knowledge to impress a girl. In this case, she didn't have to feign interest to be polite. Her predicament was the man interested her just as much as the topic. She put the rock back in the box and walked over to the table in the center of the room.

Wes put the box back on the desk. "The soup is the blend of chemicals mixed with the crushed ore to extract the metal from the rock."

He joined her at the worktable, but instead of facing the table, he turned and leaned against it, so he faced her. To keep from staring at him, she brushed at the dust on the table. "So, Uncle Frank was lucky his bookkeeper quit instead of his chemist."

"Right. After your uncle, and the engineers who oversee the mechanical equipment, the chemist is the next most important man."

She cast a glance at the man beside her, wondering where he would put himself in the order of importance. She'd suspected he tended to underrate himself. Obviously, his knowledge of smelting was fairly extensive. "So how does one assay the ore?"

He turned and drew a small mortar full of gray-looking dust and a large flask toward him. "First the ore is reduced to fine particles. That's what the stamps do. They're what's making the constant noise." His words made her aware of the muffled thumps she'd grown so accustomed to hearing; she hadn't consciously heard the noise until he mentioned the stamps.

He stirred the dust with his fingertip. "This is silver ore. An assay is a matter of percentages. How many ounces of gold or silver per ton or ore. The witch-doctor keeps careful track of all the weights and percentages." He pulled a small, shallow pan from the confusion on the table, and uncorking the flask, poured a scant half-cup of the contents into the pan.

She had never seen anything like what came from the flask. The liquid was shiny and silver, and of all things, looked heavy. "What is it? It looks almost alive." Instead of flowing thinly into the bottom of the pan, the liquid bunched together, more like the consistency of cold molasses.

"It's quicksilver. Mercury." He tilted the bowl, and the silver dollop flowed easily around the pan, always staying in one clump. "You mix it with the crushed ore." He dumped a handful of the gray-looking dust on top of the quicksilver and stirred the mixture with a wooden spoon.

"Looks like you're making mud pies."

Wes looked at her curiously.

"You know," she explained, "mud pies." She made patty-cake motions with her hands. "When you were little? Making pies made out of dirt and water?"

He shook his head, a half smile on his face.

Once again, as she had over the sarsaparilla, she wondered about the childhood of this man. "I made about the best mud pies, even if I did have to go to my room without supper once because I got my Sunday pinafore all muddy."

He smiled, making her feel very distant from that little girl in braids and ruffled pinafore. "Maybe you better stand back. I don't want to get you in trouble again."

Then he'd better stop smiling. The smile made his green eyes twinkle and his mustache twitch up at the corners. Anything that reminded her of his kiss was trouble. "Now what?" she asked to distract her thoughts.

"We separate the quicksilver and silver from the ore." He did this by pouring the mixture through a wire screen. "The amalgam, the quicksilver combined with the silver particles from the ore, goes into the pan. Here," he handed her a handkerchief sized square of soft leather, "take this and wet it."

She carried the square to the sink and worked the pump to thoroughly wet the soft leather. She twisted it to get rid of the excess water and returned to the table. Wes took the cloth from her. He draped the leather across another shallow pan and poured the amalgam into the cloth. He picked up the corners and twisted them together, gathering the mixture into a lump in the center of the cloth, and held it over the shallow pan. "Now, watch."

In fascination, Julie watched his strong, brown hands squeeze down the neck of the leather bag.

"Oh," she gasped. Small beads of mercury began to appear through pores in the cloth. As he continued to squeeze, the quicksilver droplets splashed to the pan below, each individual drop drawn immediately to another to make a silver puddle.

After a final squeeze, he untwisted the leather bag. "Don't ask me why, but the mercury goes through the wet leather and leaves the silver behind." He laid out the damp leather. In the center of the wrinkled cloth lay a tablespoon of bright, shiny grains of silver.

"You're a magician," she exclaimed.

He shook his head, embarrassed. "The mercury's the magician."

"Doesn't it get on your hands?" She glanced at his hands, remembering his wounded palm.

Wes shook his head. "Just leaves an oily coating on your skin." He held up his right hand, the one without the bandage, the palm looking greasy. A few steps took him to the pump. She resisted the impulse to help him. Obviously, he didn't need her help as he unwound the bandage, washed his hands with soap and water and rewound the bandage. He turned from the sink and picked up his hat.

A stab of disappointment went through Julie at the realization the lesson was over. He gestured to the door, and they went back outside. She cast about for something to keep him from depositing her back in her office with nothing to do but think about him. "Is that all there is to smelting?"

"It's more complicated on a large scale." He stroked his mustache, as if debating, before going on. "If you think your uncle won't mind, I could walk you through the mill."

"I'm sure he won't mind. In fact, he said something about showing me around when he had time. Where do we start?"

Wes crossed the office and opened the door for her, wondering how big of a mistake he was making. He already liked being with her too much. But what the hell, what could happen just showing her around the smelter?

"This way," he gestured for her to walk around the corner. From the corner of the chemist buildings they could look down at the smelter.

"I'll give you the layout from here. Once inside it's too noisy for much conversation." He gave a brief description of crushers, stamps, vanes, amalgamating pans, and settling tanks the ore passed through on its way down the smelting process. He pointed out the last building, "That's where the steam boilers are. They supply the power to run the whole show."

"Hope I can keep everything straight."

"Don't worry, it'll make more sense after you've seen the equipment." He turned back toward the office and she followed.

"Where did you learn so much about smelting?" she asked as they went back into the main office.

"I worked in a smelter for a couple of months when I was seventeen. I did odd jobs, helped the witch-doctor, worked some with the engineer. Just general labor." Working in the smelter had been his first undercover assignment for Wells Fargo. And just as Dan Challenge had told him, a kid could poke his nose into anything and everything without arousing suspicion. Back in those days, investigations had been fun and exciting, more than just a job.

She gave him a skeptical look. "You remember all this from that long ago?"

He shrugged. "I've spent the past two weeks in Durango smelters. Helps the memory."

In the hallway, Wes took a duster from the peg and held it out. As she turned and slipped her arms into the duster, he leaned forward slightly, taking a surreptitious deep breath. Damn, but she smelled good, all soap and a white floral scent. He pulled a handkerchief from his inside coat pocket. "You might want to use this as a scarf, it's clean."

Smiling her thanks, she folded the bandanna into a triangle tying the ends under her chin. Would her hair leave its scent on the handkerchief, he wondered? Then cursed for hoping so.

He hoped he wasn't making another mistake by taking her through the smelter. Smelting was dirty and loud, but she seemed interested and rather impressed by his knowledge. Now there was an odd thought, a girl impressed by knowledge. He'd known women impressed by money, power, a man's speed with a gun, or even by his ability to drink. He couldn't remember when a woman had ever been impressed by what he knew.

"Let's go." He took her elbow, just to help her on the rough flooring of course, and led the way into the smelter.

Once inside the smelter, they stopped on a railed platform. He moved to stand half in front of her, partially shielding her against the din and dust. The high ceilings and huge, open barn-like structure echoed with the thump of the stamps and the rumble of the crushed ore moving from one level to another. Dust hung in the air like a faint mist, making half-seen haloes around the lights. On the top level, ore poured down a chute and into the Blake jaw crushers, which turned the raw ore into fist-sized chunks.

"Crusher!" he shouted. "Big rocks into little ones!" He pointed to the chute where the ore rumbled down to the next level twenty feet below.

She nodded, her blue eyes open wide as she watched. Several men armed with metal poles patrolled the crusher, making sure any jam was quickly cleared. Wes nodded to the men and they nodded back. "All right?" he asked Julie. Now that she'd seen and felt the dirt and the heavy, almost physical pounding of the noise, he wondered if she'd change her mind.

"Do you want to go on?"

"Oh, yes!" she answered, and flashed him a smile.

He guided her down the stairway leading to the next level. Here the stamps reduced the ore to dust. "Stamps!" He watched while she studied the line of stamps, each with five vertical pulleys and cams as high as a man's head, raising and lowering five piston-shaped stamps in a non-sequential order. On a gangway in front of the constant perpendicular motion of the pulleys and cams, several men walked back and forth, checking the dies into which the pistons pounded the ore to sand. The pulverized ore ran down chutes toward the next level down. "The whole thing is so big," she shouted over the constant thumps. She glanced down at the next level, where workmen walked between rows of waist-high tables.

"Down there are the vanning tables," Wes told her. She nodded, seemingly content to stand and watch. Her gaze went back to the stamps in front of them.

"What's that man doing?" She gestured to one of the men, who stopped in front of one stamp and pulled a hand lever.

"Hanging the stamp!"

Again she nodded, seemingly willing to wait until shouting wasn't necessary for a complete explanation.

With a lever, the workman had disabled the cam, holding the stamp in the raised position while he bent to inspect the die into which the stamp smashed. What was the problem? He touched Julie's arm with a stay-here motion, and then ducked under the railing onto the gangway.

As he approached, the workman stood. "What is it?" Wes shouted. He recognized the workman as Reynolds, one of the shift leaders.

"Don't rightly know! Just don't sound right somehow!" He scratched at his head in puzzlement, threatening to tip his hat off the back of his head as he stared at the stamp. After a moment he again bent to his knees. A high-pitched metallic screech, barely audible over the steady thump of the other stamps, jerked Wes's gaze up.

Quickly, he searched for the origin of the odd noise. Again the distressed screech. Reynolds stretched his hand under the stamp to inspect the die.

Head cocked to the side trying to pinpoint the noise, Wes searched back and forth. There! The cam. A hair-line fracture. With a metallic shriek the crack began to widen. Swearing, he grabbed Reynolds's collar and pulled just as the cam broke in two, the lever flying back.

With a yell of indignation, Reynolds fell backward. His bulk slammed into Wes, knocking him to his knees. Shouts of panic rang in his ears along with the thumps of his heart. Panicked, Reynolds scrambled back, knocking Wes off balance. His legs slipped sideways over the edge of the walkway. Swearing, he grabbed for the lip of the walkway. His fingers brushed the wood. As he fell toward the floor below he heard Julie scream his name.

Chapter Eight

Horrified, Julie watched Wes fall toward the vanning tables on the level below. For an endless second the world stood still. She clutched the railing, a second scream stuck in her throat as he thudded on to one of the tables and slid heavily to the floor. He lay motionless, like a discarded rag doll.

Men yelled. Whistles sounded. The heavy throb of the machinery broke rhythm. Her mouth dry and her heart thumping, she hurried down the stairs. At the next level, she ducked under the railing and ran onto the work floor. Several men already clustered about Wes. He lay on the dirty floor between two separating tables.

As she hurried over one workman took Wes's shoulder to turn him on his back.

"No!" she shouted. "Don't move him. You could hurt him worse."

The man looked at her with obvious disdain, whether at her suggestion or over the fact a woman told him what to do, she didn't know, didn't care.

"I'm a nurse," she exaggerated as she edged the man out of the way and knelt beside Wes.

Wes lay on his right side, arm under his chest, his back toward her. With trepidation, she laid her hand along the angle of his jaw and neck. Her fingers felt his pulse and she saw his chest rise and fall. He groaned. For what seemed the first time in minutes, her heart started beating and she let out a sigh of relief. An appalling urge to weep clogged her throat. She bit her bottom lip fighting back tears.

Voices around her shouted questions, suddenly loud in the silence. The machinery had stopped.

"He all right?"

"What the hell happened?"

"He fell. Fell from the stamps."

Concentrating on Wes, Julie summoned all she'd learned by listening to Cory and Mark talk over the day's events at the clinic. She carefully felt down Wes's arm. The muscles under the corduroy jacket felt normal. She quickly ran her hands down his denim-clad legs, ignoring a surprised snort from one of the workmen.

"Nothing seems broken," she announced. She ran her hand over his scalp and discovered a large lump behind his left ear. Just then he groaned again and rolled onto his back.

His eyes stayed shut. His face looked paler than the coating of gray dust that covered half his face where it'd been in contact with the floor. His hair fell over his forehead. The corners of his mouth turned down in pain, mustache drooping.

She wanted him to wake up and be all right. At the same time she hoped he'd remain unconscious to escape the pain while they moved him, until they could get him to a doctor.

A commotion brought her head up. Several men moved back, making way in the crowded area between the tables. Uncle Frank appeared.

"Are you all right?" Uncle Frank's gaze swept over her as he went down on one knee beside Wes. "How about him?"

"Nothing seems broken," she said again. "I'm fine." Thank goodness her voice sounded steady.

Uncle Frank looked at the men who had gathered. "What happened?"

"One of the stamps blew."

"Saved Reynolds's life. Pulled him out of the way just in time."

"Think he hit his head."

Uncle Frank waved them silent. "Tommy, go for the doctor. Hope he's in town today, not off somewhere. We'll move Wes to my house. You can tell the doctor to meet us there." A young man nodded, turned and left.

Thank goodness Uncle Frank was here. She took off her scarf, actually Wes's bandanna, to wipe the gritty gray dust from his face, away from his eyes and mouth.

"Atkins," Uncle Frank continued. "Get the engineer. He went home for lunch. I want to know how long we'll be down." Another man nodded and left the crowd.

Uncle Frank turned back to look at her. "Can you see to taking Wes home? I'd better stay here."

"Of course." Thank goodness Uncle Frank saw her capable of handling the task. She didn't intend to leave Wes in any case.

"Arneal, Beach, you two help Julie get Wes home. She'll tell you what to do."

Two men moved forward. Julie was relieved to see neither of them were the man she'd reprimanded earlier.

"What ya want us to do?" the tall one asked.

"Is there a wagon?"

The short man scratched his head. "Reckon we can use the one the witch-doctor uses."

Following her directions, the men were surprisingly gentle as they moved Wes to a plank and carried him back up the stairs. He moaned and mumbled once in a while, but his eyes remained shut. She walked behind, praying he'd stay unconscious.

They emerged into the sunlight and the men loaded Wes in the back of a wagon. One of the men helped her in beside Wes while the other one climbed into the driver's seat. Someone else handed her the bandanna, now damp. The wagon rumbled off.

She used the damp bandanna to wipe the perspiration from Wes's forehead. "Don't worry," she crooned, stroking the damp cloth over his eyes and down his cheeks. "Everything will be all right. We'll get you home and the doctor will be there. You'll be fine."

His head rolled back and forth. He shifted slightly, and groaned, his hand moving to his side. She kept up the reassuring patter as she continued to bathe his face.

His eyes flickered open. "W-What..."

"You fell. You're all right," she reassured him, praying it was true.

"Hurts," he mumbled, and shifted again. His right hand went to his left side. Wondering if she'd missed an injury, she pushed back his corduroy coat. Something shiny and metal in leather rested under his arm. She frowned in puzzlement. What in the world? Then she gasped. A gun!

His hand touched the gun and with a sigh his hand slid back to his side. For a moment he lay quietly as though reassured by the gun's presence. Then his pain-clouded eyes flickered open and sought her face. "Julie?"

She'd worry about the gun later. "I'm here," she answered, taking his hand. His hand closed around hers, his grip limp.

The wagon turned, making Wes bounce. He flinched and momentarily tightened his grip on her hand. Sweat beaded his forehead and she gently wiped his forehead with the bandanna.

When the wagon turned again she glanced up, surprised to see they were almost at the Lawson house. Ahead she saw Tommy jump up from the front step and run toward them.

"Doctor's here,' he shouted.

She breathed out a sigh of relief.

Tommy waved his arm toward the driveway, "Doc said to take him round back." The driver waved and turned into the driveway that led around to the back of the Lawson house. The wagon bumped to a halt.

Tommy helped Julie down from the wagon. Under the doctor's supervision, the men unloaded Wes.

"Where do you want him," the doctor called over his shoulder as she hurried ahead to open the back door.

"In here." Julie showed the doctor the small bedroom at the back of the house, just off the kitchen. The room would have belonged to the cook, had the Lawson household employed one. She glanced anxiously at Wes as the two men carried him past. His eyes were shut tight and his jaw clenched against the pain of movement. A moment later they placed Wes on the small quilt-covered bed.

"Help me get him undressed, boys," the doctor ordered. Behind him, Wes moaned as the short man pulled off one of Wes's boots. The doctor looked over his shoulder to where she stood in the doorway. "Bring hot water and some bandages if you have them," the doctor ordered. He closed the door, leaving her alone in the kitchen.

She hurried to dip warm water from the boiler. The doctor would probably call on her once Wes was decent if he needed her help. A few moments later, the two men came out of the room.

"Don't worry, Miss," the tall one said. "Wes will probably be fine. He's just busted up a bit."

The men carried the basin of water and the bandages back into the room and closed the door. She wondered what her brother-in-law doctor would say to the medical term "busted up a bit." Sounded more like a vase than a man, and she stifled an impulse to giggle or cry. She sank gratefully into a chair and sent up a quick prayer Wes would be all right.

A few minutes later the two men came out. She offered them coffee, which they accepted, and just as she filled their mugs, Uncle Frank arrived.

"How is he?" Uncle Frank asked, door banging behind him. The door to the cook's room opened and the doctor came out.

"Well?' Uncle Frank asked.

The doctor rubbed his chin. "He's got two broken ribs and he was knocked out. He may have internal injuries, but I can't tell for sure." The doctor heaved a sigh and plopped into one of the kitchen chairs. She placed a cup of coffee in front of him.

"Thanks," he said and took a sip. He leaned back in the chair. "I'll be back round about supper time to check again. I think he'll be all right, but we'll know for sure by then. Just let him rest for the time being."

The remainder of the afternoon passed in a kind of daze for Julie as people came and went. While she kept busy at the back of the house, she sent Clare to answer the front door.

Staying in the kitchen, she made what seemed like gallons of coffee and stacks of sandwiches for the numerous people who passed through the kitchen. She fed Tommy and the men from the Rio d'Oro. The doctor was only halfway through his sandwich when he got a message and left, sandwich in one hand, medical bag in another. Sometime during the afternoon Sheriff Rickman and Landham Kennedy dropped by to talk with Uncle Frank.

As the lady of the house in Aunt Marie s absence, she should answer the door. But the steady stream of Uncle Frank's friends and neighbors were simply curious. If she answered the door they wanted to come in and talk, but as the girl, Clare could simply answer, yes, a man had been hurt, and, no, he wasn't dead, and send them on their way.

Even Mrs. Peterson came by, "Just to see if you need any help, my dear."

In any case, she had to keep an eye on Wes as the doctor said, and she couldn't be doing that and running to the front door all the time. At first she checked on the sleeping Wes every five minutes or so, but as he seemed not to get worse, she was reassured. He lay quietly, and as the afternoon wore on, his gray coloring faded as his skin took on its more natural tone.

* * *

The heat of the day dissipating with the setting sun. Julie stood on the back porch, savoring a moment of calm. Behind her, the house was quiet for the first time today. On the doctor's return visit he'd pronounced Wes out of danger.

The sound of carriage wheels interrupted the evening stillness. A dark horse drew a simple, black carriage into the backyard. A woman in a somber black dress stepped down. She looked familiar for some reason. The woman walked toward her.

"Good evening," Julie said politely when the woman was close enough.

"Evening. I heard Mr. Westmoreland was hurt in an accident at the Rio d'Oro today. Is he all right?"

"Yes. He'll recover."

Relief showed on the woman's face.

Still wondering why the woman seemed familiar she said, "The doctor just left. He says Wes'll be fine in a couple of days. Just some broken ribs and a bad bump on the head."

The woman nodded, taking in the news. Unlike the rest of the merely curious visitors who had arrived at the front door she obviously was concerned about Wes. But why hadn't the woman come earlier? Who was she?

Answering the unspoken question, the dark-haired woman said, "I'm Kate Valdez. I'm an old friend of Wes. We knew each other back in California."

"Oh." She didn't know what else to reply. "I'm Julie Lawson," she added, still wondering why the woman seemed familiar. Then the realization of where she'd seen the dark-haired woman fell into place. The woman next to Wes at the dance.

Kate Valdez stood still and straight as she watched recognition dawn on her young face. Kate wondered how much Miss Lawson might know and how she would react.

"You were at the Fourth of July dance with Wes," the young woman on the porch said. Her words were polite, conversational.

"And you're the girl in the peach-colored dress. Wes danced with you. Then both of you disappeared from sight for a few minutes," Kate added, fishing for information.

Even in the deepening twilight, Kate saw the blush creep up the young girl's face. Ah, so it wasn't just a coincidence both Wes and Julie were absent at the same time. So that's the way the wind blows. She looked at the girl more critically. She could see why Wes was attracted to her, for she was young and pretty even if she was a little on the skinny side. And judging from her blush, this Miss Lawson was also attracted to Wes.

Kate suddenly remembered how just the other day she'd seen Wes dismiss Rhonda with a smile and a pat on the butt when she'd offered to show him upstairs. Now she knew why conversation was the only thing Wes made with the saloon girls.

Realizing neither she nor Julie had said anything for several moments, Kate cleared her throat. "Is he really all right?"

"The doctor says so. Wes is sleeping right now. Uncle Frank said he'll sit with him tonight."

Good. This girl seemed to really care about Wes. But how much did she really know about him? Kate gave a mental shrug. That was between Wes and the girl. "How long will he be here? Did the doc say?"

"The doctor said he should stay in bed for a week, between the blow to the head and the broken ribs."

"If he's going to be here a week, I guess you'd better have his things." She turned toward the buggy.

"Things?"

"Yeah. His gear." Kate returned to the buggy, and pulled a pair of saddle bags from behind the seat. She suspected she was about to give Julie some information she might rather not have about the injured man sleeping in her house. She walked back to the porch, noting her puzzled frown.

"These are all of Wes's things. Clothes, razor, and such. He's been staying at my place." She handed the saddle bags to Julie. Now we'll see if she's as delicate and fragile as she looks.

"You run a boarding house?" the girl asked as she took the bags.

"I own a saloon." Kate let the bald statement lie, watching for a reaction.

Julie's eyes grew round, her mouth started to fall open. Kate could practically see the wheels going around in the girl's mind. Of all the things Kate imagined the girl might say, what she said came as a surprise.

With only polite interest showing on her face, she said, "I think I've seen your establishment. Kate's Double Eagle"

Kate nodded.

The girl straightened her shoulders. "You have a lovely sign over the door."

Kate threw back her head and laughed. "You might do, sweetie." The girl had starch all right. Kate suspected Wes was in bigger trouble than just a headache and broken ribs. "Tell Wes to take it easy and come by for a drink on the house when he's better."

Julie watched Kate Valdez calmly climb into her buggy and drive away.

Inside the kitchen, Julie noticed her hands shook as she hung the heavy, leather saddle bags over the back of a chair. Wes lived in a saloon? She remembered him dashing out the swinging doors the morning he'd bought her the sarsaparilla. That answered the question of what kind of man came out of a saloon in the morning: one who lived there. She'd never imagined people actually lived in saloons.

She glanced at the saddle bags. Did these leather pouches hold all of Wes's possessions? She came to Durango with a trunk full of clothes. He came with a pair of saddle bags and a gun in a hidden holster. She sank onto a chair.

Uncle Frank's words about a man like that would be called a gunfighter echoed in her head. Her heart thumped harder now than any time since he fell. She didn't even know anyone who owned a gun.

What was she to think about Kate Valdez? The woman owned a saloon. But what was her relation with Wes? Somehow she suspected the relationship was more than one of tenant and landlord. Of course, Kate had said she and Wes were old friends, whatever that might mean.

She remembered how unsophisticated and naïve she'd felt when she had compared herself to Kate at the dance. But Kate's comment and laugh somehow made Julie feel as though she had the older woman's approval.

But what was she to do about Wes and how she felt about him? She relived the heart-stopping moment when Wes fell. In retrospect, the strength of her terror frightened her even more. For it told her she already cared a great deal about this man.

This man she now realized she knew so little about. This man with whom she was beginning to fall in love.

She could no longer kid herself by thinking she could make the problem of Wes Westmoreland go away simply by avoiding him. That hadn't worked the last time, and it certainly wouldn't work this time. The man was right here in the house.

* * *

"But, Uncle Frank, I can't take care of Wes," Julie protested as she sat at the kitchen table the next morning. Her incautious claim of being a nurse the other day was coming back to haunt her. She wasn't ready to test her newfound feelings for Wes in such close quarters. As she'd entered the kitchen a few minutes ago, she'd heard muffled male voices behind the closed door to the cook's room. She'd gotten only a brief glimpse of the foot of the bed as Uncle Frank came out.

"Sure you can." Uncle Frank sat across from her at the kitchen table, sipping his coffee. "I told Doc we'd take care of him. He'll need a little assistance for a few days. Clare's much too young. She's only fifteen," he pointed out.

"Someone has to take care of Wes. Doc said you did a good job in bringing him here without further damage. I reminded him your sister's husband is a doctor. That was all the reference he needed. Besides, Wes was hurt at the Rio d'Oro. That makes him our responsibility."

She gave in with what she hoped was a reluctant sigh. She leaned forward and patted his hand. "You're right of course. Just don't let Mrs. Peterson find out, or we'll both be sorry."

"Don't worry. I know it's not strictly proper, you being single and all, but Clare will be here." Uncle Frank put down his cup and stood to slip on his suit coat. "I've got to get up to the Rio d'Oro." With that, Uncle Frank leaned over, kissed her on the cheek, and went out the back door.

Julie slumped in her chair. Her impetuousness had indeed come back to haunt her, even though, as Uncle Frank pointed out, she'd probably be assigned the job in any case. Now she had to take Wes his breakfast. She'd have to find some way of dealing with her feelings for Wes, and quickly.

Deciding to make the best of an inauspicious situation, she stood and set about making Wes breakfast. Coffee and toast seemed a good start. Using the breadboard as a tray, she assembled the coffee pot, a cup and saucer, buttered toast, and a pot of jelly. She walked the few steps to the closed door. Balancing the tray on her hip, she used her free hand to knock. "Wes? It's Julie. I have your breakfast."

Silence.

Taking a deep breath, she knocked again. "Wes? May I come in? I have your breakfast."

This time her response was one of those peculiarly male grunt-growls that men used to indicate grudging assent. She turned the knob and with her hip pushed the door open. She took two steps into the room and stopped dead.

The crumpled white clump of Uncle Frank's spare nightshirt Wes had worn yesterday lay halfway between the bed and the door. Propped up by a pile of pillows against the headboard leaned a bare-chested Wes, his eyes closed, the sheet pooled around his waist.

For the moment, she could only stare. His hair, still dusty from the smelter floor, stood out in all directions. His eyes, which remained closed, looked pinched at the corners. Additional lines of pain and fatigue etched his face, pulling his mustache down. Golden whiskers blurred the angle of his jaw.

Embarrassed and enthralled, her gaze drifted down from his face. Seeing him without a shirt, she realized her earlier thought that he was skinny wasn't quite on the mark. Even in repose, the muscles of his shoulders and upper arms stood defined, displaying his strength. Dense, curling golden hair, a shade darker than on his head, covered his chest, the thicket only partially concealing flat, dark male nipples. A few inches lower, strips of white bandages swaddled his ribs down to disappear under the sheet and quilt.

With a gasp, she realized the rest of him was probably just as bare as his chest. She jerked her gaze back to his still closed eyes. Act professional, like a nurse. Loudly, she cleared her throat. Not an easy task with her tongue stuck to the roof of her dry mouth.

His green eyes opened slowly. "What?" His voice sounded gruff, slightly surly, his eyes squinting, as if the effort of opening them hurt.

"Breakfast," she answered briskly, forcing herself to walk toward the bed. "Uncle Frank's gone out to the smelter and he asked me to bring you breakfast." She pulled up a vacant chair and placed the breadboard tray on the seat, hoping her manner exuded cheerful efficiency instead of the odd mix of chagrin and fascination that churned in her stomach.

To occupy her hands, she straightened his corduroy jacket where it hung over the back of a second chair. "How do you feel this morning?" She turned to see his eyes closed again.

"Like sh..."

She gave him a concerned look, not sure what was wrong.

"Sorry," he said, and she wondered what he was apologizing for. He opened his eyes and glanced at her face. Whatever he found there seemed to reassure him, for he sighed and closed his eyes again.

"I feel like my head's caught in a stamp, and there's a hot knife in my side. Go away," he added ungraciously. His voice and expression reminded her of Mrs. Gilbert's four-year-old nephew in a fit of the sulks. Her worry about his condition moderated as she decided gravely injured people seldom pouted like small boys.

"Wouldn't you at least like a cup of coffee?" She poured coffee from the pot, releasing the aroma of the dark liquid.

He made an indecipherable sound, keeping his eyes closed. Unexpectedly, the sight of a big, strong man acting like a little boy struck her funny. She remembered her sister Cory saying her husband Mark carried on like he was dying the time he had a toothache. The trepidation she felt drained away. If he was going to act like a small child, she'd just treat him that way. Maybe by seeing and thinking of him as a small boy she could nurse him without further difficulty.

"Open your eyes and take this coffee," she ordered. Scowling, he took the offered cup and saucer. Looking suspicious, he took a sip and then another.

"Do you want the rest of this?" She indicated the tray.

"No. Just coffee for now."

As she debated what to do, she heard Clare call her name. "I have to see what she wants. I'll leave your breakfast here if you change your mind. I'll be back in a few minutes."

Balancing the awkward cup and saucer, Wes watched Julie swish out the door, leaving it half-open. A moment later he heard her calling to Clare. He dropped his head back and heaved a sigh of relief. A sharp pain rebuked him for the deep breath.

His head throbbed. Damn. If he could only think straight. His brain felt like oatmeal and that was dangerous. He'd been caught up in hazy, pain-filled nightmare when Frank woke him this morning. Only then did Wes realize the accident he'd thought a dream had really happened.

After several minutes' conversation and help with a few necessities, Frank had left. As soon as Frank closed the door, Wes had gotten rid of the nightshirt. How the hell did anyone sleep with something like that trying to strangle them? Over the protest of his ribs he stripped off the offending garment.

Only then had he seen his shaving gear and saddle bags on the small bureau. Even now his heart pounded, as he re-lived the moment when someone had knocked on the door. He'd been wildly digging in the saddle bags for the leather case that held his badge. His hand closed over the worn leather just as her knock sounded at the door. The jump back into bed had jarred his ribs, bringing sweat to his face.

He gave another sigh, this time remembering to keep it shallow. Thank God Clare called Julie away. The tormenting ribs and throbbing head kept him from realizing he'd been naked and in the same room with Julie. But once the thought snaked into his mind, the pain wasn't enough to drive the idea out.

Wes took the last swallow of coffee and made a face. Cold. He wondered if he could reach around for the coffee pot without intensifying the pain in his side. Just then Julie appeared at the door. Wes pulled the quilt more securely around his waist.

This time Julie didn't smile as she entered. Without asking, she refilled his cup. "Sheriff Rickman is here," she said, her voice all business. "He wants to talk to you about the accident."

Chapter Nine

Wes lay quietly, watching through slitted eyes as Julie opened the door to allow Sheriff Tom Rickman into the room. He held his hat in his hand. Black hair and droopy black mustache matched his black coat and pants, the darkness relieved only by a white shirt and the silver star on his lapel.

"You can only stay a few minutes," Julie warned as she picked up the tray. "The doctor said he was to rest."

Rickman didn't bother to answer as he sat in the vacated chair. The stern-looking sheriff wasn't the type to take orders from a young woman.

Wes glanced at Julie to see how she'd take the unspoken rebuke and saw her glare at the back of the sheriff's head. "I'll let you know when ten minutes are up," she said before she turned toward the door and left. Wes bit back a smile when Rickman turned to scowl after her.

Rickman turned his attention to Wes. "What the hell happened?" He leaned forward, elbows on knees.

"Don't know," he answered truthfully. The last thing he remembered was helping Julie on with the duster in the hallway before entering the smelter. Maybe when his head quit hurting, he would remember more. With the constant throb in his head, he felt lucky he didn't have to come up with or maintain any consistent lie. "They told me I went out on the walkway to check something with Reynolds. That's all I know."

The sheriff snorted in disgust.

While Rickman glanced around the room, Wes tried to organize what he knew of the sheriff. Kate had said Rickman was honest, didn't try to hold up the saloon owners for more than the monthly fines. He was a close friend of Kate's, probably her lover, for Rickman always made it a point to put his arm around Kate's shoulders or her waist whenever Wes was around. Maybe his friendship with Kate was the reason Wes felt the Sheriff didn't like him or trust him.

The thing that bothered Wes the most about the sheriff was his friendship with Landham Kennedy. The two of them were often in the Double Eagle together. For that reason alone, he didn't trust Rickman. What he couldn't figure out was why Rickman was here. He could have gotten more information about the accident from anyone at the smelter yesterday.

"You don't remember anything?" the sheriff asked again, leaning forward in the chair.

Wes started to shake his head, but the motion reminded him not to. "No," he said instead. "I remember going into the smelter, and after that, just hazy dreams until Lawson woke me up this morning."

Rickman's shoulders slumped just the slightest bit. In exasperation or in relief? Wes momentarily closed his eyes against the throb of his headache.

Rickman leaned back in the chair. "Don't it seem a mite funny to you that there was an accident in the Mineral King while you were working there. And now you're working for the Rio d'Oro there's an accident there, too." The sheriff s voice sounded deceptively mild.

With a slow, deep breath he fought the unexpected anger. Damn man was accusing him! He kept his own voice mild, "You forget. Kennedy hired me because there'd already been accidents in the smelter." And, he wanted to remind Rickman that Kennedy might have been able to avoid another accident if he'd listened to his advice.

Rickman still looked relaxed, as if not getting a rise out of him wasn't a surprise. "Well, if you remember anything, let me know." With that Rickman rose and left the room.

Through the open door Wes heard the sheriff s deep voice and Julie's higher pitched one, then their footsteps moving toward the front of the house.

What was Rickman after? Wes pinched the bridge of his nose, but it didn't help his headache. Maybe the next time he telegraphed San Francisco he'd ask if they had any information on a Tom Rickman. Fortunately, he'd telegraphed a no news yet message yesterday morning before going to the smelter. He shifted carefully, setting up a minor protest from his side. At least he had a couple of days to get up and about before he needed to contact his boss again.

A yawn caught him by surprise so he carefully shifted position to lie down. He closed his eyes and sighed, sleep beginning to drift over him. He heard the swish of skirts entering his room, but didn't open his eyes. The swishing stopped beside his bed. Gentle fingers brushed the hair from his forehead. He sighed, or maybe only thought he did. A moment later even gentler lips touched where the fingers brushed. Or did he imagine that, too?

Julie softly closed the door to Wes's room behind her. Clare waited in the kitchen, looking earnest and curious. "How's the patient this morning?" Clare asked.

"He's sleeping. I hope the sheriff's visit didn't overtire him."

"Suspect he'll be fine. Mr. Frank said the doctor plans on stopping by again this afternoon."

"Good. In the meantime, we have work to do."

She sent Clare off to do the Saturday shopping. The list included the dry goods store, the drug store, and the grocery. Clare practically ran down the driveway. With a list like that and the inside track on the latest topic of gossip, Julie surmised she'd have the whole morning to herself before the girl returned.

Even though her hands kept busy with the daily chores, she couldn't keep her thoughts from Wes. She remembered finding his gun, thought about him living in a saloon, and the fact that all his gear fit into a pair of saddlebags. A western man drifting from job to job and an eastern city girl. She sighed, knowing the differences were part of what attracted her to him.

So she was attracted, but that was all. Where could it lead? He'd drift away from Durango. She'd return to Philadelphia and what? She couldn't, didn't want, to imagine the situation when she returned home. The uproar when what she'd done became known.

As she dusted the front room, Julie remembered her quiet, ordinary life in Philadelphia, surrounded by Papa, Cory and her husband. She thought of Cory, resting in the country. And prayed for the safety of her sister and her as yet unborn niece or nephew. She imagined holding Cory's baby, seeing the little girl or boy grow, the fun of being Auntie Julie. Whatever the price, Cory and the future baby were worth it. As long as Cory and the baby were safe, nothing else mattered.

She recalled how just that morning Wes had reminded her of a small sulky boy. She would stick to her plan to treat Wes as if he were a nephew, or perhaps a scalawag brother. An effective nurse could look on Wes as just another patient, treat him as an irritable, injured boy.

Midmorning she peeked in at Wes. Still asleep, the harsh lines of pain that marked his face yesterday had smoothed away. His blond eyelashes lay in pale crescents against his tanned face. He looked younger and more uncomplicated than usual, more like a boy than a man. A lock of hair fell over his forehead, heightening the small boy look. Unable to resist touching him, she once more brushed back the blond hair, telling herself it was gesture of nurse-like concern. She placed the glass of water she'd brought on the chair next to the bed in case he woke, and returned to the kitchen.

Within a few minutes of noon, Clare returned from her shopping expedition. Half an hour later Uncle Frank came home from the smelter, full of details on the repairs to the broken equipment, which he related at great length over the noon meal. After eating, Uncle Frank took Wes the soup Julie had made.

"How is he?" Julie asked, taking the empty bowl from Uncle Frank.

"Better. We talked a little about the repairs. I think his headache is better today. Said he thought he'd go back to sleep."

It was always good when a patient got better, no matter who cared for the injured person. Wasn't it?

* * *

Sheriff Rickman guided his horse up Boulevard Street toward Landham Kennedy's turreted mansion. He rode around to the back. As he tied his horse to the corral fence by the barn, Kennedy came to the back door. With visible impatience, Kennedy waited as the sheriff headed to the mansion.

Kennedy scowled as Rickman entered. "Why'd you come to the back door? You should've come to the front door. You're the goddamn sheriff, Tom."

Rickman shrugged. "Just habit." He hung his hat on a fancy iron stand by the door. "Everyone knows we're friends. Makes sense that I'd come to the back.

"Well, next time, come to the front." Kennedy led Rickman through to the front room. They entered a room heavy with overstuffed furniture and dark velvet drapes. A huge stone fireplace held old ashes. That monstrosity had come all the way from some European country. Rickman disremembered which one but he smiled as he recalled the circus atmosphere when the fireplace had arrived at the depot to be carted up to the mansion.

Splashing some whiskey from a crystal decanter into a glass, Kennedy took a drink. "So what happened? What did you find out from Westmoreland?"

Rickman snorted. "Not a damn thing. Says he can't remember." He moved to pour himself a drink. "Everyone says the same thing." Rickman swallowed a mouthful of the whiskey. The stuff tasted just like the whiskey at the Double Eagle, the same that came out an ordinary bottle rather than a crystal decanter. "Just a real accident," he reassured Kennedy.

With a grunt, Kennedy collapsed into an armchair. He raised the glass in a toast. "Here's to our good luck."

The two men drank.

"How long will the Rio d'Oro be down?" Kennedy asked.

The sheriff shrugged. "Maybe a week?" Rickman put his glass back on the side table. "Look, Land. We got lucky this time. Why don't we just back off?"

Kennedy sprang from his chair. "Back off?" he barked. He swore foully as he paced. "How the hell do you think I pay for all this?" he waved at the room. Then he spun and pointed a finger at

Rickman. "Who paid for you to be sheriff? And you got another election coming up."

"I know, Land. And I'm grateful."

"You better be grateful." Kennedy continued to pace and swear. "We were poorer than dirt."

Rickman winced at Land's shrill voice and the poor white cracker accent of their youth began to show.

"Now we got money. Folks look up to us now. I'm not givin' any of that up"

"No," Rickman agreed, "we're not giving that up."

* * *

Later that afternoon Julie opened the door to the doctor as he came by to check on Wes. The rumble of male voices, mostly the doctor's and Uncle Frank's, came from the sick room as she bustled about the kitchen making a fresh pot of coffee, setting out cups, putting sugar cookies on a plate.

The doctor and Uncle Frank came out of the room. "Ah," the doctor said, spying the cookies. "Those wouldn't be for us now would they, pretty girl?"

"They might be. Sit down you two." Uncle Frank and the doctor sat.

"He'll be fine," the doctor announced. "No internal injuries or they would have manifested themselves by now. All he needs is a few days more rest before he's up and about. His headache is almost gone, but his ribs will pain him some for a while. Starting tomorrow, he could take a little something for the pain of the broken ribs, especially at night."

"What would you suggest'" she asked.

"Whiskey, rum, whatever Frank has. And you can probably start him on regular food tomorrow. Well, thanks for the cookies." Tucking his bag under his arm, the doctor shook hands with Uncle Frank and left.

She looked at Uncle Frank who was trying for an innocent expression. "So, what sort of liquor do you have in the house? Other than the sherry and the brandy in the parlor?"

"Why, Julie," Uncle Frank said in a guileless tone. "Your Aunt Marie conceded only sherry and brandy as acceptable. And then only as an aid to digestion."

"Yes. But what else do you have to offer Wes?"

Uncle Frank smiled. "I'll get out the Kentucky bourbon your father sent me last Christmas."

She smiled, and kissed Uncle Frank on the cheek before he departed. With Uncle Frank's return to the smelter, the afternoon passed as Wes slept, and she and Clare kept busy until supper time.

Once again Uncle Frank took Wes his evening meal, and after a few minutes, reported Wes as mending and asking for another glass of water. Trying not to appear too anxious, Julie filled a glass. After all, she was supposed to be the nurse, and she hadn't had the opportunity to check on her patient since morning.

Water in one hand, she knocked at the door. "Wes?"

"Come in."

With a deep breath, she entered. Wes lay back against the pillows, once again covered by Uncle Frank's nightshirt, looking half asleep. "I brought you the water Uncle Frank said you wanted." She crossed to the bedside, placing the glass beside the bed.

"Thanks."

"Do you need anything else? No?"

Just like a young boy. Impulsively, she brushed back the recalcitrant lock of hair.

He scowled, but he was halfway asleep, and the scowl lacked force.

"Good night." With a smile, she closed the door softly behind her.

That night she snuggled into bed. Her last thought as she drifted off to sleep was that she'd spent too much time worrying about her attraction to Wes interfering with her ability to nurse him. She had everything under control.

* * *

Wes woke with a start. For a moment he wondered vaguely where he was. Then his memory came back and a second later the pain came back, too.

Once he concentrated, he could remember yesterday. He'd slept most of the day, but he recalled Julie bringing him breakfast, the interview with the sheriff, talking to Frank and the doctor. He tried to move, but something constricted his arms and legs. He'd forgotten that Frank and the doctor had put him back in that damn night shirt.

He tried to sit up and his ribs didn't appreciate the movement. He rolled to his uninjured side and pushed himself upright using his arm. Sitting on the edge of the bed, he ran his hands over his face and through his hair. He needed a shave and his hair felt gritty. Gradually, he realized that while his body felt as if he'd been run over by a team of horses, his head had finally quit thumping. He sighed in relief.

Then very carefully he worked the nightshirt off over his head. Freedom from the threat of strangulation and the absence of a headache made him feel better. He ran his hands over the bandages running from just under his breastbone to his waist. Carefully, he stretched out an arm and picked up his pocket watch someone had placed on the small bedside table. Six-thirty. Feeling better and stronger with every movement, he stood. With precise, gentle movements he stepped into his denim pants. The ache in his side became a sharp stab. When he straightened the pain subsided. He buttoned his pants. Boots were out of the question this morning. Besides, pants were all he needed to get out to the privy.

Quietly he opened the door and looked into the kitchen. The room was empty and he heard no noises from upstairs. The rest of the household must still be asleep. He let himself out the back door and in his bare feet hobbled across the yard.

When he came back he heard someone in the kitchen as he climbed the step. Hoping it was Frank, he let himself in. To his chagrin he saw Julie standing in the kitchen, her back to him. She hummed to herself as she reached into the cupboard and brought out a plate.

"Good morning," Wes said.

She gasped and whirled around. Her gaze locked on him, the plate slipped from her hand and shattered on the floor. She continued to stare, one hand pressed over her heart, the other gripping the counter.

Hell, he hadn't meant to frighten her. He stood there helpless in his bare feet. Fragments of the shattered plate covered the floor, stranding him in place. As she continued to stare at him with an odd expression, he wondered what was wrong. Her unreadable gaze traveled over his shoulders, chest and arms, then down to his bare feet. Then it hit him. He was practically naked. He felt his face heat and he shoved his hands in his pockets.

A female voice called from the front of the house, "Julie?" The voice unlocked Julie. She turned and called through the kitchen door, "Yes, Clare?"

"What was that noise?"

"Don't worry. I just dropped a plate."

"Oh. I thought maybe it might be Ryan. I'll be ready in a few minutes. If he shows up before then, tell him I'm on my way down."

"Yes, I will." Julie looked back at Wes. "I'm sorry," she apologized, "you startled me."

"Yeah," he agreed.

"Don't move. I'll have this cleaned up in a minute." She bustled about, getting the broom and dustpan, all efficient as if her moment of uncertainty had never been.

He nodded, even though with her head down as she swept, he knew she couldn't see him. He thought about apologizing for not wearing a shirt, but he couldn't think how to do it without sounding foolish. At least she'd quit staring at him.

Julie swept the last of the fragments into the dust pan. "There. You can move now." She dumped the sweepings into the trash. "I'll have coffee ready in a minute, if you'd like some."

"Fine." He crossed the kitchen and entered his room. As he pulled on his shirt he heard an exchange of female voices from the kitchen. Why had being half-naked in front of Julie bothered him so much? He'd been naked in front of plenty of women and it hadn't bothered him. Or the women.

But they hadn't been ladies he reminded himself, so just forget about how Julie looked at him. Then he recalled her expression, the way her gaze had drifted over him. He paused in buttoning his shirt. Could that look have been one of a woman intrigued by the sight of a half-dressed man?

From outside came the sound of a buggy in the drive. The back door opened and shut and a few moments later the buggy drove off. On the other side of his door, no sounds came from the kitchen.

Nothing else for him to do but go back and face Julie. He couldn't hide out in this room all day. "The hell with it," he muttered. Deciding for comfort over appearance, he left his shirttail out, looked longingly at his boots, and returned to the kitchen.

The room was empty, but the coffee pot just beginning to perk sat on the stove. He heard light footsteps coming down the front stairs. He pulled out a chair and gingerly sat down. A moment later Julie entered, her expression calm, with no remnants of the way she'd looked a few minutes earlier. He didn't know whether to be relieved or disappointed she'd so easily brushed off the moment of sexual awareness. "I brought you Uncle Frank's carpet slippers so you don't have to go around barefoot all day."

Much to his discomfort, Julie knelt gracefully by his feet, placing the slippers on the floor.

"Look," he started to protest being treated like a helpless kid, but she grasped his pant leg to guide his foot into the slipper. Without thinking he jerked his foot back. The sudden movement caused a jab like a hot poker in his side. He gasped, and the poker stabbed again. "Damn," he muttered and leaned back in the chair.

"Serves you right," she chastised with an exasperated look. "Just behave." She slid the carpet slippers on his feet. By the time she'd poured him a cup of coffee and placed it on the table in front of him, the pain had subsided to a dull ache.

"Who were you talking to this morning?" he asked. Julie looked puzzled for a moment. Then her face cleared, "That was Clare, the maid."

"She lives here?" He had a hazy recollection of the same disembodied voice calling to Julie once before.

"Yes. She has a room upstairs next to mine. Her brother came by to take her to church."

"Today's Sunday?" He felt stupid having to ask. He rubbed a hand across his forehead. "I hadn't stopped to think what day it is."

She sat in the chair across from him. "I see how that could happen. Are you sure you should be up?"

He told himself he didn't mind that her voice showed nothing but mild concern. "I'm hurt, not sick. I don't hurt anymore sitting in this chair than I did flat on my back in that bed." Well, at least not enough to make a difference.

Looking at Julie over the rim of his cup, he took a sip of coffee. She wore the same everyday clothes she wore to the smelter, a white shirtwaist and a dark green skirt. "You're not going to church?" The minute he said it he felt like a fool. Everyone went to church, except social outcasts like the people he grew up with. Hell, even the men who spent time in the upstairs rooms at the Red Garter on Friday or Saturday went to church on Sunday.

Julie smiled at him. "Not today. Uncle Frank and I decided last night that we could stay home this morning. I told him to sleep in and get caught up on his rest."

Wes nodded. While he'd slept away the last couple of days, Frank had undoubtedly been extra busy. "How are things at the smelter? Did they figure out what happened? Did the stamp get fixed?"

"Don't worry. Uncle Frank seems to have everything under control. I'm sure he'll be anxious to give you all the details later today. But for now," she stood. "What can I fix you for breakfast?

What would be the least trouble? He'd already been enough of a burden to the Lawson household, the way they'd obviously been caring for him. "Hot cakes?" he suggested.

Chapter Ten

"Hot cakes it is." She smiled and taking an apron from a hook, tied it around her waist.

Glad his choice seemed to please her Wes sighed and ran a hand over his face. The rasp of whiskers seemed loud in the quiet kitchen. He needed a shave. "If there's any hot water, I'd like to shave before breakfast. Remind me to thank Frank for getting my gear."

To his surprise, Julie smoothed her hands over her apron as if nervous, though for the life of him he couldn't imagine what he'd said.

"Actually," she said, turning to dip water from the boiler at the back of the stove. "Uncle Frank didn't bring your things."

"He didn't?"

"Ah, no." She put a bowl of hot water on the table in front of him. "The evening you were hurt, your, ah, friend brought your saddle bags by."

For a moment he wondered if his head injury had returned, having no idea what Julie meant. "My friend?"

"Miss? Mrs.? Valdez brought them by when she came to find out how you were."

Wes slumped back in his chair. Kate here? No wonder Julie stumbled over telling him how his gear got to the Lawson's.

Women like Julie weren't even supposed to know that women like Kate existed. He doubted Kate had done anything outrageous, for as far as he knew, the eminently practical Kate was always discreet. "You talked to Kate?" Try as he might he couldn't imagine the two of them in conversation.

"Of course I spoke to her," she replied, sounding indignant.

"But, she, ah, did she…" Now it was his turn to stumble.

She sank into a kitchen chair with a sigh. "I know some people would say that was wrong, that I shouldn't have spoken to her regardless of the circumstances." She looked at the tabletop. "I didn't know who she was at first when she came around to the back.

Then I remembered I'd seen her talking to you at the dance. She was kind enough to bring your things and she was genuinely concerned about you." Julie straightened her shoulders and Wes suddenly imagined her doing the same motion, setting herself to face Kate. "She said you should come by for a drink when you're feeling better."

She slid the forgotten bowl of water toward him. "Here, you'd better use this water while it's still warm. Breakfast will be ready by the time you're finished."

Wes stood, picked up the bowl, and went to shave. Back in his room he took off his shirt. If he lived to be a hundred, he'd never understand women. He stirred the brush around in the mug of shaving soap, working up a lather. Damn, even that movement made his ribs ache. Being this banged up irritated the hell out of him. He'd need at least another day of rest before he could move around enough to get back to work. So far, the accidents in the smelters had been at least a week apart. He hoped that standard would hold.

Moving with care so as not to provoke his ribs further, he shaved, and trimmed the ends of his mustache. There, he thought, running a hand over his smooth jaw that felt better.

He combed his hair and winced, both from the motion of raising his arms above his shoulders and from the dust on the comb. Guess a bath would have to wait until tomorrow. His stomach growled reminding him breakfast was waiting. He tugged his shirt back on and returned to the kitchen. Julie stood at the stove, her back to him, but his place at the table held a fresh cup of coffee. As soon as he sat down Julie placed a plate of hot cakes in front of him.

"Go ahead and eat while they're warm." She gestured for him to help himself from the crock of butter and pitcher of maple syrup. The hot cakes, light and fluffy, were the best he'd ever eaten. Even the syrup had been heated. Damn, he could get used to decent tasting food. He'd savor the memory of this meal some future morning when all he could get was half a cup of cold coffee and a stale biscuit.

"More?" Julie turned from the stove.

"Yes, please." Julie transferred three more hot cakes from the griddle to his plate. A decent meal fixed by a pretty girl. The unlikeliness of the event stuck him even more when a minute later she set a plate for herself across from him.

Finally full, he pushed away his plate. "That was really good. Thanks." He looked around the kitchen. "You do all the cooking around here?" If she did, it must make for a long day to come home and cook dinner after spending the day at the smelter.

She removed the plates from the table. "Clare does most of the cooking during the week. She usually helps my Aunt Marie." She turned to the sink and started the dishes.

With her back to him Wes looked his fill. The sunshine through the curtained windows gleamed off her pale hair. She had it done up in that elaborate knot that left the graceful sweep of her neck bare. The ties of her apron encircled her narrow waist, the apron s bow the only decoration on the back of her plain skirt. Maybe her dainty figure didn't have the proper hourglass form, but he found he didn't care. Her natural figure held more appeal for him than one achieved by ruffles and drapes of material in the appropriate spots.

He shifted in the chair. Damn, if just watching her do the dishes wasn't making him hard. Alarmed at the realization, he bolted out of the chair. The sudden movement wrenched his ribs, and he welcomed the pain.

She shot him a questioning look over her shoulder. "Are you all right?"

"Fine." Still looking for a distraction to both his thoughts and his physical condition, he picked up a tea towel from the rack by the stove. "Here, let me help. I'll dry."

That got him a smile and that little dimple. He moved to stand beside her. He was an idiot for offering to help. Standing next to her, he caught her faint floral fragrance under the smells of soap and coffee. Forget it, he told himself, and put his mind to drying the dishes as they politely discussed the weather and other innocuous topics.

"Thanks," Julie said taking the towel, and hanging it back over the rack. He shrugged, embarrassed by her thanks. Her gaze followed his hand as he ran his fingers through his hair. She looked toward the pump, and then back toward him. "Umm, if you think you could bend over at the pump, then maybe we could wash your hair?"

"Don't worry, for clean hair, I'll bend." Ever since he found out how good clean felt, he'd hated being dirty. He'd bend over if it killed him. Without thinking, he unbuttoned his shirt and started to pull it off. A twinge of pain slowed his motion as he finished stripping off the shirt and dropped it over the back of the chair.

Gripping the edge of the sink, he guardedly bent at the hips, keeping his back straight. A steady but bearable ache throbbed in his side. A second later he heard Julie work the pump handle and cool water ran over his head. He sighed. The cleansing dampness more than made up for the ache in his side. She moved closer, her body brushing against his arm and shoulder as the water trickled to a stop.

"Close your eyes," she said. For a second he wondered what she meant and then he felt her hands in his hair. A shudder ran through him. He thought she'd just work the pump.

"Yes, ma'am," he replied and closed his eyes. Her fingers worked the soap through his hair, caressing his scalp. He stifled a moan. The touch of her hands was bliss beyond belief. He knew about sex, but he'd never realized that watching someone do dishes or having her wash his hair could be so arousing. With another sigh, he gave himself up to the pleasure.

All too soon Julie's hands left. The pump clanked and water splashed down, rinsing away the soap. A towel fell over his head.

"You can straighten up now."

The ache in his side protested as he moved but settled down once he stood upright.

She took his arm. "Here, sit down." She guided him to the chair. Once he was seated, she rubbed the towel over his hair, obscuring his sight. After a few seconds, she let go of the towel and it fell back around his neck. From his seated position, with her standing in front of him, her breasts were right at his eye level. From this angle she didn't seem so slender. With effort, he forced his gaze to her face.

To his chagrin, he saw only a casual half-smile on her face, not the reflection of the sexual awareness he felt. Irritation flickered up to join his arousal. How dare she be unaffected when she was making him hotter than a two-dollar pistol?

Julie looked at Wes, the towel draped around his shoulders, his damp hair mussy, and congratulated herself. For most of the morning she'd kept to her goal of seeing Wes as only a patient. She'd only dropped the plate earlier because he'd startled her. Now here he sat, one lock hanging over his forehead given him that little boy look. She reached out to brush the damp strand back.

Quick as a striking snake, his hand shot out and caught her wrist. "Don't." His voice sounded low and harsh. His expression now forbidding, eyes narrowed, and mouth tight beneath his mustache. The same intense look that had caused her to draw back in fright the night of the dance. Holding her wrist in one hand, he slowly pulled the towel from around his neck, letting it drop the floor. Keeping his grip on her wrist, he rose out of the chair to stand before her. Her heart beat faster. But not from fear.

"Don't treat me like a kid," he said. With his hand still around her upraised wrist Wes pulled her toward him.

She took a half step to keep her balance and ended up in his arms. Her breathing matched the quick beat of her heart. The smell of man and soap filled her nostrils as he gently settled her against him. The coarse, curly hair on his chest above his bandage made crinkly sounds against the fabric of her blouse as he shifted her slightly to his uninjured side.

Sensations flooded over her. His surrounding warmth and scent, the sound and feel of his quickened breathing. She responded instinctively and tilted her head back, raising her face toward his. He bent his head. Her eyes closed in anticipation. The soft caress of his lips and mustache on her mouth left her legs without strength. She clung to him for support, her hands on his bare shoulders. His hand made slow circles on her back. Beneath her own palms she felt the shift and play of muscles under his hot, smooth skin.

His lips left hers and she gasped for air. Raising eyelids that weighed a pound, she looked into his stormy-green eyes and knew she was lost. No one had ever kissed her like this. She hadn't dreamed there were kisses like this. And she wanted more. She sighed his name and raised her mouth toward his. With a groan, he kissed her again, his mustache and warm mouth drifting from her lips to move over her cheeks, her chin, her eyelids.

"Damn," he muttered between kisses, "you feel it, too." Her breath came in short gasps. Of their own accord her hands stroked the contours of his back above the bandage, his skin like warm granite covered in satin. He shifted, widening his stance, and slid one hand down past her waist to her buttocks. This time as he kissed her, he pulled her hips against his. For the first time she felt the hardness of a man. The erotic sensation made her gasp. To her surprise, his mouth opened over hers and his tongue stroked the inside of her mouth. Astonished, she pushed at his tongue with hers. He made a sound deep in his throat and pulled her tighter against him.

The slam of an upstairs door made them both jump, breaking the sensual spell. Wes sucked a breath in through his teeth, his left hand going to his side. The sounds of heavy footsteps started down the front stairs as she stood suspended in Wes's half-embrace.

Uncle Frank's voice called, "Julie?"

"Answer him," Wes prompted in a soft voice, his right arm falling from her shoulders to his side.

"Yes?" Did her voice sound as shaky as she still felt?

"Is Wes up?" Uncle Frank called.

Beside her Wes made a choking sound. "Is he ever," he muttered as he turned to reach for his shirt.

Dazed, Julie shook her head. Then panic set in over Uncle Frank's imminent arrival, over the way Wes kissed her, the way she kissed him back. A flush of embarrassment heated her cheeks. She twisted her hands together.

Wes reached out and put his hand on her arm. "Pour your uncle a cup of coffee. Relax." He finished buttoning his shirt and gingerly bent to pick up the towel. As if the whole thing had never happened.

She tried to follow his advice. Relax and put the last few minutes out of her mind. At least for now. Maybe when the dizzy, fuzzy-headed feeling went away she'd be able to think. By the time Uncle Frank entered the kitchen, she hovered at the stove pouring a cup of coffee. Wes stood across the kitchen, facing the pump, rubbing the towel over his head.

"Morning," Wes said as soon as Uncle Frank entered the kitchen. Wes winced as he lowered his arms, bringing the towel around his neck.

Uncle Frank smiled at Wes. "You look better today."

"Yeah, I might live. How are things at the smelter?"

"Not too bad, considering." Coming to Julie's side, Uncle Frank kissed her on the cheek. Good morning.

"Morning," she replied, but he was already moving toward the table, his thoughts obviously intent on discussing business. The mundane exchange of pleasantries made the day settle into its normal pattern. "Breakfast?" she asked, putting a cup of coffee in front of her uncle.

Uncle Frank shook his head. "Coffee will be fine. I'll wait 'til lunch." Both men pulled out chairs and sat. Wes rubbed his side. She took the coffee pot from the stove and refilled Wes's cup.

"Did you eat?" Uncle Frank asked Wes. He gave an affirmative reply. Uncle Frank smiled, nodded, and said, "Glad to see Julie's taking good care of you."

The comment made her cringe inside. Her gaze shot to Wes's face, but he didn't bat an eye.

"You find out any more about how the accident happened?" Wes asked.

She turned to put the coffee pot back on the stove. How could he act as if nothing had happened? What kind of man concealed his feelings as well as his gun? She shook off the unsettling thought and turned her attention to the conversation.

Wes ran a hand through his damp hair. "I still can't remember anything about the accident. What did Reynolds have to say?"

"He says the stamp didn't seem right, and that's why he was checking it. You came out to see what was going on and the whole thing just exploded." Uncle Frank rested his arms on the table, hands around his cup. "We had to shut down that section of stamps. Cut us to about seventy percent of capacity."

"How about repairs?" Wes asked.

Julie watched him shift, his right hand reaching across to press against the broken ribs on his left side.

Uncle Frank leaned back in his chair. "Took most of Friday to clean up and assess the damage. We hope for full production within ten days. I sent the engineer to California yesterday to arrange for the spare parts we can't have made here." He glanced briefly in her direction, then back at Wes. "He's also going to talk to a couple of friends of his to see if they've had any similar accidents."

She recognized the man-to-man look between Uncle Frank and Wes as one that said let's not upset the ladies. Both men were obviously itching to say more, but her presence kept them from speaking, which struck her as silly since Uncle Frank had explained about the suspected accidents when he told her he'd hired Wes.

However, here was the perfect excuse she needed. She'd give the men a few minutes alone, take a few minutes to get herself together as well. She took off her apron and hung it over the back of her chair. "There's still coffee left. Serve yourselves."

Julie went down the short hallway to the front parlor where she sank with an unladylike collapse into the wing chair. What in heaven's name had she been thinking of, she wondered wildly, letting him kiss her like that. Thank goodness she was sitting down. Her knees grew weak just remembering. His scent, his taste, how her breasts tingled when held hard against his chest. The way his kisses made her light-headed.

What must he think of her? He'd even put his tongue in her mouth. Mortified, she dropped her head and covered her face with her hands. She should have been repulsed by something that sounded so vile and loathsome, but she'd felt only brief surprise then....What would have happened if Uncle Frank hadn't—no, she wouldn't think, wouldn't wonder. She straightened and glanced around the parlor.

The heavy curtains cut the daylight to a murky gloom, making the room much too dreary. She pulled back the curtains, allowing in the light to bring out the colors and textures of the overstuffed arm chairs and couch. Unable to sit still, she wandered the room, idly fingering the assorted whatnots and knick-knacks that crowded every flat surface. She moved a china shepherdess, and straightened a fringed lamp shade. Moving back to the window she watched the thunderheads of a summer storm boiling over the western mountains covering most of the sky. In the distance, thunder rumbled. Would they get rain?

"Julie?" Uncle Frank called. "Could you bring the brandy decanter?"

Uncle Frank must have noticed the way Wes's side bothered him and offered the doctor's suggested prescription of a drink for the pain. She picked up the heavy glass decanter. She straightened her shoulders and hurried toward the kitchen.

As she approached she heard Uncle Frank ask, "You sure? Doc said it was all right."

She stopped in the hallway, out of sight of the kitchen. Wes's curt voice explained, "I'd rather hurt than have a drink in my hand this early in the day. Reminds me too much of my old man. Never out of arm's reach of the whiskey bottle." The very lack of feeling in his voice made the words themselves sound even worse. Realizing her knuckles were white, she relaxed her grip on the decanter. She took a deep breath and entered the kitchen.

Wes watched out of the corner of his eye as Julie entered the room, the heavy cut glass decanter in her hands.

"Here you are." She set the brandy on the table. Wes eyed the whiskey with distaste, but Frank saved him from saying anything.

"Thanks, Julie," Frank said. "Maybe Wes will need some of the medicine the doctor prescribed tonight to help him sleep."

"Maybe tonight," he agreed after a moment. He glanced at Julie, noting her color had returned to normal. How could he have been such an idiot to kiss her like that? He looked away, afraid the memory of how sweet she'd tasted might show on his face. He shifted in his chair, the memory affecting another part of him.

Just then the clop of hoof beats and the crunch of gravel in the driveway announced the arrival of a buggy.

"Who could that be?" Frank wondered aloud.

Wes shifted to see Julie peer through the kitchen curtains as another roll of thunder rumbled louder and closer than before.

"It's Clare and her brother," Julie announced at the sound of the buggy pulling to a stop in the backyard. She hurried to the back door and opened it just as a panicky-looking young girl hurried through. One hand clutched her skirts, the other held her hat, which perched precariously on brown curls.

"Goodness," the girl exclaimed. "Did you see the size of that thunderhead?" Another peal of thunder boomed, and she shuddered.

Clare, the maid, Wes guessed.

"I thought you planned to go out to the fort with your brother after church," Julie remarked.

Before the girl could answer, another figure came through the back door. An army lieutenant. He took off his hat, and flashed Julie a smile.

Wes's jaw clenched. He'd last seen the too handsome, too respectable-looking officer waltzing with Julie at the Fourth of July dance.

"Lieutenant Sullivan," Julie greeted him. She returned his smile complete with dimple.

The dimple had him grinding his teeth.

"Come in, come in," Frank said.

"Sorry to interrupt your day, Mr. Lawson, Miss Julie. But you know Clare." Sullivan smiled with fond exasperation at his sister. "Once we came out of church and she saw that storm...."

"I can't help that I'm afraid of thunder storms." The girl's tone held a mixture of chagrin and defiance.

"It's all right, Clare," Sullivan said. He turned and smiled at Julie again. "Last time, we were already out at the fort when the storm came up. Clare had to spend the night with Sergeant McNeally and his wife."

Thunder boomed overhead. Clare shivered and blurted, "Excuse me," as she dashed from the kitchen. The sound of her footsteps running up the stairs followed by a door slam.

Lieutenant Sullivan sighed and shook his head, but the fond smile lingered on his face, the love between brother and sister clear. The lieutenant and his sister were obviously as close as Julie and her uncle. Wes suddenly felt the outsider he was. The relationships between these people was a world away from the way he grew up.

"Wes," Frank spoke his name, jerking his attention back to the present.

Frank gestured between Wes and the lieutenant. "Lieutenant Sullivan, this is Mr. Westmoreland. He's staying with us while he recovers from an injury."

Wes carefully stood and offered his hand. Although he knew nothing showed on his face, he was deeply conscious of standing there in borrowed carpet slippers, his chambray shirttail hanging out over his denim pants, while the lieutenant was all decked out in a crisp-looking blue uniform with shiny gold buttons and gold bullion braid.

The two men shook hands. Wes took satisfaction in seeing Lieutenant Sullivan's expression mirror the same façade of polite neutrality as his own.

"Didn't I see you at the dance, Mr. Westmoreland?" Sullivan asked.

Chapter Eleven

Wes smiled. "I was there." He'd bet money Sullivan had seen him dancing with Julie, just as he remembered Sullivan dancing with her. Looked as if the thought jacked Sullivan's jaw the way the same memory bothered Wes. Maybe he didn't look as much like some stray as he thought.

Thunder boomed, closer than before.

"Would you care to stay for lunch?" Frank asked.

To Wes's relief, the lieutenant shook his head. "Thank you for the invitation. If I leave now, I'll get back to the fort before the storm breaks. Tell Clare I'll see her next Sunday." Then to Wes's disgust, Sullivan took Julie's hand and sketched a slight bow. "Perhaps I'll see you at church next week, Miss Julie?"

"Perhaps," she answered with a smile.

Did she sound hopeful or just polite? He waited while Sullivan put on his hat and went out the door. Once the door closed behind the lieutenant, Wes sank back into his chair. His ribs ached. But he'd be damned if he'd have appeared an invalid in front of the respectable and handsome lieutenant. He wondered how much longer he could sit here before he had to excuse himself and lie down.

To his relief, Frank asked Julie to fix them some sandwiches for lunch. By the time Julie had made the thick ham sandwiches and taken one up to Clare, the summer storm passed overhead. The rain lasted only a few minutes, enough to settle the dust but not enough for mud. The perfect summer storm, the thunder now a distant boom in the east.

He looked at the half-eaten sandwich in front of him. Just eating took more effort than he wanted to admit. He'd done nothing but sleep for the past two days, and here it was only noon and he felt as if he'd done a full day's work. Julie kept casting him covert glances. He wondered if he looked tired, or if there was another reason. One he'd be smart not to contemplate.

"Just stack the dishes in the sink," Frank told Julie. "You and Wes both look tired. Julie, you go on up and take a nap. I'll get Wes settled."

"But—" she started to protest.

"Don't worry about me," Frank reassured her. "I'll have a cigar and read the newspaper in the parlor."

"You most certainly will not have a cigar in the parlor. You know Aunt Marie wouldn't allow that."

Frank smiled. "Darn, thought I could get away with it. Oh, well." He stood. "Go on up and rest. I'll smoke on the back porch."

The sound of Julie's footsteps going up the stairs faded as Frank offered Wes his arm. He gripped Frank's arm and used it to pull himself from the chair. Frank gave him a nod and said, "You're the one who needs the rest. This is your first day up. Go take a nap." He glanced at the decanter. "I'll put this in your room so it will be handy if you need it."

Too tired and too achy to protest, he made his way to his room. Frank set the decanter on the small bureau. "Rest," he ordered as he closed the door.

Gingerly, he sank to the bed. He kicked off the slippers, and holding his breath, he swung his legs up on the bed. "Damn," he breathed as he lay down, spent by the small effort. He wiped the sweat from his forehead as he waited for the pain to settle down. He glanced at the brandy decanter, deciding that getting up wouldn't be worth whatever relief the brandy might bring.

After a few minutes of lying still, the pain subsided to a manageable ache. Unfortunately, without the aggravation of the pain, his thoughts turned to Julie. What the hell had he been thinking, kissing her like that? If Frank had caught them, he'd be justified in kicking Wes's butt all the way to Denver, if not worse.

He tried to remember Julie was the niece of a possible suspect. He'd seen her dressed in widow's weeds at the train station in St. Louis, when she wasn't a widow. There were too many pieces of the puzzle that didn't fit. But all he could remember was how good she felt in his arms, her breasts pillowed against his chest, her soft hands on his naked shoulders. He groaned. If he kept thinking about this, he'd never get to sleep.

He shifted slightly. Damn, but he was tired. His eyes closed, and before he knew it he was asleep.

* * *

Julie waited on the landing until she heard Wes's door shut and Uncle Frank go out. She entered her room and closed the door behind her. She leaned back against it and rubbed her temples with her fingertips. When would she ever learn to think before she acted? Gran had warned her time and again. That one impulse to wash his hair had seemed innocuous enough, but look where it had led.

She remembered the heat and power of his bare arms as he held her, shivering at the intensity of the memory. She pulled herself from the door and hurried across the room, as if by moving she could escape the recollection.

Uncle Frank was right about her being tired. She felt as if she'd lived a lifetime since this morning. Perhaps she should follow his suggestion and take a nap. She stood at the chest of drawers and took the pins from her hair. Yes, a nap might be just what she needed to restore her equilibrium.

She unbuttoned and removed her outer clothing, laying each article over the rocking chair by the bed. Clad only in her chemise and pantaloons, she plaited her hair into one long braid. But once she lay in the bed, her thoughts turned to Wes.

The way he'd kissed her. She groaned and wrapped her arms around herself. Somehow it seemed even more upsetting to think of those kisses in her present state of undress.

Now she knew the real reason girls were warned about letting a man take liberties. Because when the right man took liberties, it made your heart pound, your knees weak, and your breasts tingle, and you stopped thinking.

She rolled over and stared at the cabbage rose wall paper. What should she do if he tried to kiss her again? Or did she really have a decision to make? Maybe he wasn't really interested in her specifically. Maybe he kissed any girl silly enough not to protest. Her heart sank at the thought. After all, he certainly didn't seem to be as affected as she. Even now, just the memory made her tremble. But Wes had, without apparent effort, treated her with polite indifference the rest of the morning. She sighed.

It was just as well if he wasn't interested, as she had more important concerns to deal with. She didn't need to turn and look at the armoire, didn't need to look to see the small valise tucked in the back of the bottom drawer. Her presence in Durango was because of Cory and her unborn child.

Even if there could possibly be something between herself and Wes, discounting their diverse backgrounds, she wasn't free to pursue that interest. The protection of Cory and the child she carried were her first concern. Not a good-looking blond drifter with a devastating smile and kisses that made her tremble and long for more.

* * *

By the next morning, Julie had convinced herself she'd overreacted to what was after all, just a kiss. The late Monday morning sun streamed through the kitchen windows, shining on piles of clothing and tubs of water as she and Clare attacked the week's worth of laundry. Her sleeves rolled up to her elbows, she ran one of Uncle Frank's white shirts up and down the corrugations of the washboard.

She glanced through the screen to where Wes sat under the cottonwood in the backyard, casually rolling a cigarette. Uncle Frank had carried a kitchen chair out to the shade before he left for the smelter, telling Wes he'd be safer out of the kitchen during laundry day. There had been nothing in his behavior yesterday afternoon or this morning that even suggested he remembered kissing her.

"Isn't it exciting?" Clare asked.

Confused, she stopped scrubbing and looked at Clare as she rinsed another shirt. "What? Laundry?"

"Of course not. I meant him." Clare nodded her head in the direction of the open kitchen door. "Don't you think it's the least bit scary, having a gunman in the house?" Before she could answer, Clare leaned over and whispered confidentially, "Do you suppose his picture is on a wanted poster somewhere?"

"Clare," she admonished. "He's certainly not wanted." At least she's didn't think he was wanted. Of course it was possible for a person to be exciting and trouble, without actually being wanted by the law. Still she felt compelled to defend him.

"He's working for Uncle Frank," she rationalized. "Just because a man goes from place to place to find work doesn't mean he's an outlaw."

Clare sighed in what sounded like disappointment. "I suppose you're right. Mr. Frank's a good judge of character. He wouldn't hire an outlaw." She brightened and went back to vigorously rinsing shirts. "I bet he's a gunman, though."

Oh yes. She looked out to where he leaned back in the chair with his long legs stretched out before him. Though just in shirt sleeve this morning, she recalled the gun he usually wore under his coat.

She'd have to remember that. She shook her head and said to Clare, "You've been reading too many dime novels. What would your brother say?"

"He'd agree with you," Clare giggled.

A few minutes later Julie carried a split willow basket of clean shirts out to the three strands of clothesline which ran from the side of the stable to a cross bar nailed to the cottonwood tree. A row of white bed sheets billowed gently from the farthest of the three lines.

Out of the corner of her eye she watched Wes stand and crush out his half-smoked cigarette with his boot heel. The sight of those boots had her mentally shaking her head at male stubbornness. At breakfast this morning, she'd been worried when he'd come from his room, his face pale, a sheen of perspiration on his forehead. But then she noticed he'd not only tucked in his shirt tail, but wore boots. Apparently being caught *en dishabille* by Clare and her brother yesterday had bothered him. Today, he obviously hadn't intended on looking like an invalid, even if he did move very carefully when he sat at the table.

Carrying her basket to the stable end of the clothesline, she started hanging shirts on the closest of the three strands, leaving the inside line vacant for the moment. After shirts, blouses, and skirts, she would hang the unmentionables on the inside line so as to be modestly unobservable.

As she hung the second shirt, Wes came to stand beside her. Her emotions ambivalent, she said nothing as he reached up and took the sack of clothes pegs from where it hung on the line. Instead of handing her the bag, he reached in and offered her one. "Here."

She took the peg, giving him a tentative smile, unsure of how to react after he'd virtually ignored her since yesterday morning. She pegged the shirt tail to the line, and he handed her another peg. "Thank you," she said, and received a shrug in return.

She hung two more shirts with Wes handing her the pegs. He must be trying to be helpful, she decided. He'd probably have offered the pegs to Clare if she'd been the one hanging clothes. She was his employer's niece after all and perhaps he felt he owed them for the care after his accident.

Having him help her should be no different than having anyone else help her. Only there was a difference. As much as she tried to dismiss it, awareness of him gripped her. His strong, tanned hand that handed her the clothes peg, his worn but polished boots that nudged the basket along as they worked their way down the line.

The silent partnership continued until the willow basket was empty and a line of white shirts waved in the morning sun. She picked up the empty basket, balancing it on one hip, meeting his eyes directly for the first time. Surprisingly, he looked deep in thought, his eyes slightly narrowed, his mouth unsmiling beneath his blond mustache as he returned her gaze.

With poise she didn't feel, she nodded and said, "Thank you for your help."

He nodded again, then still without a word, headed back toward his chair in the shade.

How peculiar. She walked back to the kitchen, accompanied by the rueful knowledge that his presence had a definite effect on her.

As she exited the kitchen with the next load of laundry, she glanced in his direction, wondering, or was she hoping, if he'd assist her again. From his seat under the cottonwood, he merely glanced over at the squeak of the screen door. But he didn't offer to help with this basket. Oh well, perhaps he felt he'd done his duty by helping with the first basketful. She should be relieved. She began pegging the clothes to the line. Yes, that was relief, not disappointment.

When she left the kitchen with the final basket of laundry, she went straight toward the clothesline. She maneuvered her way through the gap between two shirts to get to the inside line where she hung two pair of pantalets on the line. She held her chemise in her hands when a shadow fell across the basket. A moment later, Wes stepped into the cotton cavern created by the two outside lines of laundry.

She smothered a gasp. The area between the two lines of gently swaying laundry grew suddenly smaller and the air a whole lot harder to breathe in his presence. He glanced at the pantalets, then the chemise in her hand. She felt a blush stain her cheeks but resisted the temptation to hide the garment behind her back.

Gathering her scattered wits, she said, "I don't need your help. Thank you, anyway."

He shook his head. "I didn't come to help." After another glance at her reddened cheeks and back to the laundry basket at her feet, he said, "And I've seen women's under things before."

Not mine, she wanted to snap at him, but bit her tongue in time to keep the incautious words unsaid. As casually as she could manage, she dropped her chemise back in the basket. Then was sorry as her fingers trembled without something to clutch.

"This isn't proper. You have to leave." If he left, maybe the air would come back and she could get her breath.

"I've never been proper." He took a step closer. She thought about running but stood her ground. Slowly, as if giving her a chance to protest, he reached one hand toward her, the way a man might reach to touch a stove, uncertain whether or not it was hot. Gently, he laid his hand at her waist. The heat of his touch made shivers run up the backs of her legs. She felt the flex of his fingers, and the shivers turned from cold to hot.

"Damn," he breathed his eyes half-closed as he gazed at where he touched her. "I was right. You aren't wearing a corset." He lifted his head, his sea-green gaze intense.

She took a quick breath, and then another one, seeking enough breath to answer. "M-my brother-in-law," she stammered.

A frown creased his forehead.

"H-he's a doctor. Very progressive. He forbade my sister and me to wear one when we do laundry or other heavy work. It's not healthy he said." But maybe not wearing a corset was even more unhealthy. Without the barrier of a corset, the heat and strength of Wes's hand radiated a warmth that made her heart beat too hard, too fast. Made breathing an effort.

With a sigh, he dropped his hand. Without his touch, thinking became possible again. She clutched her hands together, wondering at the outrageous conversation. She should have fainted, or wept, or something.

Her heartbeat calming, she noticed Wes run a hand through his hair. The intense look faded and he gazed at her quizzically. Whatever could he be thinking?

With a look of bafflement he asked, "Why did you let me kiss you?"

Astonished, she blinked. "You surprised me."

"Maybe at first. But why didn't you slap me afterwards?"

Again, the heat of embarrassment flooded her cheeks. She looked down. Her honesty and impulsiveness had her answering without thinking. "Because I liked it."

He groaned as if in pain. "You're too damn honest," he said with a shake of his head.

Her chin came up. "You think people should lie?"

"People do lie. Some tell lies as easily as they tell the truth."

"Honesty is the best policy," she quoted.

He snorted. "Honesty is for people who can afford it." She started to protest, but he continued, "In some cases honesty can be downright dangerous. It can get a man shot or killed. Or it can get a woman in trouble."

"Trouble?"

With a look of total exasperation, he took a step forward. "You're not supposed to say you liked it when I kissed you. You're supposed to slap my face to keep me from trying again."

Her heart did a double thud at the thought of kissing him again. Her hand went to her throat as if to keep her heart from jumping out. "Why would you want to kiss me again?"

"Because," he practically growled, his voice suddenly low and rough, "I liked it, too."

Her heart jumped in delight. She wet her lips and tried to think. He took a half step closer and put his hands to her waist. Across the smallest of spaces that separated them, she felt the heat and tension radiating from him. Her ragged breaths drew in the mingled scents of soapy laundry and warm male.

She saw his pulse beat in his throat. Her gaze dropped a few inches lower, to the spot where the open button of his shirt revealed the golden hair on his chest. She wondered what the coarse curls would feel like and impulsively put her hand against his chest.

His face took on the hard, intense look that should have frightened her, his eyes narrow and his lips compressed beneath his mustache. But she couldn't seem to pull away from his touch, not even when he lowered his head. Her face tilted up to his, her heart wild with expectation.

Then he stopped, his lips just a touch away from hers. "See," he whispered, "I told you honesty could get a person in trouble." He exhaled and stepped back, taking his hands from her waist.

She swayed a little before regaining her balance. The fierce look was gone from his face and he was in control again. "The only thing that can come from us kissing is trouble. We'd both better remember that."

He swore under his breath, but she didn't catch the words. He shifted his feet and ran his hand through his hair. "Think I'll go out for a while. Tell Frank I'll be back in time for supper." He turned and strode toward the kitchen.

Dazed and confused, she took a few steps and leaned against the barn. She closed her eyes. When he'd kissed her before, she'd been frightened. But this time she'd learned something. She'd not been afraid of him but of what he made her feel, of her reactions to him.

And she'd learned something else. She resumed hanging clothes. Now she knew Wes was affected by the tension between them.

She wanted to rejoice in the glory of his admission, the validation that she appealed to him, that he saw her more than just a girl. But an uneasy disquiet forced her to acknowledge he was correct to say only trouble would come from their kissing.

They had nothing in common except being in Durango temporarily.

But she couldn't stop herself from wondering about the possibility of another kiss.

Chapter Twelve

Wes walked down H Street, heading for the corner of Main. He'd gone into the Lawson house only long enough to slip on his gun and coat and grab his hat. He discovered the lump on his head from the fall was still sore when he put on his hat. Readjusting his Stetson, he tried to find a normal angle while avoiding the sore spot.

Hell, he must have hit his head a whole lot harder than he thought, because he sure wasn't using his brain much these past two days. He'd been an idiot to kiss Julie in the kitchen yesterday, and today he'd practically assaulted her right out in the yard. Nothing like trying to create scandal by ruining a woman s reputation. He cursed again and slowed his pace.

He forced himself to remember the trouble his attraction to a woman had caused him in Tucson. He'd been Tom O'Malley's partner for four years when Challenge had sent them to find the culprit behind the rash of Wells Fargo robberies in that area. While Tom worked as the hostler at the livery stable, Wes got a job dealing cards in the saloon. He'd been young enough, stupid enough, to be flattered when one of the saloon girls treated him like a person, rather than just a customer. He'd been in her room the night O'Malley got shot up.

He felt a twinge of guilt every time he remembered how he'd let his partner down, even though O'Malley never held it against him. Tom always maintained he shouldn't have gone after the robbers by himself. And who would have guessed the saloon girl was in cahoots with the gang, and that her job had been to make Wes unavailable?

He reached the corner and turned onto Main, heading toward the Double Eagle. Maybe his weakened physical condition made him soft in the head. He hadn't thought, just reacted to the sight of Julie bending and stretching as she hung the wash. The knowledge she wasn't wearing a corset had tantalized him into touching. He remembered how she'd felt. Warm, soft and feminine, smelling like soap and sunshine. She was too good for the likes of him. Too honest and straightforward for a saloon kid who made his living pretending to be someone else.

He shrugged his shoulder, settling his .32 into place. She should be interested in a man like that army lieutenant. Someone honest, steady, reliable. That description surely didn't fit him. And in any case, he had to concentrate on the job at hand, his investigation. He couldn't afford to let a pretty girl distract him. Not a second time.

Wes pushed though the bat-wing doors of the saloon. Only when the large noontime crowd all turned their heads in his direction did he realize the force of his shove. The doors still flapped behind him. "Sorry," he said, feeling sheepish as he tossed his hat on the bar.

Before he could say anything else, Kate appeared. With a frown, she looked him up and down and announced, "You look like death warmed over. Come and sit down." She nodded toward a table. "Jake," she called to the bartender, "bring the kid a whiskey."

"No, thanks." He eased himself into the chair and with a deep exhale, relaxed and stretched out his legs. "I'd take some coffee if you've got it, Kate." He tried a half smile.

She gave him a disgusted look and flounced back to the kitchen. He stroked his mustache to hide his smile. Kate always did treat him like her little brother who needed looking out for.

In a minute, Kate was back with a mug. She thumped the mug down in front of him. "There, now drink."

He took a drink. The coffee slid warm down his throat, but a secondary warmth lingered. "Kate," he said with exasperation.

She sat down in the chair next to him and rested her hand on his arm. "So I added a shot of whiskey in the coffee. It'll do you good. You can't see how pale you look and how carefully you're moving. And having a drink just because you hurt don't mean you'll be like Sam. Your old man drank for different reasons."

Startled by her perception, he didn't know what to say. But with Kate, you didn't have to worry. She just took over.

"Jake," she called, "make us a couple of sandwiches." She turned back to Wes. "You, drink the rest of that," she ordered. "Think of it as medicine."

"Yes, ma'am," he answered with false timidity before she stalked away. But he obeyed. And damn, if she wasn't right. He did start to feel better.

He looked around the saloon. The noon hour was in full swing, the saloon crowded. Merchants, clerks, a few miners, and cowboys all helped themselves to the free lunch set out at the far end of the bar. Jake kept busy at the beer tap. The sounds of conversation, music of the player piano, and the click of the faro wheel made it clear the Double Eagle did a good business as a well-liked place. Kate brought him another cup of whiskey-laced coffee which he sipped as he sat and watched, and thought about smelters and accidents.

"Hey, there's Westmoreland," a man called. Several men who looked vaguely familiar to Wes came over to the table. They pulled out chairs and sat down, asking him about the accident at the Rio d'Oro. He gave them the same answers he'd given the sheriff that he didn't really remember. Trouble was it was the truth.

"You think Kennedy is right?" asked one of the men. "That there's some sort of plot against the smelters?" Wes just shrugged, not wanting to say publicly what he thought.

Several other men in the group took up the conversation, speculating who might want to sabotage either the Rio d'Oro or the Mineral King. One man with a handlebar mustache suggested it might be some sort of union plot. Another man put forth a theory that it was the Utes, angered somehow by the white man's digging in the earth and making noise and smoke.

Kate arrived with a plate of sandwiches, putting an end to the speculation and the men drifted away to let him eat.

"Thanks," he said, as Kate deposited the plate in front of him before she returned to the bar. He reached for a dry-looking ham sandwich, but the scraping sound of a chair being pulled back made him look up. The sheriff.

Rickman's dark eyes looked Wes over as the sheriff settled himself into a chair. "You're out and around mighty soon."

"Man's got to eat," he answered, and took a bite of the sandwich.

The sheriff leaned back in the chair, his thumbs hooked into the armholes of his black vest. The relaxed pose didn't fool Wes, for the sheriff's eyes remained hard. "This ain't no restaurant. Maybe it's becoming one though. Never seen Kate serve anyone else before." He shot a caustic glance in Kate's direction.

Wes put the sandwich down with an internal sigh. So that was the sheriff's problem. He was jealous. "Look, Sheriff, like Kate said, I'm an old friend of hers. We grew up together."

Rickman looked slightly mollified. He stood and looked down at Wes. "You still look peaked to me. Maybe you better get back to Lawson's and rest."

Although he understood the order, Wes couldn't bring himself to meekly agree. So he just nodded, saying, "Perhaps you're right. But I'll finish eating first."

After another hard look, Sheriff Rickman ambled over and put his arm around Kate. Wes took another bite and chewed the mouthful of day-old bread and salty ham.

He'd thought about stopping at the telegraph office and sending a message to Dan Challenge in San Francisco today. But with the way the sheriff kept casting sharp looks his way he decided not to press his luck.

Wes washed down the last bit of sandwich with his loaded coffee. He'd have to leave now. At least his conversation with the men earlier told him he probably had learned all he could today. The general population still thought the problems in the smelters a series of accidents.

With one more hard look in his direction, the sheriff left the saloon. As soon as Rickman left, Kate headed in his direction. She pulled out the chair next to him and sat down.

"You still look like death warmed over. That Lawson girl's gonna chew your hide for coming out so soon."

He gave a noncommittal grunt. He did feel bad, but there was no point letting Kate know she was right. Turning the conversation he asked, "What did you say to her the other day?"

"Nothing, just brought your stuff over." Kate smiled. "She sure is pretty. Bet she doesn't take any sass from you either."

"No," he agreed. "She's just like another woman I know."

Kate chuckled. "Thanks." Then she leaned back in her chair, waiting until he started to take the last swallow of coffee before she said, "There something between you two?"

He almost dropped the cup. "Yeah," he sneered, hurt that a friend like Kate would josh him so. "We have so much in common."

Kate waved away his reply. "All it takes is for one of you to be a man and the other a woman." She took something from her pocket and passed it to him under the table. "Here."

He felt something soft tucked into his hand. He glanced down at the small purple satin bag she'd given him. "Jeeze, Kate," he hissed. He hurriedly pushed the bag into his pocket, the flush of embarrassment probably climbing up his neck. "I've got a rubber."

"Better safe than sorry, as we always say."

"I remember." And a memory he didn't want came back.

Something must have shown on his face, for suddenly Kate's gaze turned sad. "Sorry. Didn't mean to stir up the past." She patted his hand then stood. "Go back to Lawson's and get some rest."

That sounded like a good idea. He picked up his hat, and with a wave to Kate, left the Double Eagle. Once on the boardwalk outside, he stopped to look up and down the street. Midafternoon sun made him squint after the dimness of the saloon, and the light breeze held the usual mixture of smelter smoke and pine from the mountains.

Better safe than sorry. The words almost made him wince in memory. He'd been thirteen, a tall and skinny kid, when Sam and Rita had an argument. Sam, looking down his nose, had called Rita poor white trash. It was true, but Rita didn't like it, and as Sam was the boss there was nothing she could do. Wes hadn't realized until later that he'd been the mechanism that Rita had chosen for her revenge.

Rita had waylaid him as he'd walked by her room on the second floor. Before he knew what happened, she talked him inside and was offering to make a man out of him. He'd been scared and excited. She'd done things to the boy he'd been that still made him blush. She'd taken him to bed and into her body. As the climax hit him, he'd thought he was dying.

And later, as Rita bragged to Sam what she'd done for his brat, Sam had laughed, and cuffing his mortified son upside the head, told him to always wear protection. Better safe than sorry, Sam had said. Wes shook away the old memories.

He stayed on the west side of Main as he walked south, but in the next block, he caught himself glancing across the street at Tiffany's Drugs. Unbidden, the memory of sharing a sarsaparilla with Julie engulfed him. How sweet and young she'd looked in the rose-colored walking dress, how she'd smiled at him.

Forget it. Remember instead the suspicious look Mrs. Peterson had given him. Remember that while Julie belonged in the soda parlor, he belonged in a saloon like Kate's place. He'd be better off thinking of a way to keep Julie away from him, since he was doing such a damn poor job of staying away from her.

Disgusted with his thoughts, he waited to cross F Street. Of all the stupid things he'd done in his life, and there had been a few, kissing Julie had to take the cake. Kissing her was bad enough, but he'd really screwed up today by touching her again. If he wasn't on a public street he'd smack himself in the forehead for that stupid stunt. Up until then the situation wasn't so bad. She'd acted as if the kiss at the dance hadn't happened, but after today's stunt he'd didn't know what to expect.

All his experience with women had been with working girls, or ones no better than they ought to be. But Julie was a lady, even if she didn't wear a corset all the time. If only she'd responded with anger, then maybe he could have resisted temptation. But he'd dug himself a hole and he had to figure a way out. He watched another freight wagon go by and then started across the street.

Maybe he could make her mad, that way she'd understand a kiss didn't mean anything, wasn't the start of something special between them. Hell, how could he even think there might be something between them? A saloon kid with no home had nothing to offer a well-bred girl from Philadelphia. In a day or two he'd be back at work, and when he finished here Challenge would send him someplace else. She'd go back East and in a couple of months wouldn't even remember his name.

He'd have to make her angry. Keep anything else from happening. The decision made, he rubbed at the peculiar ache in his chest. It couldn't be regret. But it was the first time relief had hurt.

The tobacco shop was in the next block. Wes decided to make a quick stop for cigarette makings. The bell over the door rang as he pushed open the door.

"Just a minute," the tobacconist called from the behind the curtain.

But before the man appeared, the bell rang again and Landham Kennedy entered. He gave Wes a sour look as the tobacconist pushed the curtain aside and stepped up to the counter. "May I help you?" He looked from one man to the other.

Kennedy shouldered past Wes. "My cigars come in yet?"

"Yes, sir." The man turned and pulled a box from behind the counter. "Here you are sir," he placed the box on the counter.

"Thanks," Kennedy said. He picked up the box and headed for the door.

"Ah, Mr. Kennedy," the man called.

"Put it on my tab," Kennedy called over his shoulder. The bell tinged and he was gone.

Wes turned to the tobacconist. "Expensive cigars?"

"Oh, yes. I get 'em especially for Mr. Kennedy," the man replied as he pulled out a paper tablet. "He don't even like me selling 'em to anyone else in town." The man sighed, and pulling a pencil from behind his ear, added to a long line of figures under the name Kennedy. He looked up. "Now then, what can I do for you?"

Wes bought papers and tobacco and then he started back north and east toward Lawson's. He wondered if Frank had heard anything from the engineer he'd sent to San Francisco and how the repairs were coming. His ribs ached. He'd be sore tomorrow from all the walking today. But at least his mind felt clearer, more focused on his job. He figured maybe one more day's rest and then he'd go back to the Rio d'Oro with Frank.

* * *

Julie pulled the curtain aside and looked out the kitchen window. With all the laundry now hanging on the line, the kitchen had ceased to be the laundry room and was ready for the start of the evening meal in another hour or so. She told herself she was silly to be worrying about where Wes might be and what he was doing. But still it was only three days since he'd fallen, and today would be the first day he'd been up all day.

After Wes left and her heartbeat had returned to normal, she started to think again. Then she got irritated. After all, what kind of man admitted he wanted to kiss you and then didn't? Now she was angry with herself for fretting about him. She let the curtain drop, dratting him for going out, and dratting herself for caring.

She turned her attention to dinner. From the front parlor, she heard Clare singing to herself as she went about dusting the knickknack cluttered room. The rattle of a buggy in the driveway had her going to the back door.

Uncle Frank pulled the buggy to a stop a few feet from the back steps and called, "Look what I found on Main Street." There sat Wes next to Uncle Frank on the buggy seat.

Wes climbed down from the buggy, his extra careful movements betraying he hadn't fully recovered. Once on the ground, he kept a grip on the buggy as he stretched himself fully upright. Uncle Frank clucked to the horse. The buggy started toward the barn, jerking Wes off balance. He staggered and clutched at his side.

Alarmed, she hurried down the steps. In a second, she was beside him. Still hunched over, his arms wrapped around his midsection, his breath whistled between his clenched teeth.

Wanting to comfort, to ease his pain, she put her arm around his shoulders. "It'll be all right," she reassured him.

He jerked away then cursed under his breath. Shocked, she nonetheless reached for him again. He straightened, and the hard look he gave her stopped her

"Don't touch me," he practically hissed, his green eyes blazing

Stunned, she froze. "I just wanted to help."

"I don't need your help." He bit off the words. "Just leave me alone." He pushed past her toward the back steps and into the house.

Unexpectedly, she felt the prickle of tears. How could he be so deliberately cruel? She'd only wanted to ease his pain, and he'd acted like, like she didn't know what. Blinking back the unshed tears of hurt, she glanced over her shoulder toward the barn. Uncle Frank had yet to reappear. She took a handkerchief out of her pocket and blew her nose, determined not to let anyone see her upset.

How dare he treat her like this? How dare he admit earlier he was attracted to her and then just now say he lied? He'd obviously taken Kate Valdez up on her offer to have a drink. She'd also caught the unmistakable odor of whiskey on his breath as he'd pushed past her. In Kate's saloon. And after refusing Uncle Frank's offer of brandy.

She looked down at her own slim figure, dressed in plain shirtwaist and skirt. She remembered the well-endowed Kate, and imagined her dark coloring flattered by something red, shiny, and low cut. By his actions today, he'd had made it apparent he had no use for a young, unsophisticated girl like herself.

How dare he make me feel inadequate? The thought fueled her anger to crowd out the hurt he'd so callously inflicted. How naïve she'd been to be so concerned with a few silly kisses. She squared her shoulders. Well, if he thought he could insult her he had another think coming. She'd show him. Show him that he and his kisses meant nothing to her.

The sound of footsteps made her turn as Uncle Frank came from the barn.

"Evening, sweetheart," he said as he kissed her cheek.

"Evening, yourself," she answered. She struggled for normal conversation. "Everything all right at the Rio d'Oro?"

"Everything's good as can be expected. Just a long day is all." He sighed, and put his arm around her. "But no longer than your day, I imagine. I can't tell you how lucky I am that you came to visit just now while Marie is in San Francisco. You've been a big help."

Uncle Frank's words of praise had her blinking back tears for the second time in as many minutes. The positive comment, so soon on the heels of Wes making her feel worthless, seemed all the more valuable. She gave Uncle Frank a quick hug, whispering her thank you into his vest.

"Now," she said, standing back, "let's go see what's for supper after our long day."

Uncle Frank smiled. Going up the steps, he opened the door for her. Determined to be the competent person Uncle Frank had complimented, she marched up the back steps and into the kitchen.

The evening passed without event. Supper was a quiet meal. Neither she nor Clare had much to say, as laundry didn't inspire conversation. Uncle Frank carried the conversation as he and Wes talked about how the repairs were progressing. Darn her for noticing the lines of pain that bracketed Wes's mouth. Or the way he constantly shifted, as though unable to find a position that didn't hurt. She didn't care, of course she didn't. Immediately after the dishes were done, she excused herself and went to her room.

* * *

The sunlight shining in his eyes woke Wes. He rolled over and groaned, his body protesting the exertions of the day before. He sat up on the side of the bed and ran his hands over his face feeling the scrape of whiskers. Damn, but he hadn't hurt this much since that stagecoach accident back in '85. He lifted his head, realizing by the slant of the sunlight it was probably past eight o'clock. No sounds or breakfast smells came from the kitchen. He'd overslept. He glared at the empty glass beside the bed

He'd let Frank convince him to take half a glass of brandy last night. To help him sleep, he said. And with the way his ribs were hurting, it seemed like a good idea. The brandy had been for the physical pain. Not for the hurt he'd seen on Julie's face when he'd snapped at her. Not for the way she'd made a point of not looking at him during dinner. With a sigh, he scratched the bandages around his waist, which was all he wore. Then he reached for his pants.

After dressing, he headed for the kitchen. On the table lay a note, written in a feminine hand.

Mr. Westmoreland, I have accompanied Uncle Frank to the Rio d'Oro. Clare has errands to run this morning but will be home to fix you lunch. Should you decide to go out again, please leave a note to tell Clare if we should expect you for the evening meal.

Not only was he now Mr. Westmoreland with no salutation, she hadn't even signed the note. He rubbed the back of his neck, thinking he should be happy his plan had worked so well.

He dropped the note on the table.

Obviously the girl Clare had already left. Yesterday he'd noticed that she seemed skittish whenever he was around, so he doubted she'd show up again until lunchtime. The room was empty, the house filled with the quiet of people absent. The stove was cold, and a damp towel hung on the rack.

He went to the cupboard and pulled out a mug. In the coffee pot on the stove he found three-quarters of a cup of cold coffee. Then he cut himself a slice of bread from the loaf he found in the breadbox. The solitary breakfast, one he'd once have considered pretty good, today seemed only adequate. Funny how quick a man could get used to good things like a breakfast fixed just to please him. Disgusted with his thoughts, he downed the coffee and stuffed the bread in his mouth as he put the cup on the sideboard by the sink.

Being alone in the house was too good an opportunity to miss. Just because he thought Frank Lawson's operation was on the up and up, that wasn't a reason not to look around. Wes went down the hall and into the library off the parlor. In addition to one wall lined with books, the room contained a desk and a cabinet. Looked like Lawson did some of his smelter paperwork here at home.

He had already looked through the office at the Rio d'Oro, just as he'd gone through Kennedy's office when he'd been at the Mineral King. Since the smelters operated twenty-four hours a day, nobody thought anything about him hanging around long after office hours. And when it came to investigation, a locked door didn't keep him out.

None of the drawers in Lawson's desk were locked, which could be an indication there was nothing to hide, or perversely, a façade of innocence. A thorough search revealed nothing more than a stack of letters postmarked San Francisco. Wes opened the top one and read the salutation, *my dearest Frankie*. Obviously from Lawson's wife in San Francisco, Wes skipped to the signature *your loving Marie.*

Feeling vaguely guilty, Wes refolded the letter and placed it back on the stack. In a lower drawer, he found several letters dealing with smelter business, which he skimmed. Nothing of interest in the cabinet, just a few ore samples, several bottles of liquor, a deck of cards. He closed the cabinet and left the library.

At the foot of the stairs he paused. If Clare came home from her errands, he could easily explain why he'd been in the library, but there wouldn't be any reason for him to be upstairs. Maybe he shouldn't. He cursed, knowing he was only looking for an excuse. The vague guilt he'd felt in the library nagged at him. This was part of his job, why should he care that the Lawsons had taken him into their home? He swore under his breath and started to climb.

He was good at his job. The best, Challenge had once said. The job was all he had. All he was.

Lawson's room, at the front of the second story, overlooked the street, the graciously furnished room done in rich browns and creamy yellows. A huge tester bed took up the south wall. An overstuffed chair and chaise sat near the fireplace. A comfortable looking room, where a man and wife could sit and talk before a fire on a cold night. He made a quick search through the armoire and dresser. Funny, how this room spoke of companionship. In his world, the relationship between a man and woman was business. He felt like an intruder into some private sanctuary. He found nothing suspicious, and then cursed the feeling of relief.

A quick glance out the front windows showed no one on the street.

Down the hall, he paused in front of Julie's room. Go on, Westmoreland. What's so special about this room? You've searched plenty of rooms. Still cursing himself, he slowly reached out and turned the glass door knob.

Chapter Thirteen

The fragrance of Julie's room hit him first. The clean, fresh scent with the underlying hint of Julie herself. He took a deep breath, inhaling the faint, tantalizing aroma. Guilt stabbed at him.

Even though he knew Julie was only visiting, the place suited her. The pale peach walls reminded him of the faint taste of peaches when he'd kissed her that first time at the Fourth of July dance. Even then he'd wanted her. He sighed and rubbed a hand over his aching ribs. Best get on with the job.

The large cherry wood closet on one wall matched the small dresser and table. A damask bedspread in shades of blue covered the bed. A rocking chair, a white piece of material draped over it, sat next to the window. He crossed the room to look out the window. Julie's view toward the back of the house showed the backyard with a glimpse of the barn, and of course the clothesline. He twitched the curtains back in place, closing off the sight and memories that flooded his mind.

Turning back to the room, the bed caught his gaze. What would her silvery hair look like spread over the dark blue bedspread? Pulling his eyes and imagination away from the bed, he looked at the rocker, only to realize the white thing draped over the chair was a nightgown. Feeling like a scoundrel, he couldn't stop himself from picking it up. The fine lawn material draped softly over his hand. He envisioned the garment warm from her skin as he held the gown to his face. Eyes closed, he inhaled the sweet womanly scent of Julie. Blood rushed hot through his body.

His physical reaction was natural and he accepted it. What bothered him was the intense longing, the wanting of something more, of something unnamable that filled him whenever he thought of her. He carefully put the nightgown back and moved to the wardrobe.

The doors were slightly ajar, and inside hung a row of clothes. Wes recognized the peach-colored walking dress, and one of the skirts looked like one she'd worn the day Kennedy had taken him to the Rio d'Oro. He closed the doors and pulled open the deep drawer underneath.

His mind still on the unidentifiable longing he felt, it took him a moment to recognize the black silk garment stuffed in the drawer as widow's weeds.

What the... He'd almost forgotten. He began to think. His professional investigator's cold calculations sprouted unanswered questions. Why had she been dressed as a widow when she'd bumped into him on the railroad platform in St. Louis? Why was this dress stuffed into a drawer when all the rest of her clothing was neatly hung up? Why would she need a disguise?

He pulled the weeds from the drawer. The familiar hint of camphor came from the folds of the material. Beneath the dress, a small valise rested. He shifted his shoulder, remembering when she'd fallen into him, knocked him off balance. The valise had thumped his shoulder leaving a bruise. He pulled the valise from the drawer. A quick look inside revealed folded sheets of newspapers and ledgers.

Damn. He needed time to go through all this.

Valise in hand, Wes hurried back to the front bedroom. A brief look out the window showed no sign of Clare returning. He moved a small table over to the window and pulled the contents of the valise out onto the table. Quickly he flipped through the papers, glancing out the window every so often.

The ledgers bore the legend Bradley House on the front page. He frowned. Wasn't that where she and her sister worked? The ledger appeared to be a cash account record. Money in from donations, money out for books, pencils, doctor's visits, medicines. Another ledger dealt only in foodstuffs, a third, laundry services.

He turned to the newsprint. He unfolded the sheet to reveal the front page of a Philadelphia newspaper. *Disastrous Fire Consumes The Hatten Shirt Company And Seamstresses* read the headline on the first article. The sub-heading continued, *Young Women Scream As They Jump To Their Death To Avoid Raging Flames. Five Seamstresses Dead In Desperate Leap From Fourth And Fifth*

Floors. Others Perish In Inferno. Valiant Effort By Fire Department Keeps Blaze From Devouring Adjoining Buildings.

Conscious of the time, he unfolded another sheet. It, too, dealt with the fire. Several articles, dated the day after the incident, bore headlines such as, *Engulfed Building Had Recently Passed Inspection, Girls Panicked, Owners Deny Unsafe Working Conditions Survivors Claim, Inspector Who Passed Building Suddenly Called Out Of Town.*

Wes noted the dates and name and address of the factory.

Still working quickly, he replaced the papers in the valise making sure they were in the same order as before. He returned the table to its original position and hurried back down the hall.

In Julie's room he replaced the valise, then stuffed the widow's weeds back in approximately the same manner as before. Three minutes later, he sat on the back step smoking a cigarette and thinking. Why would she be in disguise? Why the clippings of the fire? She obviously wasn't the type to be working in a factory. Did all of this tie in with the Bradley Center? And, more important, did it tie in with the smelters.

Because he'd liked the way she looked, the way she felt and tasted, he'd let himself forget the suspicious circumstances when he'd first met her. Angry with himself, he ground the half-smoked cigarette out under his boot heel. After lunch he'd walk down to the telegraph office and send a cable to his boss. Challenge could get him some more information on what happened in Philadelphia.

He heard footsteps on the gravel drive, and Clare, shopping basket over her arm, came around the corner and toward the back steps.

* * *

Late afternoon sun slanted across Julie's desk at the Rio d'Oro. With meticulous care, she made the final few entries in the journal for the day. That done, she put the pen down and blew gently on the column of figures, then cleaned the pen and recapped the inkwell.

She leaned back in the chair and rubbed her eyes. In a few minutes, Uncle Frank would be ready to return home, and she would face the prospect of seeing Wes again. The way he'd treated her yesterday still hurt. How he'd made her realize she wanted him to kiss her. How he'd lied when he said he'd wanted to kiss her before, pushing her away with cruel words.

She leaned forward, resting her elbows on the desk and massaged her temples with her fingertips as if she could rub Wes out of her thoughts. Think of something else. Think of Cory and the baby. Mentally she calculated the time, as she did every day.

She'd been in Durango for almost a month now, half the time she'd calculated she'd need. That she'd gone this long without detection was a good sign. Every day that passed was a day closer to her goal.

Please God, she prayed, keep Cory safe. She couldn't worry about what might happen afterward. She prayed only for her sister and the unborn child. And thank you, she added, for letting this plan work. I know I did wrong, but it was the only way I could think to keep Cory safe. And besides, Gran always said, the Lord helps those who help themselves. That's all I'm trying to do.

With any luck, in another month she'd be able to go home to Philadelphia, to take up her regular life. Somehow the thought didn't bring as much comfort as it should.

Before she could wonder why, Uncle Frank came out of his office. "Ready to go?"

She and Uncle Frank chatted on about nothing in particular as they drove. As usual, she marveled at how a road she knew to be heavily traveled just before and after the change of shift, could seem so peaceful and quiet the rest of the time. In certain places, the pines' clean scent blotted out the acrid smell of the smelter and it seemed as if she and Uncle Frank were alone on a quiet country lane.

She immersed herself in the slow, even clip-clop of the horse, the unhurried pace, feeling herself relax. Eventually, the buggy wound to the bottom of the hill, the road leveling out. They crossed the bridge, then just a few minutes through town and home.

As Uncle Frank pulled the horse and buggy up to the front of the barn, she spied Wes. He sat on the back step, whittling. The low angle of the sun struck flashes from the long knife blade as he shaved small curls from the wood. Dressed in denim pants and a chambray work shirt, surrounded by wood shavings, he looked very much at ease. His relaxed air irritated her. Why did she have to work so hard to appear unconcerned when he made it look effortless?

Uncle Frank pulled the horse to a stop. "Evening Wes," he called with a wave.

Julie wondered if she should also acknowledge Wes. Would Uncle Frank think it odd if she didn't? Before she could decide, Wes waved back and then turned and called, "They're home," through the kitchen screen. And that seemed to take care of her dilemma. The buggy rocked as Uncle Frank got out. While Julie waited for him to come around and help her down, she watched Wes.

He brushed a few errant wood shavings from his denim pants, then tugged up the hem of his right pant leg and slid the knife into his boot. The action, which only a few days ago would have shocked her, now came as no surprise. After all, she'd seen the gun he carried under his jacket. Just another reminder of how incompatible Wes was with her world.

Uncle Frank assisted her out of the buggy. While he led the horse into the barn to be unhitched, she straightened her shoulders and walked toward the back porch and Wes. As she approached, Wes stood and came down the porch step. Be polite, she reminded herself. After all he was her uncle's guest.

"Evening, Miss Julie," Wes said. He, too, was being polite. The slight nod accompanying the greeting would have had his fingers going to his hat brim, had he worn a hat.

"Mr. Westmoreland," she answered. He stood between her and the kitchen door. He didn't seem disposed to move, and she lacked the resolve to push past him. "Are you feeling better today?" The question sounded inane, but that was his fault for being in her way.

"Getting better every day."

"Why are you out here on the back step?"

He gave a slight grin. "Well, I don't think Miss Clare would want all these wood shavings in the kitchen, do you?"

She commanded herself not to be charmed by the way his mustache kicked up on one corner to reveal his white teeth.

"She said she wanted to start dinner, and I thought I'd get out of her way. I make her nervous."

She just bet he did, remembering how Clare'd wondered if Wes were an outlaw. "Perhaps, Mr. Westmoreland, your reputation has preceded you."

His relaxed air disappeared as he stiffened. "Right. You know how many people judge somebody by their reputation? Regardless of whether or not the reputation is true? How about you, Miss Julie?" he asked, his voice carrying an undertone of suppressed anger. "Do you judge a man by his reputation?"

She remembered the disparaging look and remarks Mrs. Peterson had given him that day in the soda fountain. But her own hurt, hurt caused by his actions, swamped any sympathy she might feel for him. Her desire to strike back had her giving him the same down-the-nose look Mrs. Peterson had.

"Not everyone prejudges people by their reputation." She paused and watched some of the stiffness fade from his stance. "Some of us," she asserted, "judge a man by his actions."

She gave him her best cutting look. "Now, if you'll excuse me, Mr. Westmoreland, you're in my way." She swept past him and up the back steps. She noted with satisfaction the expression on his face, one of a man who d grabbed a butterfly, only to have it sting.

The rest of the evening, he unobtrusively kept out of her way. They were like two duelists. Each had drawn blood, and were now willing to step back, calling the duel a draw. The next morning, he was in the kitchen with Uncle Frank when she came downstairs. She hesitated at the sight of him drinking coffee with Uncle Frank as Clare fixed breakfast.

"Wes is going to the Rio d'Oro with us this morning," Uncle Frank announced.

"Don't you think it's a little soon?" she commented in her best neutral voice, not sure she liked the idea of Wes being at the smelter where she would be. She took the teapot from the cupboard and opened the tin of tea leaves, an action that had her facing away from the table.

Behind her, Wes's voice echoed her neutral tone. "Figured if I managed to go out Monday, and was up and around all day yesterday, I'm ready to go back to work. See how the repairs are coming."

She moved to the stove to check the kettle. She resisted the temptation to point out that it had been less than a week since he'd fallen. What did she care if he took a chance on hurting himself again? By the time she'd poured the boiling water into the teapot and returned to the table, Uncle Frank and Wes were deep in a technical discussion of the repairs underway at the smelter.

The next two days were, in fact, trouble free. Wes and Uncle Frank were always busy somewhere in the smelter, leaving the office to her. Everyone in the smelter, from stamp operators to the witch doctor, treated Wes like a returning hero. If Wes had strutted and preened, she could have ignored the whole thing. But he waved off any acclaim, seemingly self-conscious at the praise.

And at home, in the evenings, she noticed Wes spent a lot of time out in the yard or in the library with Uncle Frank. Whether to avoid her, or to stay out of Clare's way she wasn't sure. She noticed Clare, indeed, acted timid around Wes. He avoided speaking directly to the girl whenever possible, as doing so made Clare fidget and stutter, in spite of the gentle tone of voice he used. And, for her own peace of mind, Wes disappeared right after supper, either going out or to his room.

Whenever his good behavior with others caused her to question her judgment, she had only to remember how he'd treated her to see him for the miserable wretch he undoubtedly was.

At noon on Friday, Uncle Frank went down the hill from the smelter to have lunch with friends at the Strater Hotel. Content to stay in the office, Julie ate the sandwich and apple she'd brought while reading the latest issue of Harper's Monthly Magazine.

The sound of a wagon pulling up outside the office made her look up. A few moments later, Uncle Frank came in.

"Back so soon?" Julie asked.

"Meeting broke up earlier than we anticipated." Uncle Frank hung his hat on the rack by the door. "I went by the post office and picked up the mail." He took several letters from his coat pocket on the way to his office. To her surprise, he simply laid the letters on his desk and came right back out. "Have you seen Wes?" he asked, seeming preoccupied.

"Not since we arrived this morning."

"Think I'll see what he's up to. Go on and finish your lunch." He put on his hat and left.

Julie shook her head. Must be something to do with the meeting. Uncle Frank would probably tell her about it at dinner. Only a little concerned, she went back to her reading.

Forty-five minutes later, when she was once again entering figures in the ledgers, Uncle Frank returned. With no sign of worry on his face, he kissed her cheek before going into his office and closing his door. Whatever minor problem had been bothering him apparently had been settled by seeing Wes. She went back to work with a shrug, the uneventful Friday afternoon stretching ahead

When boot heels thumped in the hallway and hour or so later, she looked up. The door opened to reveal Wes. Surprised to see him, she gave him a cool stare. He'd avoided this part of the smelter since his return to work. At her look, his gaze slid around the room. He remained standing in the doorway. She hoped the haughty look hid the sudden leap her traitorous heart took at the unexpected sight of him.

"Frank asked me to come by," he explained, as Uncle Frank came out of his office.

"Julie," Uncle Frank said. "I asked Wes to take you home." Julie shot a look at Wes, but his gaze was on her uncle. All three of them would normally be going home together. She glanced at the clock on the wall.

"But..." she started to protest.

"I know it's a little early," Uncle Frank continued, "but I'm going to be held up here for a while. You and Wes run along."

Having no choice, she stood. "I'll be ready in a minute."

Uncle Frank nodded, saying, "See you at home later tonight," and returned to his office.

"I'll wait by the buggy." Not bothering to shut the door, Wes disappeared down the hall.

She concentrated on the small duties of straightening the desk. Anything to keep from thinking about being alone in the buggy with Wes. She neatly stacked the ledgers on the desk. Don't be silly, she reminded herself as she pinned on her hat, a small straw boater with floating ribbons, and picked up her gloves.

Once outside, in the bright afternoon sunshine, Wes lounged against the buggy. As she walked toward him, he straightened, moving with less of the stiffness of the past few days and more of the easy grace she remembered. She would have liked to avoid having him touch her, as he would have to do to help her into the buggy. But to avoid his hand on her arm would be an admission that he affected her. Unwilling to give him the satisfaction of knowing she wasn't indifferent, she simply walked up to the buggy.

She didn't glance at him when he took her elbow as she climbed into the buggy, or when he walked around and climbed in beside her. Neither of them said a word as he clucked to the horse and the buggy started down the long, twisting road to town.

She sat as far away from him a possible, but there didn't seem to be much room to spare on the seat. Every so often their shoulders brushed together as the buggy bumped and swayed, his corduroy coat against her starched cotton blouse.

Julie studiously watched the scenery, the afternoon sun bright on pines and aspens, the occasional outcropping of rock. Wes let the horse set his own pace down the hill. He hadn't realized in time what Lawson's request to take Julie home would mean. Close enough to touch. Close enough to catch brief whiffs of her perfume. The sweet scent made him want to lean over and bury his face in her hair. If he did, she'd probably push him right out of the buggy.

At least then she'd have to acknowledge him instead of looking right through him like she had for the past two days. He cleared his throat, glancing over to her. "Tell me about your family." The question surprised him as much as it did her. Her brows pulled together in a puzzled frown.

Just as he decided she wasn't going to answer, she said, "Why would you want to know about my family?"

He shrugged. "Better than getting frostbite."

Her frown deepened and she cast a quick glance around the sunny hillside. She looked back at him, giving him that down-the-nose look she did so well.

"Brrrr," he said, and gave a pretend shiver under her glare. Her frown faded as she took his meaning.

Suddenly, what started out as joke to shake her out of ignoring him became important. He didn't want her angry at him anymore. He held his breath for her reaction. Her lips pressed together. Not to frown, he realized with relief, but to keep from smiling. The tension eased out of his shoulders. He gave her a half smile. "Come on," he prompted, "tell me about your family."

"Oh, all right." She sounded exasperated rather than angry. "But I'm sure you'll find us very boring." She shifted on the seat, marginally relaxing in his presence for the first time in several days. "Besides, I told you most of it before." Her voice trailed away, and she turned to look back out at the unchanging scenery.

"Tell me again." Now that he had her talking to him, he didn't want her to stop.

"Well, you know Uncle Frank is my father's younger brother. And Aunt Marie is in San Francisco with my cousin, Grace, for a few months. I think I told you my father's touring Europe with Mrs. Smith, but of course, she's Mrs. Lawson now." She said with a faint smile on her face, so he gathered her father's remarriage pleased her. "He'd been alone for such a long time, Cory and I were glad when he remarried." She turned and looked at him. "What about your parents?"

"What about them?" he hedged.

"Well, your father, for instance."

He sure as hell couldn't tell her exactly how he grew up. Maybe this conversation would help remind him that he and Julie came from completely different worlds. He shrugged and kept his voice indifferent. "Sam may have been my father, but he didn't do much in the way of upbringing except to see I didn't starve."

She cleared her throat and asked, "Your mother?"

He guided the horse around a curve, pulling back on the rein. "Never knew her. She died when I was born." And Sam never forgave him for that. "What about your mother?" he asked to turn the conversation back to her.

"She died, too. But I at least have good memories of her. And, then I had Cory to help raise me."

"She the one married to the doctor?" As soon as the words were out he wanted to bite his tongue. Afraid he'd reminded her of how he'd manhandled her by the clothesline, afraid she'd give him the cold shoulder again. That's what he should have hoped for, but his luck still held. She still had that a smile on her face, the one that showed her dimple. He could only wonder if it was good luck or bad luck she hadn't frozen him out again as he guided the plodding horse around yet another curve.

"Yes, Mark's a doctor. He's one of the doctors who volunteered their time at the Bradley Center. He'd give inoculations, or help Cory teach nutrition. It was the funniest thing," she said, and shifted sideways on the seat to face him. "I could tell Cory and Mark were attracted to each other, but neither of them did anything about it."

"Then how did they get together?" That wasn't the question he should have asked. He was getting stupid in his old age. He should be asking about the Bradley Center, trying to find the connection with the ledgers and newspaper clippings. But a mischievous smile played across her face, and he felt his heart thump.

"I arranged it." She looked so smug, her blue eyes laughing, her pink lips smiling.

He wanted to pull the horse to a stop and kiss her silly. He cleared his throat. "How?"

"One day when Cory and I were leaving the Center, Mark was coming up the front steps as we were going down. I accidentally-on-purpose stepped on the hem of Cory's skirt, and she tipped right into Mark's arms. I think she realized I'd tripped her, because she gave me a sharp look and then complained of a twisted ankle. So he carried her back inside, examined her ankle, and asked her if he could call on her." She shrugged and spread her hands. "Simple, huh?"

Wes chuckled, both at her story and at the false innocence on her face. "Where's your sister, now?" To his surprise, the happy expression faded, and she suddenly glanced away from him, her expression grim. "What's wrong?"

"Nothing, really. It's just that she's, ah, that is...." Her voiced faded.

He frowned. What could be wrong with her sister? "She sick?"

"Oh, no. It's just that she and Mark, they want children, and now she's and the last two times...." Again her voice trailed off. She looked flustered and made a gesture with her hands. The light dawned.

"She's pregnant," he guessed.

She flinched, blushed, then nodded, telling him he'd guessed correct. He cast around for something else to say, sorry he'd been so blunt. But pregnant was the nicest word he knew to describe the condition. He heard a lot less polite descriptions of that condition where he'd grown up.

"They want this baby so much," she half-whispered to herself.

Her distress for her sister made him feel even more deeply how incompatible the lives he and Julie led. She was hurt and worried for her sister, who wanted a baby. In the world he grew up in, a baby was the last thing a woman wanted.

He didn't know what to say, and apparently neither did she, for they both fell silent. The horse plodded along, the buggy slowly bumping over the dirt road.

He felt Julie turn toward him and open her mouth to speak when a rabbit shot out of the bushes and streaked under the nose of the horse. Startled, the horse neighed and reared.

Chapter Fourteen

The rearing horse jounced the buggy, throwing Julie sideways. She threw out both arms, grabbing whatever was handy. The same instant, Wes's arm shot across her, pressing her back against the seat.

"Whoa! Easy boy!" he called to the animal. He pulled on the reins. The horse's front legs thumped down. The buggy bounced like a small boat in a squall as the animal danced in panic. In alarm, she wondered if the horse might bolt down the steep trail.

Wes called, "Steady now, steady." Reins in one hand, he controlled the horse. His other arm still pinned her securely back in the seat. Bit-by-bit, the animal's fright calmed. Finally, all four hooves were on the ground. The animal gave a shudder and blew gustily through his nostrils. His tail switched and he stood still.

After a long second, Wes relaxed the reins, still crooning to the animal. The pitch and roll of the buggy settled into a mild sway. Turning to look at her, he asked, "You all right?"

"Fine." Her voice sounded breathless. She inhaled, preparing to give a sigh of relief. But neither she nor Wes had moved and her deep breath pressed her breasts against the barrier of his arm. The breath stuck in her throat.

How close they were! The solid muscles of his arm pressed against her tingling breasts as his hand gripped the buggy rail next to hers. His unique, warm, masculine scent filled her nostrils, and she looked up at him. His chest rose and fell with heavy breaths. Her own breath matched the rhythm of his.

Through half-closed eyes, the heat of his gaze burned her. In reaction she unconsciously flexed her hands. His breath whistled in between clenched teeth. He blinked and looked down. She followed his gaze, amazed to see her hand clutching his thigh.

Heat flooded her cheeks. Instead of jerking her hand back as her training commanded, she simply relaxed her grip. Compelled by curiosity, and something else she couldn't define, she slid her hand down along his thigh. The warm, soft denim of his trousers over the hard muscles fascinated her. Recklessly she ran her hand back up his thigh, impulsively willing to hazard his reaction.

She got more than she bargained for. For an instant he froze. Then, as if she'd unleashed a tornado, he wrapped the reins around the brake handle and shot out of the buggy pulling her behind him. Her feet barely hit the ground before he flipped his Stetson back onto the seat, spun her into his arms and kissed her.

With a moan, she sank into his embrace feeling the whole world disappear. Only she and Wes existed, isolated by the lonely road, the midafternoon sun, the slight breeze wrapping them in a sensual cocoon.

Her hands rested against his shoulders. She closed her eyes to take in the delightful sensations. The way his soft mouth and velvet mustache moved on her lips. The ache in her breasts that found relief and a deeper longing pressed against his solid chest. Her insides warmed and liquefied. Lack of air made her dizzy, but who needed to breathe?

He broke the kiss with a groan. "Say my name," he muttered as he started a trail of little kisses over her cheek.

"Wh-what?" How could she think when he planted kisses down her neck?

"I want to hear you say my name," he repeated. "And not that Mr. Westmoreland nonsense, like all this last week."

So he did care, she thought in elation. "Like this?" She clasped her hands to the back of his neck, leaning fully against him. "Wes," she whispered and kissed the angle of his jaw.

She felt a shudder run through him. With a groan of pleasure, he kissed her again, his hand stroking up and down her back. This time, when he parted his lips on hers, she understood what he wanted. Willingly, she opened her mouth to his invading tongue. He tasted warm, masculine, like his scent and feel. Guided by nature, she stroked his tongue with hers. He rewarded her with another low sound in his throat.

Heady in her new found power as woman, she ran her hands into his thick, golden hair. She pulled him to her as she tried to draw his tongue deeper into her mouth. A heavy shudder shook him. He shifted, his booted feet moving farther apart, as he pulled her lower body against his. The layers of denim and petticoats didn't disguise his hardness. He cupped her buttocks in his hands and rocked against her.

Sensations like the Independence Day fireworks shot through her, the sparks converging at the juncture of her thighs. Now it was her turn to moan. She threw her head back and gasped for breath. His belt buckle dug into her stomach, but she didn't care. All she wanted was more. She clutched his shoulders, remembering the last time they'd kissed, his shoulders naked, hot and smooth under her hands.

Once again he rained kisses across her face, her throat. His hands were at the collar of her blouse. Before she could wonder at his intent, the backs of his hands brushed her breasts. The brief contact shot more sparks. Then his hot hand closed gently over her breast and she realized he'd unbuttoned her shirtwaist and camisole. The thought of his hands inside her clothing, with only the fabric barrier of her chemise was almost as exciting as his touch.

"So soft, so sweet," he murmured against her throat as he caressed her breasts. A tremor rippled through her, and her nipples hardened against his palms. He must have felt them, too, for he gave a self-satisfied hum.

There was no air left in the world, her knees trembled and threatened to buckle, her head spun. She felt out of breath, weak as if she'd been running up a mountain. He ran kisses down her throat making her bones melt.

Her grip on him loosened and she swayed. Then, through her chemise, she felt the hot, wet heat of his mouth on her breast. Her world spun out of focus. She grabbed for a hold, clutching him hard around his waist.

He gave a sharp cry of pain. His body jerked. She thumped back to earth.

He wrapped his arms around his midsection, his shoulders hunched over in pain. Bereft of his support, she staggered slightly before regaining her balance. She turned her back, engulfed by humiliation and embarrassment. Dear God, what had she been doing?

He must have sensed her sway, for he caught her elbow to steady her. "Careful. You all right?"

Tears of mortification blurred her vision. How could she be all right? Maybe they were in the middle of nowhere, with no one and nothing in sight, but it was still a public road. She'd let a man she hardly knew take liberties. Her head bowed, her fingers fumbled with the buttons of her camisole and shirtwaist.

"Julie?" His voice at her shoulder sounded so concerned, so gentle.

Tears trailed down her cheeks and she choked back the sobs that made her chest hurt. "Go away," she mumbled, not looking up. She attempted to shake his hand off her elbow.

His answer sounded suspiciously like a snort of mild amusement. She saw his boots as he moved to stand in front of her. "Here," he said, holding out his handkerchief.

She wanted to take the offered hankie, but her fingers still grappled with the uncooperative buttons. The dilemma seemed insurmountable and she wept all the harder.

"Ah, sweetheart," he sighed. He took her trembling fingers in his warm hands. "Here, wipe your face." He pressed the handkerchief into her hands. Then with great tenderness he did up the buttons she'd been unable to manage. With another sigh, he took back his handkerchief and tipping her face up, wiped away her tears. His gentleness and concern unnerved her and she stood quietly under his ministrations. Even when he held the linen to her nose and ordered her to blow.

"There," he said, "feel better now?" He gave her his charming half-smile.

She took a deep breath. "Why?" she didn't understand the myriad emotions that whirled through her.

He smiled and gave a little shrug. "Because I'm a man and you're a woman. We're drawn to each other."

"But you said," she started.

"Yeah, well, I lied." He looked down and scuffed his boot across the dirt. "Look," he raised his head to look at her, "I thought if I made you mad at me, you'd treat me just like you have for the last week. I thought then I could stay away from you. So I lied to you on Monday, when I said I wanted you to leave me alone."

"But why did you want me to leave you alone?" she asked, her embarrassment turning to affront as she remembered how his words had hurt.

"Because."

Incredulous at his answer, she snapped back. "Because? What kind of answer is that!"

"Because, I didn't want this," he made a vague gesture with his hand, "to happen. I told you that us kissing would only lead to trouble."

She couldn't dispute that, not after the recent demonstration. She blushed, and looked away, her embarrassment returning. In desperation she whispered, "Why couldn't you have just kept your distance?"

"You ever see what a magnet does to iron filings?" he asked, his voice sounding strangely resigned.

She looked back at him, wondering what little shreds of iron had to do with anything. She nodded.

"Well," he bit out, "I feel like those iron filings when I'm around you."

Beyond embarrassment now, she simply stared at him. The afternoon sun burned golden highlights into his rumpled blond hair. Under her gaze he shifted slightly then winced, his hand going to his ribs. His unsmiling mouth concealed by his mustache, his stormy sea-green eyes met her gaze. If they were attracted to each other, then maybe, just maybe....

"Come on," he said abruptly, taking her elbow again. "We'd better get going."

She allowed him to guide her toward the buggy. Thank goodness no one could be expected to come up or down the trail to the smelter at this time of day

The horse stood quietly between the shafts, head down, looking half-asleep. She wondered how long it had been since Wes had pulled her from the buggy. Still shaken by what had passed between them, she looked down to check her buttons again, then put a hand to her head. Her hat wobbled on her loosened chignon. How disheveled did she look?

"Wait." She stopped beside the buggy. "I have to do something about my hair." She pulled out the hat pins, and took off her hat, placing it on the seat next to his Stetson.

To her surprise, he turned her around, and with her back to him, he started to take out her hairpins. In a second, she felt her hair fall free down her back. "Got a comb?" His words were mumbled, as if had the hairpins in his mouth.

Too stunned by his actions to say anything, she simply shook her head.

"Okay," he muttered, "then this will have to do." She shivered as he ran his fingers through her hair. Then with amazing dexterity, he twisted the mass around and around and up. Then she felt him re-pinning the chignon.

"All set," he said, his words now clear.

She whirled around, her hand verifying her hair was once again in place. "How did you know how to do that?" She'd never guessed a man would know such things

He shrugged. "I grew up around a lot of women." Intrigued, she let him help her into the buggy. He settled his Stetson and she re-pinned her hat. He clucked to the horse and they were off down the road again.

She thought back over what he'd said. "Did you have a lot of sisters?"

Wes turned to look at her. She sat with her back straight, her hands folded together in her lap. How could a woman who looked so prim and proper turn him inside out so quickly. If she hadn't grabbed his mending ribs…. The attraction between them was stronger than he'd realized. Innocent, inexperienced Julie made him hot. But scarier still was that she made him long for things he'd never longed for. Things he'd never thought to have. A home. A family. Not to be alone.

Now here she was asking him more questions about his family. Ten minutes ago, when he'd looked for a way to remind himself of the unbridgeable chasm between them, he'd glossed over the details. And now, when he wanted her close to him, he was going to answer her question. His hands tightened on the reins momentarily. He was going to tell her information that might convince her that the distance between them was indeed as unbridgeable as the Grand Canyon. He took a deep breath. "No, no sisters. No brothers either. Just me and Sam."

He saw her questioning look. He turned his attention back to the horse and drove, not wanting to see her reaction. "I grew up around a lot of women, because after my mother died, my old man made his living as a gambler. He ended up running the Red Garter saloon in San Francisco." He hazarded a glance in her direction. Puzzlement knit her brows.

He pulled the horse to a stop. "The saloon had rooms upstairs, and women who worked there." He didn't know how else to put it.

For a long moment she continued to frown at him. Then understanding dawned, her eyes going wide and her mouth dropping open.

"Yeah, that kind of women."

Her mouth closed and she blushed scarlet. "Oh, my," she breathed, staring at him.

He flicked the reins to get the horse moving again. "Don't feel sorry for me," he said sharply, wanting to forestall any pity. "It wasn't as bad as you probably think." At times it had been worse than he hoped she could imagine.

But his upbringing hadn't been all bad. "When I was a baby, they took care of me. When I was five or six, one of them taught me to read and write. I learned arithmetic from a roulette wheel and playing cards. I was always underfoot and, mostly, they treated me like a kid brother. There's not much privacy in a place like that. I probably knew as much about any of them as you know about your sister."

He shot her a sideways glance. She looked intrigued rather than horrified, and he felt some of the tension leave his shoulders. "And that's how I know about hairpins and parasols and corsets and such," he concluded.

"And, I suppose," she said in a dry tone that surprised him, "that's where you've seen women's under things, too."

He remembered her startled look when he'd stepped between the lines of laundry to catch her holding her chemise and he chuckled. "Right. I've seen more unmentionables on the line than..." he started to say than you've worn, but changed it to "than you can imagine." He gave her another sideways glance, starting to say something about seeing her under things. But the flush on her face told him she wasn't ready for that kind of intimate banter.

Her embarrassment reminded him she was a lady, and deserved to be treated like one. The buggy rounded the last curve in the road and the bridge loomed ahead. Wes pulled the horse to a stop.

He couldn't deny the attraction between them, but they couldn't risk flirting with disaster this way. He mentally cursed himself for his lack of discretion. Turning toward her, he cleared his throat. "I was out of line with what happened back there. I'll talk to Frank tonight and tell him I'm moving back to the saloon."

Without giving her a chance to answer, for what could she possibly say, he clucked giddy-up. The horse, with a toss of his head as if to say make up your mind, once more started home.

The rest of the drive was completed in silence. He turned the buggy on to the gravel drive toward the stable at the back of the house. The horse came to a stop in front of the stable door.

With the way he'd treated her, he wouldn't have been surprised if she'd jumped out of the buggy as soon as it came to a stop. But she sat there, her hands together in her lap. Damn if she wasn't a plucky little thing. There she sat, still willing to let him touch her, willing to let him help her from the buggy. Stifling a groan at the twinge in his side, he climbed out the buggy and walked around to help her down. He held out his hand, noticing with a mental wince she still looked a might peaked. She took his hand, steadying herself as she stepped from the buggy.

"Go see about supper," he told her, "I'll take care of the horse."

She nodded and started toward the back door. He watched her walk, head held high, shoulders square, the bewitching hint of a sway in her hips. She was some lady, all right.

Hand to his sore side, he took a deep breath. But she deserved better than someone like him, a drifter, a man who was always pretending to be somebody else. And that was why he had to leave. He turned to lead the horse and buggy into the barn. He'd best get to work, for he still had to pack his things and move back to the saloon.

He worked steadily, moving carefully as he unharnessed the bay, grunting now and then as a movement pulled at his side. The task occupied his hands, but not his mind. Maybe he should have made some excuse for what had happened, but he sure as hell wasn't sorry. His only regret was the time and place. No woman had ever turned to liquid fire in his arms the way Julie did. He'd been pretty hot and hard himself. At least the time and place had kept them vertical when things had been pretty close to getting horizontal.

The bay snorted, and he realized he was just standing there. "Sorry, fella," he apologized to the horse, and started brushing again.

But who would have thought she would have responded like that? Especially, since she was a lady, and all she probably knew was the polite claptrap about how a good woman did her duty by her husband.

He shut the horse into the stall, fed, and watered him. Wandering out into the backyard, he reached into his pocket to check his watch. About half an hour until Frank showed up, provided he came home at the regular time. From the kitchen, he heard Clare's voice, rattling on about something punctuated by Julie's replies.

Reluctant to parade through the kitchen to his room to pack, he strolled over to lean against the cottonwood. For something to do, he rolled a cigarette.

In the short time he'd been here he'd gotten used to seeing her, talking to her. Sharing the buggy ride, the meals and conversation with her. Once he moved back to the saloon he'd only see her at the smelter, exchange polite greeting. In a few weeks, he supposed, she'd return to Philadelphia. A pretty young thing like that, she'd probably be engaged, married before much longer. He realized he was frowning, and took another drag of his smoke. So what was it to him, if she married some Philadelphia stuff shirt? Some stuff shirt who would only expect his lady wife to grant him his husbandly rights.

He shook his head. He'd never understood why some so called decent men wanted a wife who didn't like sleeping with them, men who would be shocked if she even acted as though she liked sex. The same men who were regular customers at places like the Red Garter.

He ground the half-smoked cigarette out under his boot heel. Men like that didn't deserve a woman like Julie, couldn't appreciate her passion, her fire. Not the way he did. Julie deserved a man who would kiss her like he wanted her. A man who would make sure her first time was a dream to remember. Not a nightmare to forget like Rita had done to him. Julie deserved a man who would really want her. And by God, he did want her.

At least, he looked toward the kitchen again, if he made love to Julie, it'd be because she desired it, not just some wifely duty to be endured for the creation of children. And he knew better than some stuffed shirt how to protect her, keep her from getting children until she was ready. Growing up the way he did made him very aware of the possible consequences of sex.

Maybe wanting her wasn't correct or polite, but at least what he felt was genuine. He pushed back his hat, the evening seeming much warmer than before. God, he did want her. His imagination took him boldly across the yard to throw open the screen door, and scoop Julie up in his arms.

The fierce ache in his fingers from where he gripped the trunk of the cottonwood stopped the dream. He released his grip on the gray-brown bark and flexed his hand. He definitely had to pack and get out of here before he did something stupid.

The sound of a horse on the gravel drive brought Wes's head up.

Chapter Fifteen

Thankful for something to distract him from thoughts of Julie, Wes walked toward the barn as a worried looking Frank Lawson rode into view. What had happened since he had left the smelter to drive Julie home?

"What's wrong?" He asked, taking the horse's bridle as Lawson dismounted.

"There was an accident at Kennedy's smelter." Wes's belly tightened like he'd been kicked. "When?"

"About forty minutes ago."

A week to the day since his own accident. His scalp prickled, his sixth sense telling him the answer to his investigation had gotten closer.

Lawson took off his hat and wiped his brow with his handkerchief. "We heard the alarm. By the time we got over there, Kennedy said he had things under control."

"So Kennedy wouldn't let you in the Mineral King?" Wes verified.

"No. Said they didn't need help."

He snorted. "Wonder what they didn't want you to know?"

"Struck me as odd, too," Lawson acknowledged.

"Well," Wes said, thinking out loud for Lawson's benefit. "Kennedy'd never let me in to look around, either. But too many people were there for Kennedy to keep what happened under wraps." He drew the reins back and forth between his hands. "It's about time for the shift change. I'll go down to the Double Eagle. Enough men from the Mineral King will be there who know me. And they'll be talking about the accident. I'll find out exactly what happened." He gave the reins back to Lawson. "I'll just go pack my things first. Time I moved back to the saloon."

"No!" Lawson looked back toward the house, the chatting voices of the two women fixing dinner, the smell of fried chicken drifting on the evening air.

"No," Lawson repeated, this time without the urgency. He turned, but didn't look Wes in the eye. "Don't move back to the saloon just yet. I have to go to Denver tomorrow for a meeting."

Wes raised his eyebrows. Then he remembered Lawson's distraction when he'd returned from lunch. And then he'd asked Wes to drive Julie home early. He shoved his hands in his pockets, forcing his memory away from that drive home and back to the explosion at the Mineral King. So maybe Lawson's trip wasn't connected to the explosion. "A meeting on Saturday?"

"I have a ticket for tomorrow morning's train. I'll be back on the first train Monday morning. I need you to stay here with the women while I'm gone."

Wes rubbed a hand over his face. He glanced to where the soft light from the kitchen window spilled out into the deepening twilight. Damn. Now he was stuck, temptation right in front of him. "Okay, I'll stay until you get back."

A relieved expression crossed Lawson's face, so Wes knew nothing untoward showed in his voice. He pushed all complications from his mind to concentrate on the smelters as he pulled his watch from his pocket to check the time. "I'll go down to the saloon now."

"I'll go with you," Lawson offered.

He shook his head. "The men will talk more freely if I'm alone. No need reminding them I work for you. I'll be just another fella who got hurt in an accident. Later, I'll go out to the Rio d'Oro for the rest of the night. If I find out anything, I'll let you know." After all, Lawson thought Wes worked for him.

Lawson sighed. Then nodded his acknowledgment for Wes's plans.

"What time's your train?"

"Nine," Lawson said.

Wes stuffed his watch back in his pocket. "I'll be back in time to drive you to the station if not before."

"Good luck," Lawson called as Wes swung into the saddle.

"Thanks." He turned the horse and headed for the Double Eagle.

* * *

Julie took a stack of plates from the cupboard and turned toward the table. She tried to pay attention to Clare's idle prattle. But thoughts of what had happened with Wes tumbled over and over in her mind leaving her feeling dazed and bewildered. She didn't even know what to call the incident. It was far more than a kiss; less than what could have happened. How willing she'd been. Her cheeks warmed with the heat at the mere memory.

Until now she thought she'd understood the knowing looks she'd seen Cory and Mark exchange when they thought no one was watching. Could a man kiss a woman with such passion if he didn't care for her? Her own eagerness, while embarrassing, told her how deeply she had come to care for Wes.

But now what were they to do?

Thoughts a muddled mess, she laid the plates on the table. A few minutes earlier she'd heard Uncle Frank come home and peeking out the window had seen him talking to Wes. The sound of hoof beats made her pause.

Before she could wonder, Uncle Frank pushed open the screen door and entered the kitchen. He greeted her as he took off his jacket.

Expecting Wes to be behind Uncle Frank, Julie glanced at the empty doorway. "Where's Wes?"

"Gone." Uncle Frank draped his jacket over the back of the chair.

"Already?" In confusion, she glanced toward his room, knowing he hadn't come in to pack. "Gone where?" Her voice must have sounded odd, for Uncle Frank gave her a curious glance.

He paused, rubbing the back of his neck, he gave a sigh. "There was an accident at the Mineral King this afternoon."

"Oh, no," Clare exclaimed.

Wes has gone to investigate.

"How can he investigate," she asked, "if the accident was at the Mineral King?"

Uncle Frank pulled out a chair and sat down. "Actually, by this time, the men who were at the smelter will be at the saloon, so Wes will talk to them there."

She frowned. She didn't like the thought of Wes, the man who had just turned her world upside down, spending the evening with the beautiful and sophisticated Kate. Of course, there were plenty of saloons in Durango, but somehow she knew Wes would be in the Double Eagle.

* * *

Friday evening the Double Eagle, along with every other saloon on the block, teemed with miners, cowboys, merchants, and smelter workers. Letting the conversations surge around him, Wes slumped in his chair at one of the tables while he absentmindedly twisted a half empty beer glass to make wet rings on the tabletop. All the talk centered on the explosion, and everyone had a story to tell. While every man had his own version, the basic facts remained consistent. One of the boilers supplying steam power for the smelter had sprung a steam leak. And after two hours in the Double Eagle with the haze of cigarette and cigar smoke, the constant din of tinny music and loud talk, smell of whiskey and beer, and the way redheaded Rhonda kept draping herself all over him, he was more than ready for some fresh air. He took a sip of beer, looking around the saloon. What should feel like home no longer did.

The hell with it. He drained the beer. He had work to do and best get on with it. The only odd thing about his evening was that he hadn't seen Sheriff Rickman or Kennedy around. Wes stood and made his way to Kate through the crowd.

He borrowed a pen and paper from Kate, and in the kitchen scribbled a brief report to Lawson, writing the date and time at the top.

A boiler sprang a leak, and escaping steam badly burned three to ten men, depending on who's telling the tale. Best estimate probably five hurt. Mineral King without power as whole boiler room shut down, the coal fires swamped by hot water flooding when someone opened the relief valve on the broken boiler. Smelter capacity is down approximately fifty to sixty percent. Repairs to take two to four days, depending on inspection and repair.

He gave the note and a coin to Jake, knowing the bartender would find some kid who would deliver the note to the Lawson house.

Between the nearly full early-rising moon and Lawson's horse, which must surely have the road memorized, he made the nighttime ride up to the Rio d'Oro with ease.

After talking to the night manager and filling him in on the news from the Mineral King, Wes sent a man to make sure the water barrels on the roof were full. Starting at the top with the crushers, he walked each level of the smelter, ending up in the Rio d'Oro boiler room at the lowest level.

Hot and dank, the boiler room was only marginally less noisy than in the main smelter area. Three massive boilers, stoked with coal, generated steam needed to power the smelter. Although Wes was sure the door closing behind him didn't make enough sound to carry over the enveloping noise, the boiler room supervisor immediately left the gauge he'd been studying and ambled toward Wes.

"Howdy," McCarthy greeted him. "What do you hear about the Mineral King's accident?"

"I hear it was the boilers." Wes kept his voice mild, knowing the aged Irishman's protectiveness of his beloved boilers.

"So you thought you'd check out my boiler room?" McCarthy tipped his head down and gave Wes a narrow-eyed look over the top of his spectacles. "Well, won't find any problems here, young feller." He spit, the tobacco probably making a small ping as it hit one of the spittoons scattered around the boiler room.

"Didn't think I would. But it couldn't hurt to look, now could it?" He gave McCarthy a man-to-man smile.

The old man conferred one more suspicious look on Wes before deciding to cooperate. "Guess you gotta do your job. Here," he said, pulling a plug of tobacco from the hip pocket of his dirty overalls, have a chaw."

"No, thanks. I already have enough bad habits."

McCarthy guffawed, then followed Wes as he checked the boilers

When he heard what Wes recounted of the Mineral King boiler leak and consequent flood of the boiler room, McCarthy spit again. "Gotta be careful around boilers, ya know? Me, I been with boilers all my born days. Started in steamboats on the Mississippi when I was still in short pants." He stopped to pull a rag from his pocket and polish the glass face of a pressure gauge. "Kennedy, he shoulda known better than to use old equipment like that."

"What do you mean?" A sixth sense crept up the back of his neck at old man's words.

He'd gone through the receipts and bills of lading in the Mineral King's office when he'd worked for Kennedy. He remembered the price Kennedy paid for the boilers, because when he'd gone through Lawson's study, he'd compared the price against what Lawson's records showed what the Rio d'Oro paid. Both men had bought their boilers from the same Denver company at the identical price.

"It's the same as this equipment as here," he said.

"The hell it is!" McCarthy punctuated the statement with another spit of tobacco. "Boilers have number plates, ya know?" He stooped over and pointed to a small brass plate nearly concealed by the outward curve of the boiler's cylindrical shape. "I was at the railroad station the day Kennedy's boilers come in. Number on his boilers was low, meaning they'd not be new manufacture. Maybe them boilers was all cleaned and painted up pretty, but they was old." McCarthy nodded, as if confirming his own statement.

"You certain?"

"Hell, yes, I'm certain. I looked at the plate. Less'en someone put old number plates on a new boiler. Ain't no purpose in that now is there?"

No, but there might be a purpose in putting a newer plate on an old boiler. "Thanks for your help, McCarthy." Wes shook his hand. "I'd better get on with my tour." McCarthy nodded, and turned back to his beloved boilers as Wes left the boiler room.

Outside, the position of the moon high in the sky, told Wes the night was more than half over. Instead of fatigue, energy flowed through him as he began to pace, thinking about what he'd just learned.

From the start, the problem with this investigation was that both smelters were having accidents. Who would benefit if both smelters went out of business? No one that he could see. He leaned against the boiler room wall, and absently rolled a cigarette as his mind turned the problem over and over. What if some of the incidents he'd been sent to investigate were truly accidents, while others were the result of sabotage? Where better to hide a tree than in a forest?

Both smelters had steady business, but his peek at the records in the Mineral King and the Rio d'Oro told him that the volume wasn't what it had been two, three years ago.

He considered sneaking into the Mineral King to check the busted boiler's plate himself but discarded the idea. Not only could too many people there recognize him, but there was no way to tell if the number plate now on the boiler was the original one McCarthy had seen when the boiler arrived in Durango. And since Wes often saw Kennedy in the company of Sheriff Rickman, something told him a trespassing charge might land him in jail quicker than spit. Since the accidents always occurred several days apart, he had a little time. The wisest course of action was to have the Denver office do the checking for him.

He tossed aside his un-smoked cigarette, and made his way back up to the witch doctor's office. The chemist wouldn't be in until the morning shift started so his office was empty. He pushed aside a scale and mortar and pestle to make a clear space on the work bench. Then he dug around in a drawer to find a pen, inkwell and paper. He wrote a request to the Denver office, asking them to check with the boiler company to see what their records showed. What was the original boiler plate number on Kennedy's and Lawson's equipment, and what had each paid the smelter company? The invoice in Kennedy's office had been for new equipment, but if his boiler was old. If the boiler company confirmed what McCarthy said, then Wes almost had proof of who, and why, there was trouble in the Durango smelters.

* * *

Low in the sky, the dawn sun cast a yellow glow over the back of the Lawson house as Wes, slumped in the saddle, rode his equally tired mount up the gravel drive. He stifled a groan as he dismounted. The barn door creaked as he pushed it open, letting the light into the dusky interior. He looked back toward the kitchen. No movement. No clink or clatter. No one up yet.

He led the horse inside. "Long night, huh, fella," he asked as he undid the cinch. The gelding blew gustily down his nostrils in agreement as he lifted the weight of the saddle from the animal's back. "Yeah, me, too."

But the long hours had been worth the effort. He brushed, then fed and watered the horse. In a few hours from now, when he took Lawson to the train, he'd telegraph the Denver office. Then, within a couple of days he'd have the answers he'd been sent to find.

As he left the barn and walked toward the house he noticed the back door was now open and through the screen came the sounds of water splashing and then the clank of stove lids. Someone was in the kitchen. All of a sudden, he seemed less tired. His pace quickened. He climbed the back steps and peered through the screen door into the Lawson kitchen.

Clare stood at the counter measuring coffee beans into the coffee mill.

His shoulders sagged as disappointment hit him. He'd anticipated seeing Julie, and the realization made his stomach churn. He watched Clare without seeing her, imagining instead how Julie's silver-blond hair would look in the early morning light streaming through the window. He couldn't stop himself from remembering how fine and cool her hair had felt in his fingers. Couldn't stop from imagining how that silky hair would feel if trailed across his body. He suppressed a shiver of delight.

Damn. What was wrong with him? He should be too tired for such thoughts. The burst of energy had lasted through writing to Denver. Now his eyes were gritty and he felt the effects of being up all night.

He reached out to open the door but hesitated a moment. Knowing how nervous he made Clare, he considered going back to the barn for a few minutes. No, he was too tired. He'd just call out before he went in.

Just then, he heard Julie's voice. "Clare?" she called, followed by something indistinguishable.

"Coming," Clare called. Drying her hands on her apron, she left the kitchen, her heels tapping down the hall and up the stairs.

With a grateful sigh, he entered the kitchen and hung his hat on the rack. He dropped into one of the chairs, glancing around the empty kitchen. The quiet room wrapped him in an odd feeling. He searched for the words. Comfort? Contentment? No, more than that.

Home.

Where had that thought come from? Why did this house, this kitchen where he'd only spent a week seem so much more like home than a saloon where he'd spent practically his whole life?

* * *

After setting Clare on an upstairs task, Julie headed toward the kitchen. She'd spent last night contemplating yesterday's ride home with Wes.

The way he'd kissed her, the way he'd touched her yesterday left her frightened, exhilarated and confused. She should have… have what? Shouldn't she have been outraged? Shouldn't she have screamed or slapped him or demanded Uncle Frank throw him out of the house?

But she'd done nothing. Not even later. Wes had been the one to suggest he leave, not her. And what would she do when she saw him again? She reached the doorway to the kitchen and came to a sudden halt.

Wes. His chair turned sideways to the table, he slumped back, one arm across the table top. Eyes closed, head resting on the chair back, one booted foot rested on the neighboring chair. His other foot braced against the floor, apparently the only thing keeping his slack body from sliding out of the chair.

An up rush of tenderness at the sight of him had her gripping the doorway for support. She wanted to hurry to his side, touch his face, comfort him, fetch him coffee and breakfast. Help him take off his boots. Wes. Oh, Wes. She wanted to do all the little things for him that she had seen Cory do for Mark. She wanted to have Wes do for her all the things Mark did for Cory. The little things that marked a man and woman as belonging to each other. She wanted to let her hand trail across his shoulders as she walked past where he sat, proclaiming to anyone watching that he was hers.

She loved him. The wonderful, warm feeling threatened to make her knees buckle.

Then cold panic intruded and the warmth fled. My God. She pressed her hand to her throat.

She loved him.

Chapter Sixteen

She loved Wes.

But she couldn't. Not now.

Beneath her hand at her throat, her pulse raced. She loved Wes, but her first priority was Cory and her unborn baby. She had to return to Philadelphia.

What was she to do?

A soft thump sounded as Wes's booted foot slipped from the chair, and she jumped. Sitting upright, both feet on the floor, Wes stroked his hands down his face, as if to wipe away the sleep. Then he turned and looked at her.

Just his sleepy glance was enough to make her heart leap. She squared her shoulders, silently adhering to Gran's advice to keep up appearances. Smoothing her hand over her skirt, she pasted a smile on her face and walked into the kitchen.

"Sorry, guess I fell asleep," he said as he stood. "I, ah, just got here. Clare had gone back upstairs, so I let myself in." His voice had a slight upward cant at the end, making his statement a question. Ah, he'd waited until Clare had left before he entered the kitchen. One couldn't have missed the way Clare sidled around when in the same room with Wes. Though he'd never let on, he obviously noticed.

Finding her voice, she answered, "Uncle Frank said you'd be back this morning." She cleared her throat. "To drive him to the station." Don't just stand here and stare. Go finish the coffee, keep your hands and mind busy with everyday things.

She crossed the kitchen to the counter. As she turned the crank on the coffee mill, he moved to stand behind her. Thank goodness her hands were occupied, otherwise he might notice them trembling.

Would he touch her? She both wished for and dreaded his touch. She held her breath, and fortunately after a second or two, he moved a short distance away.

He leaned back against the counter so that they were side by side, facing in opposite directions. She turned the handle, the steady grinding noise filling the silence. From the corner of her eye she saw him rub the back of his neck. Then he took a deep breath.

"Look, I'm sorry," he said, apologizing to the kitchen. "I can't leave like I said I would."

She cleared her throat. "I, I, ah, Uncle Frank explained about his trip to Denver." The grinding noise faded away. Opening the mill, she started to measure the coffee. To fill the silence, she said, "Uncle Frank will be down soon. He was pleased to get your note about the Mineral King boiler last night." She practically winced as she realized she was babbling as badly as Clare sometimes did.

Why didn't he say something? If she asked a question, then he'd have to make this a conversation. Without thinking further, she asked, "Do you think you might stay in Durango?"

The question fell like a brick and the silence thickened. Finally he shrugged. "Who knows how long a job will last?" He pushed off the counter and took a seat at the table.

She bit her lip at his implied rebuff. Why had she blurted out the first thing that came into her head? The next spoonful of grounds missed the pot, ending up on the counter. Quickly she cleaned up the mess and put the coffee on the stove to perk.

She glanced at him as she went about preparing breakfast. What was he thinking? His shaggy blond hair looked like he'd combed it with his fingers. The golden stubble of his overnight beard blurred the outline of his jaw and the weary slant of his shoulders made her hands itch to rub away the fatigue. She busied her hands with tying on the apron she'd forgotten until now.

Impulsively, she took a chair across the table from him. Did you really grow up in a saloon?" she asked unthinkingly.

He frowned, as if puzzled by the question.

"Oh, not that I didn't believe you. It's just, ah, well. What was it like?"

Again he shrugged. "Like I said, not as bad as you probably think. It was just where I grew up."

But by the look on his face, the memory of childhood wasn't all that pleasant.

"What was it like for you?" he asked. "Growing up in Philadelphia?"

How could she explain? And why did she feel slightly guilty that her childhood had been happy, secure in the knowledge she was loved. "Nice. Comfortable."

Wes raised an eyebrow, as if the terms had no meaning for him in this context.

She sighed and tried to explain further. "We have a nice house in the Germantown section of Philadelphia. A big yard, with a swing in the tree. Cory and I each had our own rooms. Papa would read us a story at bedtime, and them Mama would take us upstairs and tuck us in." She pictured it in her mind, remembering how she and Cory had played together, how Cory had cared for her and loved her after their mother died. A quick glance at him showed an odd mixture of wonder and disbelief on his face.

She hurried on with her explanation. "I remember once there was a big party at our house. I must have been about four or five, but I remember Mama and Papa all dressed up, the house full of flowers. Cory and I were on the upstairs landing, waiting to watch the guests arrive. Mama and Papa came into the foyer. Papa took Mama's hands and held them out to her side and cocked his head as he looked at her. 'You're just as beautiful as ever, Caroline,' he said. Then he leaned over and kissed her. Cory and I giggled. Mama and Papa looked up. Mama blushed like a school girl, but Papa just laughed." She smiled at the happy memory.

Wes stared at her with a curious look of amazement on his face. His expression confirmed what she had guessed the day they had sarsaparilla together. He'd had a cold lonely childhood like the children she saw at the Bradley Center. She may have a slight idea of what his childhood was like, but he obviously couldn't imagine what hers had been like.

"Cory and I had such good times together. I can't imagine what it would be like to grow up without a sister."

"Didn't you do anything alone?"

Now Julie chuckled. "Of course. I got into trouble all by myself."

He gave her a sideways look. "You in trouble?"

"Oh, yes, Mr. Westmoreland, I most certainly was capable of misbehaving." She gave him a mischievous smile that flashed her dimple. "The time I remember best was one winter. There was a pond not far from our house where we went ice skating. I was forbidden to go alone. But Papa was busy, and so was Cory, so they said wait a day or two, then they would have time to take me skating.

"I woke up early the next day and got my skates and snuck out of the house and over to the pond. Just as I got there, it started to snow. Lovely big flakes drifting down. The air was quiet and cold and still. My skates left the first tracks over the unspoiled ice. The blades hissed in the morning stillness. It was beautiful. Just me and the ice and the quiet gray and white world." She couldn't describe the incredible feeling of freedom and lightness any better.

"Where's the trouble?" he asked. He leaned back in his chair his eyes held the look of a small boy hearing a fairy tale for the first time.

She sighed, dramatically she hoped. "It was mid-morning by the time I got home, and the whole household had been frantic with worry. Mrs. Bates, the cook, was crying in the kitchen, sure I'd been kidnapped. Papa was out searching. Mama grabbed me and gave me a big hug, then a swat for worrying her so. I was sent to my room for three days to contemplate my sins."

"And what did you learn from this?" A smile accompanied his reproving tone, telling her he was teasing.

She assumed a serious expression and folded her hands on the table. "Unfortunately, I learned that the memory of that solitary morning skate was well worth the price. I still remember skating, I don't remember the three days confined to my room."

He smiled and shook his head. "You, Miss Lawson, are some girl." The wonder in his voice warmed her. Slowly his smile faded away. He straightened. Then abruptly stood up and crossed to stare out the window. His broad shoulders flexed under his chambray shirt as he pulled the curtain aside.

What had caused her to tell all those stories? Who knew that love made you stupid? Why had she asked him those embarrassing questions about staying in Durango and the way he grew up? No wonder he wanted to move back to the saloon. He probably thought her a naïve, silly girl.

Still looking out the window, Wes said, "I'm only staying because your uncle asked me to. And I'll be leaving, moving back to the saloon as soon as he gets back from Denver."

The words could have been a cruel dismissal, but the way he said them sounded as if it hurt him to say them. Dare she hope?

The sound of footsteps coming down the stairs drew her attention away from Wes at the window. Within a few minutes the kitchen filled with the normal business of four people having breakfast.

Scooting back from the table, Uncle Frank pulled his watch from his vest pocket. "We'll have to hurry to make the train."

Wes stood and nodded. "I'll hitch up the buggy." He took his hat from the rack by the back door, and the screen banged gently behind him as he left.

Julie stifled an inner sigh. Even walking away he looked good to her. "Well," she said briskly, "we'd better hurry with these dishes."

Uncle Frank left to get his bag, and the two girls started on the cleanup. "Tell you what," Clare suggested. "Why don't you go to the station so you can say goodbye to Mr. Frank. Then you can do the shopping on the way home, and I'll stay and finish here and get started on the cleaning."

She hesitated. Was it to avoid being alone with Wes after Uncle Frank took the train? Even then she and Wes wouldn't really be alone but out shopping in public. What could happen? "Good idea," she told Clare, and took off her apron.

A few minutes later, she sat squashed between Uncle Frank and Wes as he drove the buggy down the drive and turned south toward the train station. The train stood panting next to the depot, passengers already boarding; a few lone businessmen and several families apparently on their way to Denver.

When Wes pulled the rig up, Uncle Frank reached behind the seat and pulled out his bag. "No, don't bother to get out." He kissed Julie on the cheek, and then to her surprise, shook hands with Wes. "I'll be back Monday."

The train whistle shrilled, and she watched her uncle hurry across the platform. He paused at the doorway and turned and waved. She waved back. He disappeared as a massive shudder shook the train and it gradually began to move. The whistle tooted again, and Uncle Frank was on his way to Denver.

And she was alone with Wes. The realization she loved him made her feel suddenly self-conscious and awkward.

Wes flexed his hands on the reins and from the corner of his eye saw Julie clasp her hand together in her lap. Neither one looked at the other. He stared off to the west, where clouds like cotton bolls had already formed over the mountain peaks.

Not knowing what else he should do, Wes clucked to the horse and headed back north on Main. Although he didn't look at her, he was aware of her next to him. She'd scooted over when her uncle got out of the buggy, but she was still close enough that her skirts brushed against his boot. Small wonder she hadn't scooted practically out of the buggy, not with what happened the last time he drove her any place.

Damn, but she looked good. She wore a plain shirtwaist with the rose-colored bodice and walking skirt, the one that went with the stubborn parasol, he recalled. All his thoughts about how wrong he was for her were about as useful as dipping water with a sieve when he was near her.

Thank God she seemed to have more sense. All those questions this morning about growing up in a saloon and was he going to stay, were obviously her way of reminding herself he had nothing to offer her. She was out of his class. His mind may have known it but his body sure didn't. All he wanted to do was pull her over his lap and kiss her until she was breathless.

Julie cleared her throat, interrupting his thoughts. "You can let me off by the grocery."

"Let you off?"

"Clare offered to stay and start the cleaning if I would do the shopping. You can let me off here," she gestured to the line of retail stores that lined this block of Main Street. "I'll walk home when I'm finished."

He hated how tense she sounded. The way she stared straight ahead not looking at him was beginning to make him angry. Did she think he'd attack her here in the middle of town? He pulled the buggy up next to the boardwalk. "You, ah, don't want me to wait?"

"It's not necessary." Her voice had that ultra-polite quality that grated on his guilty conscience.

"Fine," he snapped. He flipped the reins around the brake handle, jumped out of the buggy to walk around to help her down. As impersonally as possible, he helped her from the buggy. As soon as she was safely on the boardwalk, he climbed into the buggy and scooted over to the driver's side. He couldn't help one more glance at her, as she stood there, twisting her hands together. "I'll see you back at the house."

A startled look crossed her face. "Oh, my," she gasped.

"What?" The question came out sharper than he'd meant it to. She looked down at the toes of her shoes, then up at him. What could be wrong?

"It's just, that is…" she flushed and looked away. She cleared her throat. "It's just that Clare is there alone, and, well, you…"

Suddenly the light dawned. Although he never even looked cross-eyed at her, that silly Clare acted like he'd pull out his pistol and shoot up the countryside at the least provocation. He'd noticed how Julie always tried not to leave Clare alone in the same room with him. So anxious had Julie been to get away from him, she was willing to abandon poor Clare. The thought had him clenching his jaw. "Don't worry about Clare. Two minutes after I get back, I'll be in my room sound asleep." He gathered up the reins. "Don't bother to wake me for lunch either," he added as he shook the reins, and left her standing there without a backward glance.

Julie watched the buggy turn the corner and disappear from sight. Now, maybe, she could think. Think about how she loved him? No. Not think, just put everything out of her mind, concentrate on the shopping to be done. Later she would try to think of something, some course of action.

All around her the bustle of Saturday in town seemed willing to occupy her. Carriages, buggies, and wagons filled the street. Foot traffic cluttered the board sidewalks. A fine summer morning, with only puffy white clouds boiling up over the western mountains. Surely on such a day, she could carry out a simple task like shopping.

But before she could head toward the grocery, a female voice called her name. She turned to see Mrs. Peterson striding toward her. The newspaper editor carried a black silk parasol to match her dress. The determined look on Mrs. Peterson's face as she marched toward Julie had her remembering Uncle Frank's words about how the editor had her pencil into everything. Like an advancing tornado, Mrs. Peterson whisked her up and into Tiffany's drugs, had them seated at a table with two gently fizzing glasses of sarsaparilla. How, she thought with disgust, was she supposed to put Wes out of her mind when the last time she'd sat at a table like this it had been in his company?

Mrs. Peterson said, "I suppose you heard all about the accident at the Mineral King yesterday. I haven't seen your uncle today. I couldn't even get a decent quote from Landham Kennedy. The man was actually rude to me." The matron practically quivered with indignation.

She hitched her chair closer to the table and leaned over, her posture inviting confidences. "What did your uncle think? Does he think there's a cause behind the accidents? What about the last accident at the Rio d'Oro?"

Julie's stomach began to churn. All these questions that she didn't want to answer. She didn't want to say something Uncle Frank might not want her to say. She took a sip of the sarsaparilla to buy a little time before answering. "Really, Mrs. Peterson, I think you should ask Uncle Frank. I don't want to answer for him."

Mrs. Peterson gave her a look, as if thinking about rebuking her for equivocating. "Well, my dear—"

"Why don't you come by and see Uncle Frank?" she broke in, wanting to divert Mrs. Peterson, and bring the conversation to an end. "Perhaps Monday afternoon at the Rio d'Oro? I'll make an appointment for you at one o'clock." She gave Mrs. Peterson her sweetest, most harmless smile then buried her nose in the sarsaparilla.

She drained the glass. "Thank you so much for the soda. Oh, my, look at the time," she glanced at the wall clock. "I simply must get on with my errands." She stood, thanked Mrs. Peterson again, and left the drug store.

Once outside, Julie walked quickly down to the grocery. A little wind had come up, and small puffs of dirt blew over the walkway. She hurried into the store, which was more crowded than usual for a Saturday morning. By the time she exited the store she was surprised to find thunderheads quickly scudding in from the west.

Thunder grumbled in the distance. She stood on the walkway and watched the shoppers duck into carriages or hurry down the walk. She shivered as the wind gusted down the street, the temperature noticeably cooler than it had been before she entered the grocery. Oh, dear, they were in for a summer storm. Thunder growled again, even closer than before. Clare! The poor girl would be petrified. Julie grasped her billowing skirts with one hand, and joined the people hurrying toward home.

Fortunately she had turned the corner toward home before large, scattered raindrops started to fall. Instead of going around to the kitchen door as she usually did, she rushed in the front door as a loud clap of thunder echoed over the town.

The clouds were now thick enough to dim the interior of the house. At the hall table, Julie stopped and unpinned her hat and pulled off her jacket. She laid the hat and jacket on the table. She called out "Clare?" just as another clap of thunder sounded. Shaking her head, she hurried down the hall to the kitchen.

At the kitchen doorway, her steps faltered to a halt.

Wes.

In one stunned instant she took in everything, the image burned into her mind. His back to her, Wes stood by the sink, dressed only in clean denim trousers. Slightly crouched over, he looked into a small mirror propped against the cupboard as he shaved. Even with her gaze locked on Wes, she noted the tub of water next to the table. The clothes he'd worn that morning thrown over a chair. A clean shirt, along with his gun and holster lay on the table. A combination of mortification and fascination held her both motionless.

The straight razor made a soft shussing sound as it scraped the soap from his jaw. She watched the bewitching play of the muscles of his back and shoulders as he shaved. A few beads of water dripped from his damp, dark, wheat-gold hair onto his wide shoulders. Absently, she noted he no longer wore any binding around his ribs. His whole back was bare to his waist. Never had she seen such an expanse of naked male skin.

She must have made some sort of sound, because he spun around, his hand going to the gun on the table even as his eyes fastened on her. He halted and let his hand slide from the gun to his side as he stood staring at her.

How could he help but hear the rapid thudding of her heart? She knew she should look away, but the sight of him, damp hair, clean shaven jaw, bare chest and bare feet, held her enthralled.

"Oh, my goodness" she whispered.

The sound of her voice made her realize she was staring. The heat of embarrassment flooded her cheeks allowing her to look away. What would he think of her? She couldn't move, couldn't think. It took all of her will power not to stare again. Who knew a man could be so beautiful?

Wes cleared his throat, and her gaze went back to him. "You're early," he said in a normal voice. "I thought you wouldn't be back until around noon."

Who could make conversation, when all she wanted to do was look? She tried not to fidget or wring her hands together.

She cleared her own throat. "I, ah, where's Clare?" she finally got out.

He frowned. A boom of nearby thunder rattled the kitchen window. He glanced out the window at the fast fading daylight. "Ah," he said. "You came back because of the storm."

She nodded, not knowing how to talk to a gloriously half-naked man, even if she did love him.

He rubbed the back of his neck. "Clare's gone. Her brother came by right after I got back. He took her out to the fort for the day."

Oh. She was staring again. Thick, curly, golden hair covered the upper part of his chest. How would it feel, soft or springy? Her own thoughts shocked her. When she was around him her sense of propriety and her common sense deserted her. Even more disturbing was the realization she was in no hurry to have them return.

She ought to leave the kitchen, but instead of taking a step back she found herself taking a half step forward.

Chapter Seventeen

Rain rattled against the kitchen window. Julie took another small step toward Wes, the compulsion to touch the man she loved irresistible. Her heart thumping she took another step. The last step brought her so near he could pull her into his arms.

But he didn't.

He held his hands clenched at his sides, his shoulders rigid, the skin over his cheekbones stretched tight. His stormy green eyes glittered from behind half-closed lids.

For a fleeting second she wondered if he were angry. Then the peculiar tingling began in her breasts and low in her stomach as she responded to his fevered gaze. The achy feeling she only experienced when he was near. Her body throbbed, remembering his embrace, his kiss, his touch beside the smelter road. The way she felt when he'd held her. When he'd kissed her and touched her. Her face grew hot, and her breasts tingled as she remembered just where he'd kissed and touched.

The physical sensations he caused had left her confused enough. Then this morning, she'd realized she loved him. Loved him in some deep indefinable way that she knew and recognized. A love so intense that it welled up, like a heaviness in her throat, as she blinked back the prickle behind her eyes.

Was that why just a narrow-eyed look from him made her so aware of his maleness and her femaleness? Because she loved him?

More important, did he feel the same way? Thunder growled and a gust of wind pushed against the kitchen door, but she hardly noticed. Her heart beating faster, she hesitated then slowly reached toward his face.

He sucked in a sharp breath, drew his head back a little and then stood stone still.

"You have soap behind your ear." She reached out and wiped a dab of shaving soap from the curve of his jaw. The warm, sleek feel of his skin made her fingers tingle, her breasts feel heavy.

He closed his eyes and blew out a breath. His right hand reached out to clutch the back of a nearby chair, knuckles pale with the force of his grip.

Could it be? Did she have the same power as he? Could she make him feel the same strange, achy excitement which coursed through her? The thought made her body pulse and to ease her throat she swallowed and ran her tongue over her lower lip.

A moment passed. He neither moved nor spoke. The excitement, the sense of daring from standing so close to him made her breath deepen and quicken.

"Wes?" Amazing how low and vibrant her voice sounded in the still kitchen.

He opened his eyes. His features taut, the fierce look of his eyes, the tightness in his jaw, the flare of his nostrils, gave his face the intense look she'd come to recognize and love.

The storm-dimmed light of the kitchen allowed her to be bold. Lured by his look, she stretched out her hand and with tentative pressure placed her palm in the center of his chest.

A compressed breath escaped him. Again his eyes closed. His jaw clenched.

Intrigued by the thicket of blond hair stretching across his chest, she flexed her fingers into it feeling the dense, springy texture. Warmth radiated from his skin while the curls under her fingers still held traces of dampness from his bath. She moved her fingers a second time and he groaned. A moment later, he leaned ever so slightly into her caress, the rapid rise and fall of his breathing evident under her fingertips, his heart beating as frantically as hers.

Yes! She could make him feel the same physical awareness that he made her feel. Enchanted, she flexed her fingers again. With a sudden movement, he caught her wrist.

"Don't." His voice was a low growl. He gazed at her through narrowed eyes. "You're playing with fire." His grip on her wrist tightened.

Knowing she stood on a precipice, she hesitated. What she felt was more than just physical. She felt it in heart, her bones, her being.

She loved Wes.

She loved everything she saw. His damp hair curling around his ears and neck, his powerful chest, his long, denim clad legs. Even his bare feet appealed to her.

Though some people might look down on a man of his background, she saw beyond his gunslinger façade. She knew him to be honest and kind. In the past weeks she'd seen him in his day to day life, seen the respect Uncle Frank gave him. The way other men at the smelter joked with him, turned to him for advice. She'd seen him hurt and angry.

In any other circumstances, she and Wes meeting or spending time together would be highly unlikely. But fate, in the form of her impulsive flight from Philadelphia had brought them together.

She'd fallen in love with him. Her body, her soul, longed for him. No other man in the world could make her feel as he did.

Lightning flashed. With the fleeting illumination came her decision. She was his. With a sigh of surrender, Julie stepped off the precipice.

She wrapped her hands around his neck and leaned forward.

Stunned, Wes momentarily froze. From the moment she'd walked toward him, he'd tried to resist, telling himself she didn't know what she was asking for. Even though he'd often resisted more aggressive sexual invitations, her innocent seduction had been more than he could withstand. Her look of wonder and desire as she'd buried her fingers in the hair on his chest pushed him to the edge of his control.

She felt so good against him, tasted so good, he needed a deeper taste. Willingly she granted the access his tongue demanded. Tentatively, she stroked his tongue with hers. At her participation, a low groan rumbled in his chest.

Julie felt, as well as heard his low sound of pleasure. A thrill pulsed through her. Delighting in her new found power to create in Wes what she felt, she stroked her hands over his bare shoulders and down the muscles of his back. He felt so wonderful. His smooth skin over solid muscles moved under her touch. The heavy, rain-damp air was laden with his musky, masculine smell and she inhaled in joy.

In reciprocation his warm, hard hands traced the curves of her body as she clung to him. His kisses moved over her cheeks, her brow, her eyelids, behind her ear and down her neck. The faint tickle of his mustache made her shiver with delight.

The familiar heaviness in her breasts increased. Silently she urged him to touch her there as he had last time. As if responding to her unspoken plea, his hand covered her breast. She sighed and gave a little quiver. The fierce tenderness with which he caressed her told her of his need. A need she'd felt for the first time yesterday. A need that increased with his every touch.

Wes trailed kisses down her throat, tasting the damp sweetness of her fair skin as the sound of rain rose and fell with the wind. Her knees must be as shaky as his, the way she clung to him. No other woman ever felt as good in his arms. Her body was soft, but he sensed an underlying resilience of her spirit. The velvety strokes of her hands up and down his back pushed his desire higher.

Even now he told himself he'd stop before things went too far. He fumbled with the buttons on her blouse. If only she'd pull away, do something to make him stop. But instead of resisting, she sighed and leaned back, granting him access. He kissed the pulse where it beat at her uncovered throat.

"Mmmmmm," she murmured, as he felt the vibrations of her purr of pleasure against his mouth.

The throb of pleasure that flashed through him like the lightning outside had him slipping his hand inside her open blouse. Even through the remaining layers of material the hard peak of her nipple burned his palm. He shoved his hips against hers, pressing her against the ache in his jeans. Her arms around him tightened and she twisted against him.

His breath hissed out between his clenched teeth. Stop and think, idiot. He tried to get command of himself.

He fought to remember that he'd seen her dressed as a widow in St. Louis, of the papers he'd found in the valise hidden in her closet. Whether that turned out to be something or nothing, he needed to consider that. And if she stopped to think, would she really choose a drifter with no prospects to make love to her? One of them had to be sensible.

He shuddered and stilled his hands.

"Wes?"

At Julie's whisper of his name, he lifted his head. What he saw almost stopped his heart.

His hand in her blouse still cupped her breast. She clung to his shoulders as if to hold herself upright, her hips firmly pressed into his. Even in his imagination, she had never looked more alluring. His breath came quick and heavy. God, he wanted her. Needed her.

"Wes?" she asked again in a half whisper. Her heavy lidded eyes filled with passion, excitement and something he'd never seen before looked at him. Before he could wonder, she tugged gently on his shoulders, offering her mouth for a kiss.

The slight encouragement was more than enough. What little control he had left vanished like a gray cat on a foggy San Francisco night. He groaned, knowing this time there'd be no stopping, no turning back for either of them.

Julie sighed as he kissed her again. She'd been puzzled when he paused, but any questions dissolved under his kisses and caresses. All the wonderful sensations she'd felt yesterday paled next to the intensity of today's.

She shivered with anticipation as his rough fingers untied the neck of her camisole and chemise.

"Sweet Julie," he whispered as his hot hand closed over her naked breast.

Oh, yes. Please, please, she silently begged. And, like yesterday, his hot mouth closed over her. Intense waves of indescribable sensations shot through her. As he suckled a heavy ache settled low in her stomach. She tilted her head back, letting the fantastic feelings wash over her.

She cried out as his fevered kisses and exhilarating touch swept her along in a swift current of wanting and needing, of passion and love.

Wes swore under his breath. He had to slow down or he'd take her right here in the kitchen. The thought of frightening or hurting her brought him a measure of control. The precious gift she offered deserved to be savored. Savored by both of them. He'd have to be the one to control the pace.

"Come on," he whispered and caught her up in his arms. Thunder rumbled overhead, and a gust of wind rattled the kitchen window.

To his satisfaction, she snuggled against him, head resting on his shoulder, her eyes closed. He carried her the few steps to the door of his room which stood slightly ajar. Pushing the door open with his shoulder, he carried her into the dim room and kicked the door shut. Stopping beside the bed, he lowered her to her feet.

Even then she kept her arms around his neck. He rained kisses over her face as he threaded his fingers through her hair, seeking out the pins and discarding them. He grunted in satisfaction as the fine, silvery mass tumbled down her back. He wanted to see her hair spread out on his pillow. Desire throbbed and he told himself to go slowly.

He ran his fingers through her hair, watching it slip through his fingers like quick silver. So fine and delicate, but with an inner strength. Just like the woman herself.

She offered him a priceless gift, one he didn't deserve, but one he hadn't the strength to turn down. The only things he could offer in return were his experience and his knowledge. His experience to go slow, not hurt her, not scare her, make her first time a dream to remember. And his knowledge to protect her from any consequences.

He took a deep breath to steady himself.

Julie sighed. Wes's fingers running through her hair sent delightful chills up and down her arms. He kissed her temple, then with gentle hands he took her arms from around his neck and they stood facing each other, her hands in his.

She heard the storm rattle and beat on the house but as though from a great distance. The wind and rain shut out the world leaving them alone in his room. Just the two of them in their own world, where all she could hear was their deep breathing, could see only the planes and shadows of Wes's face in the muted light.

"Don't be afraid," he said in a low, gentle voice.

She smiled. How could she be afraid? Didn't he know he filled her with such physical sensations, such emotions that all she felt was need? A combination of excitement and anticipation bubbled up and she bit her lower lip to keep in the giggle that threatened.

Even in the dim light, she saw the concern in his eyes that warmed her heart. She momentarily tightened her hands around his and looked into her love's face.

"How could I be afraid of you?" The concern left his eyes and his shoulders relaxed. She smiled as the intense look she'd come to recognize returned to his face. Feeling warm and wanted, she took a deep breath and opened her mouth to tell him of her love. But he quickly leaned forward and kissed her.

She closed her eyes to take in the wonderful sensations. His warm hands holding hers, nothing touching but their lips. He deepened the kiss with his teeth and tongue, and she forgot everything but just loving him.

Chapter Eighteen

In action and word, Julie's response reassured Wes. Carefully and gently as he knew how, he stripped her of her outer garments, shoes and stockings until she stood before him dressed only in her corset, chemise and pantalets. His chest labored as if he'd run to the smelter and back.

She stood pliant before him, her gaze never leaving him, her breathing quick and shallow. Her eyes filled with a longing and an absolute trust that gripped his heart. With steady fingers that belied the trembling he felt inside, he unhooked the front of her corset.

When the corset fell away she took a deep breath and sighed. Even though he wanted to see her naked, touch all of her, he didn't dare. He was too close to the edge, and he'd promised himself he'd make her first time a good memory. The thought made it easier for him to leave her in her camisole and pantalets. He reached behind her and pulled back the covers on the bed.

"In you go, sweetheart," he murmured. He rested his hand in the small of her back, but without any pressure she slid into his bed.

A shudder of anticipation racked him. Quickly, he pulled the sheet over her. The room was cool enough to warrant the gesture. But he knew he did it to help his control as well as give her a sense of security.

The only sound in the dim, quiet room was the faint drumming of the rain and their breathing.

Wes looked down at her. The sight of her pale hair spread out over his pillow hit his gut more powerfully than he imagined. His body clenched. She looked up at him through half-closed eyes.

He wanted her body. But he wanted more. He wanted her. Julie. And everything that was part of her. Her lightheartedness, her natural optimism, her impetuousness. To be able to see all the goodness and light she saw in the world through her eyes.

He wanted to shelter her, keep her safe. He needed to shield her from the evil, the cynicism, the wickedness he knew existed. He had to protect her. He turned and pulled the small, satin bag out of his saddle bag, slipping it under the pillow as he slid beneath the sheet.

"Don't worry, I'll take care of you," he whispered. Willingly, she came into his arms. God, she was a brave little thing, coming to him the way she did. She moved against him as if trying to get inside his skin. Excitement raced through him and he swore. He had to get out of his jeans before she caused him permanent damage. Muttering reassurance to her, he rolled away and pulled off his jeans, pushing them to the floor.

He rolled back, gathering her in his arms once more, enjoying the cool, slick feel of her chemise and pantalets against his naked body. The fine, delicate garments didn't conceal the way she fit to him, female to male.

She sighed, and to his satisfaction offered her mouth for a kiss. When he put his mouth over hers, she opened for him. He deepened the kiss, his tongue mimicking the action of what he really wanted to do.

Wanting her under him, he hesitated, then rolled so that instead of being on their sides, he lay half over her. She made no protest but gave a contented sigh. He continued to kiss her, his hand slipping inside her camisole to find her breast. Arching her back, she pushed into the caress. He smiled, knowing he pleased her.

He ended the kiss and heard her gasp for breath. Taking her nipple in his mouth he sucked gently, tasting the faint hint of peaches.

She moaned, her fingers digging into his shoulders. Just as gently, he suckled her other breast. Her hips began to squirm and he slid his bare leg between her thighs.

"Oh," she gasped. "Wes, I feel so..." she panted.

"It's all right, sweetheart. It's supposed to feel this way." He nuzzled her ear as he whispered reassurances. Trying to control the rising fever her response generated, he swallowed. He wanted to make her so ready that the pain he had to cause would be as inconsequential as possible.

He indulged himself in the taste and feel of her breasts as he continued to kiss and suckle, while she whimpered a little series of ahs and ohs. The way she continued to wiggle pleased him. Letting his hand drift downward, he made caressing circles from her breast to her waist and then lower. When his hand pressed over the juncture of her thighs, she jumped.

"Let me touch you," he whispered, sliding his hand between her legs. After a slight pause, her thighs relaxed.

"That's right," he whispered, warmed by her trust. He slowly slipped his hand between her thighs, feeling the heat and dampness through her pantalets. He kissed her with his tongue and mimicked the motion with his hand. Her hips flexed and began to follow his rhythm. His pulse pounded through him. Then she dug the sharp edges of her fingernails into his shoulders and made a sound deep in her throat. Need rolled through him like a flood tide.

Gasping for air, he broke the kiss. He looked down, watching as he slipped his tan finger through the open crotch of her white pantalets. Lightly, he brushed at the curls he found. She began to pant, her hips rocking harder. He heard himself groan as he found her warm wetness.

Jaw clenched, his pulse hammering, he slowly pushed his finger into her. She gasped and went wild. Her breathing harsh, her head twisted back and forth on the pillow, her face intense with pleasure. Tight nipples, still wet from his kisses, peeked through her undone camisole. The sight made him throb with a hard, fierce beat. It was time.

His hand shook as he reached under the pillow for the protection in the satin pouch. A moment later he moved over her. Claiming her mouth again, he parted her thighs with his knees.

She clung to him, her eyes closed. His blood pounding, he settled his hips between her thighs. Instinctively she drew up her knees. Sweat beaded his forehead. Supporting his weight on his forearms, his hands curled over the top of her shoulders.

Unable to delay any longer, he pushed into her. She took a deep, shuddering breath. Without giving her time to be afraid, he kissed her deeply and pushed all the way in. She flinched and her nails dug into his shoulders. Her warmth and tightness had him grinding his teeth to keep the intense pleasure under control.

"Relax, sweetheart," he whispered between kisses to her eyelids. "Relax. The pain is over." He continued to comfort her with light kisses and whispered words.

Julie lay still. The dull, burning pain of his entry had indeed faded. His weight and the totally unexpected feeling of fullness and pressure momentarily disconcerted her. His gentle kisses and murmured words of reassurance gradually eased her bewildered state.

Lying beneath him, him within her, became pleasing. She felt somehow comforted and secure with him over and around her. She sighed his name. As if he'd waited for a signal, he flexed his hips, pulling back to push again. She gasped as his movements increased the pressure and the pleasure.

"Wes?" she panted, not knowing what to ask.

"Julie," he whispered in her ear. He continued to move and she gasped for breath.

As if to enhance her other senses, her eyes locked closed. She heard his harsh breath, felt his skin like hot, slick satin over shifting muscles, smelled the intriguing muskiness of their bodies. Something coiled deep inside her. Searching for the elusive goal, she moved her hips against his.

As the internal tension coiled tighter, she felt a shudder sweep through Wes. "Ah, yes, sweetheart. That's it." His voice sounded raw, and on the edge of speech.

She wondered how he could speak at all. She couldn't have uttered a word.

"Julie," he murmured and tightening his hold, he increased the rhythm and force of his thrusts.

Unable to do anything but respond, she moved with him. And suddenly the feelings deepened, became more complex. No longer able to separate one sensation from another, she began to pant. Her eyes squeezed tighter as sensations pushed her higher. Her body, and somehow her selfness began to slip beyond her control.

"Wes?" she cried, as fear tinged the still increasing sensations.

"Don't worry, sweetheart," he panted. He tightened his grip on her shoulders, holding her securely underneath him. His strong thrusts pushed her against his solid grasp.

She clung to him and met him thrust for thrust. Dizzy, gasping for breath, Julie held on to the only tangible thing in the world. Wes.

Unable to form conscious thoughts, she spiraled higher and tighter, unknown feelings spinning through her. She began to dissolve. She fought to stay together.

In a panicky gasp, she called, "Wes? Wes?"

His voice was harsh, but nearby. "Let it happen, sweetheart." He shifted and deepened his strokes, still pushing her higher and higher, closer and closer to dissolving.

Unable to resist, she felt herself spinning apart. A tremor started deep inside.

"Ah, let go, Julie," he encouraged. "Let go."

She let the love and trust she had for him well up and join the tremor. Waves of pleasure too intense to bear surged through her, and in a multicolored explosion, she disappeared.

Wes felt the tremors deep within her. He bit his lip for control as he watched her blue eyes fly wide open, unseeing as she uttered a high, breathless wail. The bite of her nails stung his shoulders. She bucked beneath him, arching as he drove in. A fierce sense of satisfaction swept through him. Holding her close, secure, he continued his strokes.

With a shudder her eyes fluttered shut. Her head fell back and she sighed his name. He crushed his hips into hers, his strokes short, desperate. Sweat coated his body. His heart hammered like a stamp at the smelter. Within seconds, pure pleasure like he'd never known hit him. He threw his head back as he let the tide of passion sweep him to where he'd taken her. Eyes closed, Julie floated like a leaf on the surface of a lazy summer stream, in a light, insubstantial golden haze she would have believed inconceivable were she not experiencing it. Drifting, she relished each lazy sensation. The weight of Wes as he lay atop her, his face buried in the hollow of her shoulder and neck. His panting, the small tremors running though him. The hot, damp skin of his back under her hands. The air scented with rain, soap, the musky smell of man.

As her breathing returned to normal, she could finally think. Who would have thought such intense and wonderful feelings existed? How loving Wes physically was an extension, a fulfillment, of the emotions she felt for him. How love irrevocably changed a woman when she took a man into her body. By giving herself to him, he had become part of her. And in return, she had bound herself to him.

Her heart too full for words, she turned her head slightly and kissed him behind his ear.

He gave a little quiver just before a deep sigh. Sliding to one side with languid ease, he rolled, pulling her with him. His strong arm surrounded her shoulders, and he nestled her against his side.

With a sigh of her own, Julie draped her arm across his chest. The fascinating golden curls crinkled under her fingers as his chest rose and fell. His breathing slowed and deepened. The warmth of his body guarded her against the slight chill of the room. She snuggled against him. He gave a satisfied sounding grunt and momentarily tightened his arm around her.

Though she wanted to prolong the moment, she felt her body relaxing, slipping into sleep. Totally content, she rubbed her cheek against his warm solid shoulder and whispered, "I love you." And she slipped into peaceful sleep.

Her words hit Wes like a freight train.

His body went stone cold still. He lay motionless for long seconds, his heart pounding. Gradually, he became aware of Julie's even breathing, the utter repose of her body and realized she slept. He took a deep, shaky breath.

He wanted to believe he'd imagined her words, but knew he hadn't. *I love you.*

Just the memory made him shudder.

No one, absolutely no one, had ever said those words to him.

She couldn't have meant what she said.

Not to him. He scrubbed his face with his free hand and cursed himself. A good girl like Julie, of course she thought she loved him. How else would she explain away her behavior? He may have been able to protect her against the ultimate disgrace of unmarried pregnancy, but he'd taken her virginity. Taken a chance on ruining her reputation.

My God, what had he done? Guilt rolled through him making his gut churn. He carefully removed his arm from around her shoulder and slid from the bed.

She slept on.

Damn, she was beautiful. The muted light bathed her in shades of silver and white, her fair hair falling free over his pillow. Dainty white breasts half revealed by the unlaced chemise. A fairy princess. Too beautiful and too good for any mortal man. Especially a man like him.

Gently, he pulled the covers up to conceal what he never should have seen, never should have touched. Settling the sheet over her shoulders, he noticed her peaceful expression, the hint of a smile on her lips.

He jerked back his hand, cursing himself again as the guilt clutched his belly. He hurriedly cleaned up, pulled on his denim pants and took himself to the kitchen.

Chapter Nineteen

Wes stood with his arms braced against the door jams looking out the open back door of the kitchen. The wind blew mist through the screen chilling his arms, chest and bare feet. Behind him, the aroma of fresh coffee drifted from the stove.

Another puff of cool air puffed in, followed by a fading rumble of thunder from the east as the storm moved past the town. But the storm inside him stayed, pulling him one way and then another. The exhilaration of making love with Julie had him on top of the highest mountain peak shouting for joy, while his guilt for the same act cast him to the deepest pit.

He heard light footsteps and steeling himself, turned and looked at her.

"Wes?" Julie came to a halt, gazing at him.

His heart stuck in his throat at the sight of her. Beautiful. Even partially dressed, she somehow managed to appear as sweet and good and innocent as she always had. Dressed only in her chemise and pantalets, her unbound hair flowed in a quicksilver cape down her back. Her bare toes curled against the cool wood floor. She stopped to fasten her chemise, and the fabric clung to her breasts.

Heat rushed through him. He mentally cursed as he grew hot and hard with wanting her. The reaction added another brick to his wall of guilt as he watched her expression change. A hesitant look crossed her face and an instant later she straightened her spine.

He took a deep breath, preparing himself for fear, anger, and God knew what else from her.

A gentle smile lit her face, and she walked directly to him. Wrapping her arms around his bare waist, she leaned her head against his chest.

She didn't hate him.

Stunned, he heaved a ragged breath and let his arms close around her. He'd thought he could stand anything, but he knew now he couldn't have taken that. He stared out the window over the sink as rain dripped from the eaves with a steady plink-plink.

"Wes?" Her voice sounded muffled against his chest. He cleared his throat, but words wouldn't come. What the hell would he say? Apologize? His actions were beyond apology. And he'd be damned if he'd say he was sorry for something so... hell, he didn't even have a word for it.

"Yes?" He kept his voice neutral.

"It's still raining."

Looking at the drizzle through the window, he frowned. "Yeah," he answered, not knowing if it had been a question or not. A flash of lightning followed by a faint clap of thunder, this time from the west, broke the silence. Somehow, the noise released him. He eased out of her embrace and moved toward the stove. Maybe distance would allow him to think

"I made coffee. Want some?"

"Yes, please." She took a small step toward the table. Wes turned toward the cupboard. When he glanced at her the cramp in his gut eased a little, realizing she was taking the whole situation better than he seemed to be. She stood straight chin up, hands clasped in front of her. The perfect picture of a lady.

Damn, but the woman had backbone. He reached down a cup from the cupboard. The least he could do was show the same gumption. Relax a little. With a little work he could pretend she wore more than her undergarments and he more than his uncomfortably tight pants.

He filled the cup and set it on the table for her. While she sipped, he absently rubbed his hands along his ribs. He wanted, no, he needed to reassure her. If only he wasn't so confused.

After a moment, he cleared his throat then said, "There's another shower blowing up over the mountains. We're in for a line of storms this evening." Lightning flashed, and thunder rumbled closer and louder, confirming his statement. "I hear," he continued, "that when it rains like this, the bridge over the creek between here and the fort washes away."

"Yes," A slight frown wrinkled her forehead.

Did she understand, he wondered? With the rain at least she didn't have to worry about that silly girl Clare and her brother showing up. His mind formed the words about not getting caught, but the sourness they implied wedged them in his throat. His frown deepened and he resisted the urge to pace.

"Oh, Clare!" she gasped, understanding dawning. His shoulders sagged in relief.

"Yes," she said, looking at her hands. "I'm sure the bridge will be out, ah, not that Clare would, er, in this rain." Her words stumbled to a halt. Her gaze fell on him for only a moment before she glanced away.

His gaze did the same dance. He was having a hard time acting as if she were fully clothed. Every time her gaze went to his chest, he felt her fingers there.

His fists clenched in his effort to resist taking her in his arms. He'd do anything to protect her, take care of her. But how the hell could he when, more than anything, she needed protection from him. How could he shield her from the way she made him feel?

He rubbed the back of his neck. Fatigue settled heavily in his limbs. Was it only last night he'd spent at the Double Eagle and then with McCarthy in the boiler room? He'd been up too long. That's why he was having so much trouble thinking. Yeah, that was the reason. Right.

The rain increased in tempo as a hard gust of wind rattled the screen door.

Julie shivered and wrapped her arms around herself. The instinctive need to go to her, to offer comfort had him take a step toward her. She looked at him longingly. In an instant he was at her side. "You're cold," he murmured, gathering her into his arms.

"Not anymore." She sighed, and he knew he'd done the right thing.

With the warmth of Wes's bare chest and arms surrounding her, Julie relaxed. Now, everything would be all right.

She'd been so happy when she'd awakened, so joyous. She hurried from Wes's room in search of him, wanting to see him, share the joy she'd felt. The sight of him looking so sad, so forlorn, had torn at her heart.

Safe in his embrace again, she smiled against his chest at the unexpected humor of the situation. She knew she should be the one to feel guilty, should be ashamed, should be concerned and apprehensive. She should be having all the doubts and worries she'd seen so plainly written across his face when he'd turned toward her. And all the things she seen on his face made her love him even more.

She couldn't worry just now. She rubbed her cheek lightly against him, liking the sound and texture of his springy chest hair. Liking even better the way his arms tightened as he sighed into her hair. The love she'd discovered with Wes was too big, too expansive to allow doubts for the time being.

She listened to the steady patter of the rain as full night came on. Even the weather seemed willing to seal the two of them inside their own small world together. Tonight, she intended to take with both hands whatever fate provided. Only the two of them existed in the whole world, and she didn't want to lose one moment.

"Come on," he said suddenly. "It's too cold in here." He grabbed his cup from the table, and putting an arm around her waist, guided her toward his room.

"Wes," she started.

He interrupted. "Don't argue. You're shivering. You need to get warm."

She had no intention of arguing. His voice sounded light, teasing. She smiled, relieved the awkwardness between them had passed. In his room, Wes pulled back the covers and gave her a little push. Obediently, she got in the bed and settled back against the pillows.

"Drink the coffee," Wes instructed as he handed her the cup, then drew the blanket up around her. He turned to the lamp on the table and struck a match. The room flared into brightness before he turned the wick down to a soft glow.

His efforts made her feel cared for, cherished. She smiled at him, wanting him to know how she felt.

"Warmer?"

"Yes, thank you." She studied his face, trying to read what thoughts ran behind the concern in his eyes.

He ran his hand through his hair, as if he, too, felt the fragile nature of what-to-do-now between them.

Her determination to take whatever came this night gave her courage. "You must be chilly, too. Here," she scooted over and patted the bed beside her.

She almost giggled at the startled expression on his face. "Please," she asked when he hesitated.

"You, sweetheart," he murmured, sitting down on the edge of the bed, "are something else." The warm glow of the lamp made his tousled hair look like gold floss. The light and shadows played over his bare arms and chest. The intimacy of their half-dressed state created a contentment that warmed her from the heart out. This was her man. And she was his woman.

"Here, you finish this." she offered him the cup.

He finished the coffee then set the empty cup on the table. When he didn't move back, but sat half turned away, she realized he waited for her lead. Enjoying the game, and the new found power of her womanhood, she smiled and touched him on the arm. "You're cold, too."

"Yeah, a little."

She scooted over a little more, hoping he'd take the hint. He swung his denim clad legs up on top of the covers. Then settling back, he put his arm around her shoulders, bringing her against him.

Love welled up, and she wondered if her heart would burst from happiness. Totally content, she rested her head against his shoulder and sighed, "Wes."

"What?" His voice sounded tired, sleepy.

"Nothing, really, I just like the sound of your name."

"It's just a name."

His off-hand tone caught her attention. She frowned. "Yes, but it's really your last name." She sat up to look at him in the dim glow of the lamp. "What is your full name?"

He glanced away for a moment before saying, "Samuel. Samuel Jacob Westmoreland."

"Samuel," she repeated. "That's not so terrible. Why aren't you called Sam?"

He shifted, the muscles in his arm tensed. "Sam's my old man's name. Everyone called him Sam."

He certainly didn't appear happy to be named after his father. She remembered the few times Wes had mentioned him. He always referred to him as the old man or Sam. "You call your father by his first name?" The casualness and lack of respect shocked her.

He ran a hand over his face, and she noticed how tired he appeared in spite of his freshly shaven cheeks. Lines of fatigue etched around his eyes and mouth. She belatedly remembered he'd been up all last night. Maybe she should just let him rest and not pester him with questions right now.

"Look," he sat up and swung his feet to the floor. "Let's just forget this whole thing. You really don't want to know the details of my life."

Startled as much by his sudden movement as by what he said, she scrambled from under the covers to kneel next to him. In a gesture of comfort, she rubbed her hand across his tense shoulder. Distress pricked at her as he flinched from her touch.

"Wes, what is it?" What could be so awful? They had been as close as two people could be, a closeness more than physical. What had caused him to draw away? "Tell me what's wrong."

Again she stroked his shoulder. This time he allowed it. He dropped his head in his hands and mumbled an oath. Her hand on his arm, she tried to turn him to face her, but he resisted.

He took a deep breath, as if to steel himself. "I always called my old man Sam. I grew up in a saloon, remember?" His voice sounded harsh and far away. "No man who runs a saloon with sporting girls wants some snot-nosed kid calling him Pa."

He laughed without humor. "Must have been about five or six when I realized other boys call their father Pa, not by his name. Made the mistake of calling Sam Pa one night. He slapped me so hard he knocked me down."

Chapter Twenty

Appalled, Julie stared at Wes. She didn't know which broke her heart more, a father who'd slap his son, or the causal, unfeeling way Wes described it. As if it were normal, as if he were the one in the wrong.

Oh, Wes. Her hand stilled against the tension that vibrated from him. She'd known his life had been much harsher than hers. But until now she'd thought in terms of creature comforts, or lack thereof. This seemed so much worse.

Swallowing a lump of sympathy for the little boy he'd been, she resumed stroking his shoulder. What had his life been like? What had the other children thought of the way his father treated him. "The other boys? Were they friends of yours from school?"

He gave her a look from the corner of his eye. "No," he said, his voice dark with cynicism, "they weren't friends from school." He looked back at the floor, and in a voice almost too low to hear, said, "Never went to school. No one cared enough to make me go, and even if they had, what school would've had me? A saloon kid? Wouldn't want me hanging around with regular kids."

The shame in his voice brought the lump back to her throat. "But," she said without thinking, "you can read and write." To her horror, the words sounded more like a question than the statement she meant.

His head came up and he gave her a bland stare. "Yeah, I can read. Cipher, too. One of the whores," she flinched at the harsh word. His face hardened, and he went on, as though using his anger and crude language to push her further away. "One of the whores taught me. She'd been a school teacher until some good looking son-of-a-bitch cowboy got her in trouble."

Embarrassed, she started, "But, I…"

He sprung to his feet and swung around to look straight at her, his hard gaze hot in the dim lamp light. "I tried to tell you that day out by the clothesline that nothing good could come from us being together. Only trouble." Anger threaded his voice as he spoke louder. "Well, lady, you don't seem to realize it, but this," he waved his hand in a motion that took in the rumpled bed and their state of undress, "is more trouble than either of us need!"

How dare he! Exasperation and anger swept through her. How dare he call what had happened between them nothing good? How dare he be so contrite when she was so elated?

Folding her arms, she glared back at him. She wouldn't allow his anger to drive a wedge between them. "It's not all your fault. I didn't say no."

After a moment his hard gaze softened and the tension went out of him. "Ah, hell," he breathed and ran an absent-minded hand along his ribs. "Damn it, Julie," he swore gently. "I told you not to be so honest. I'm a saloon kid, someone you shouldn't even be talking to, let alone...."

His voice softer, he said, "Frank should run me out of town on a rail. Your father would be justified in shooting me for what I did." The expression on his face told her he believed he deserved such treatment.

She looked at the man she loved, her anger left her as suddenly as it had come. Because she loved him with her heart, and had loved him with her body, she understood him. She remembered thinking the day he'd bought her sarsaparilla that his life had been so much different. She'd grown up surrounded by love. Her mother and father and sister. The love they'd given her. And as a child, she had seen the love her parents had for each other. She thought of Cory and Mark and their love. Family, and the core of the love that bound them together, was the foundation of her world.

With the life he'd led, how could Wes even recognize, let alone accept, love? Had anyone ever loved him? Perhaps because what was between them was so new, so unfamiliar, he didn't know how to acknowledge it. That would come in time, but right now she wasn't about to let his guilt cloud what had happened. She had come to him out of love. A deep love that filled her soul.

She reached out and laced her fingers with his. A gentle tug pulled him down to sit on the edge of the bed. "I won't apologize for being honest. All I see are the two people in this room. You and me. And what I feel for you is honest. The man you really are, the man I know, not the child you were. What happened between us was the most honest thing I've ever felt."

Wes started to speak, but she quickly placed her fingers against his mouth, silencing him.

"No, don't tell me again about your childhood. It doesn't matter. Don't you see?" she said with a smile at his bewildered expression. "It's you, Wes Westmoreland, that I care for. All of you. How you grew up is part of what made you who you are, just as my childhood made me who I am."

He looked at her, his expression perplexed. Maybe he didn't understand her, but at least his self-reproach seemed to have run out of steam.

"Anyway," she went on, "you aren't as bad as you seem to think. If you were, you wouldn't be so upset now. And you wouldn't have, ah." Oh dear, how did one put it delicately? She nearly giggled. She'd never been delicate. "You protected me."

Wes blinked, his belly tightened, as though the floor dropped out from under his feet. In the dim light, he watched a blush creep up Julie's fair skin. Damn, every time he thought he'd made headway, she turned the tables on him.

Then she giggled, telling him the look on his face must be as stupid it felt. What should be worrying him even more was the fact that from the look on her face, she knew she had the upper hand.

"Come on," She tugged him with her as she scrambled back under the covers. "It's chilly. You don't want to catch cold."

He swung his denim clad legs up on the bed. He settled back against the headboard, his legs stretched out next to hers. She pulled the covers over them. "There, that's warmer," she said, snuggling against his side.

Instinctively he put his arm around her shoulder, settling her next to him. For a few moments the room fell quiet except for the rain pattering on the window. The lamp cast the room in a dim, warm glow.

He swallowed to clear his throat, and turned to look at her. "Ah, how did you know about... ah... protection?"

She wrinkled her nose. Oh, dear. Then she sighed. "You forget, my brother-in-law is a doctor. And somewhat of a free thinker."

"He told you about... about..." Once again words failed Wes. Hell of a thing when he couldn't even imagine her doctor brother-in-law talking about what he and Julie had just done. She shook her head.

"Oh no, Mark never said anything. I found out from Cory."

"Your sister told you?" This got more confusing all the time. Lack of sleep and closeness to her had affected his brain.

"Actually I overheard and then she had to explain." She settled back against the pillows, looking like a mischievous child. How could she appear so innocent when he could see the shadow of her nipples beneath the white linen? He jerked his attention back to what she was saying.

"...how Cory helped raise me after our mother died? Anyway, she and Mark had been trying to have children, and after the last, ah..." She looked away and smoothed the covers over her lap.

He remembered how Julie had spoken of her sister's desire for a child. He knew what she didn't say. He settled her back against his side. Growing up surrounded by women, he understood. "You told me she's expecting again now though, right?"

She nodded, looking relieved as she continued. "Last year, after," she made a gesture, "well, Great Aunt Hilda came for a visit and while I was in the kitchen making tea, I heard Aunt Hilda say at least Cory would be spared her duty for several months."

"I could tell Cory was trying not to laugh while Great Aunt Hilda looked so serious. So after she left, I asked Cory what was so funny." Julie turned to him, "You don't think Cory was wrong to tell me do you?"

"Why would I think that?" Hell, he thought it was a good idea for a girl to know as much as she could. But he certainly couldn't say so, not when good girls weren't supposed to know anything.

"Well, most people would." She leaned back. "It's just I don't want you to have a bad opinion of Cory, or think she didn't do a good job raising me."

"She did a good job, Julie." He wanted to say more. She was the best woman he'd ever known. Only he didn't know how to put that into words.

She smiled. "Thank you." Her smile grew wider. "I can just see her, trying not to snicker. She told me that in spite of what Great Aunt Hilda said, the marriage bed wasn't that much of a duty. And being a doctor, Mark knew how to..."

"I got it," he said. He could almost picture the two women giggling in the kitchen. The closeness he'd seen between Julie and Frank must be a pale comparison to the love between the sisters.

Beside him, he felt her quiver with a silent laugh.

"What?"

"I was just thinking. Cory was certainly right."

He frowned. "Right about what?"

"Well, it certainly didn't seem to be such a horrible duty. And certainly not the type of thing one would want to avoid." She gave him a sideways look of wide-eyed innocence.

He couldn't help it. He laughed out loud.

She sat up, and took his hand in hers. "It's good to hear you laugh. You're much too serious, Mr. Westmoreland." Before he could think of reply, her smile faded. She looked earnestly into his eyes. "Is it always like that? So wonderful?" Her solemn expression touched him.

"No," he said, straightening to look her square on. "It's not always like that. This was," he searched for a word, and found only an inadequate one, "special."

He ran a hand through his hair, looked at her again. "Most of the time, it's just," he made a vague motion with his hand. "I don't know how to explain."

She seemed satisfied with his vague explanation. "I think it was special between us for a reason." She wrapped her arms around him, her face in the hollow of his shoulder. He held her close. "This is special between us," she said, her voice soft, her breath warm against his neck, "because I love you."

Once again his heart stopped. She must have felt his reaction, for she quickly looked up. He opened his mouth to say he didn't know what. But she forestalled him once more by placing her fingers across his lips.

"Shhh," she said. "You don't have to say anything. I just wanted you to know that I love you, Wes Westmoreland."

His heart thudded, and his mouth went dry. She thought she loved him. Before, he'd tried to slough off her whispered words. But now she'd said them right out loud. Without reservation. Or expectation of a like reply. He didn't know how to repay the gift she'd just given him. But he had to try.

He swallowed the lump in his throat, and it settled in his gut. "You know how you asked about my name? Wes?"

She nodded.

"It's short for that Westmoreland brat. That's what they called me when I was little kid. Then it just became Wes." At least that's what Ruby had told him, and he had no reason to doubt it. "I'd never really cared for my name." He took Julie's hands in his. "Until now."

She looked puzzled.

"Because now..." He looked at her hands so trustingly in his. "When you say my name, you make it sound like something good." After a pause, he shrugged, not knowing how or what else to say. But it must have been enough.

She smiled. "Wes."

And he heard, as he knew she'd intended, the special way she said his name as if it tasted sweet in her mouth. So he did the only thing he could think of. He kissed her.

Chapter Twenty-One

Wes dreamed of Julie, soft and warm in his arms. Not wanting to wake, he tried to keep his eyes shut. But they flickered open and he stifled a groan. Incredibly, the dream remained. He was awake. Julie was real and nestled in his arms. He lay still, enjoying the reality. In lazy satisfaction the images of yesterday rolled through his memory.

After they made love a second time, hunger had driven them in search of food. Julie had made sandwiches while he'd done the evening chores. He barely remembered eating, as by then the exhaustion of being up all the previous night had caught up with him. They went back to his bed, where snuggled together they fell asleep in each other's arms.

Had it only been the night before last that he'd talked to McCarthy about boilers and then sent a telegram to San Francisco? And even longer since he'd sent the telegram after he'd found the hidden valise. What a waste of time that had been. How could he have ever suspected Julie of anything devious? She was so straightforward. Just look at yesterday.

Yesterday. Again he savored the thought and memories of the day before. So intense was the time he'd spent with Julie, he felt he'd lived a lifetime since she'd come home and caught him shaving.

And now, this morning, like spoons, they lay together. His arm around her waist held her close. He savored the warm softness of her skin, the gentle inhale and exhale as she slept. Her womanly scent filled his nostrils. The sight, sounds, scents and feel were all too good.

Again, he thought of yesterday, hoarding the memory against the crushing guilt that was sure to hit. But to his amazement, the guilt didn't come. Because of Julie. The way she'd come willingly to his arms. Her acceptance of him, of who he was, and of what he was. Her acceptance had somehow vanquished the guilt.

Tempted to kiss her awake, he hesitated. At least he could give her some privacy when she woke. Carefully, he eased out of bed, grabbed his clothes and boots and went to the kitchen to dress.

* * *

A rolling boom of thunder roused Julie from sleep. Rain dripped from the eaves, but fitful morning sunlight fought through the window. She rolled over, her muscles making small protesting twinges from yesterday's activities. She buried her face in his pillow and breathed in his lingering warmth and scent.

She stretched and smiled. She loved Wes Westmoreland. And, although he didn't know it, he loved her, too. After a few moments, she sat up, realizing Wes had gotten up earlier, allowing her to wake in private. A quick look showed that although his clothes were gone, her robe and fresh under things were draped over the back of the chair. She got up, the wood floor cool under her bare feet.

On the chest of drawers sat a basin of water, the water still warm. Her smile grew broader at the evidence of his concern. She crossed to the door and peered into the empty kitchen. Through the window, she saw the open stable door, indicating he'd gone out to do the morning chores.

Washed and in clean underwear, she went up to her room. While she dressed for church she pondered the changes in her life that loving Wes, and making love with Wes would make. As she pulled on her skirt, she purposely didn't look at the valise hidden in the armoire. What would she say to Wes when it was time for her to return to Philadelphia and Cory?

She debated sharing her problems with Wes, but somehow it seemed too soon. Because she loved him, she shouldn't burden him with her problems and concerns. After all, she pondered while buttoning her shoes he was having a hard enough time dealing with what he felt for her.

Now was all that mattered. Let tomorrow take care of itself. For now she intended to enjoy being with Wes. Carrying her hat, she went back downstairs. She left her hat on the table by the hall mirror, marveling once again at her reflection. How odd that her whole life had changed last night, but she looked just the same. She should be nervous, facing Wes after yesterday. But instead, she anticipated seeing him. In her reflection, her cheeks grew pink. She entered the kitchen. Wes stood in the back doorway, his back turned as he shook the rain from his hat. Her heart skipped a beat and a fierce surge of love filled her. What was his mood this morning?

He turned and caught sight of her. For a moment, his expression didn't change. Then a slow smile lifted the corners of his mustache and it was like watching the sun come out.

"Good morning," he said, as he hung his hat on the peg. "You sure look pretty in that outfit."

Joy rose in her heart at his cheerful mood. "Thank you. You look pretty good yourself."

Surprised, he looked down and she saw a look of puzzlement cross his face as he inspected his ordinary denim pants and shirt. He looked up. She gave him a smile and to her delight, his cheeks flushed as he realized what she'd meant.

"Sit down and have a cup of coffee," she ordered. "I'll get breakfast started. She tied on her apron and poured him a cup from the pot he'd started. As she sliced the bacon, she couldn't help but think this was the way it would be if she and Wes... but, no. She'd promised herself not to look beyond the moment. She should appreciate what she had right now.

While they ate the bacon and eggs, the weak sunshine faded. Soon came the familiar sound of thunder from the west. Wes stood up and crossed to look out the window.

After a moment, he let the curtain fall back in place. "Mud's rim deep or better. Doubt many people will be out today. But I can hitch up the buggy and take you to church." He looked back at her. "If that's what you want."

She considered. The rain shower just starting would probably keep most people from church this morning. Not only because of the mud. Most people wouldn't want the horse and rig standing in the rain, either. And, if she went to church, she'd have to answer all sorts of questions about Uncle Frank's whereabouts.

But if she stayed home? She glanced at Wes standing patiently by the window. Everyone would assume the weather accounted for the absence. Tomorrow was soon enough to start facing up to the changes in her life. She'd already decided to enjoy what today and Wes had to offer. Thunder boomed and the rain fell a little harder, as though reinforcing her decision.

She stood. "I think I'll stay here today." She turned to the stove. Grabbing the pot holder, she took the coffee pot from the back of the stove.

From his position at the window, Wes watched her turn to the table and refill his cup. She was willing to stay with him. She trusted him. That faith and trust settled like a warm glow deep inside him. He crossed the kitchen and sat back down in his chair. For a moment he was willing to let the peaceful contentment wash over him while they ate breakfast. The light in the kitchen dimmed as the thunderstorm moved overhead. He watched her clear the table, happy to watch her hands, the way her skirts swished as she turned. The way the bow of her apron, perched on her backside like a bustle bounced as she moved around the kitchen. As much as he liked the view of her backside, he couldn't sit here and watch her do all the work.

He swallowed the last of his coffee and rose to carry the cup over to where she washed the dishes. Her pinned up hair exposed the nape of her neck. He considered kissing the soft white skin there. Since when did he consider the back of a woman's neck kissable? Definitely something to think about for later. He plunked the cup into the dish water.

"Thanks," she said, giving him a smile.

"You wash. I'll dry." He reached around her and grabbed the towel. By the time they finished the dishes, the rain shower had stopped. Watery sunshine struggled through the clouds once more.

"You think it will rain again?" She peered out the window.

Leaning next to her, he scanned the sky. "That's probably the last storm. The sky's clear over the mountains to the west." He wondered if she was reconsidering going to church. But because it'd stopped raining didn't mean the roads were any better. "It'll probably take the rest of the day for the streets to dry out. Maybe by tomorrow people will be out and around." He pulled out a chair and sat.

She checked the sky one more time. She turned and gave him a mischievous smile as she dried her hands on a towel. "Guess you're stuck here with me today."

"Guess I am." As if he would complain. He could think of a lot worse things than being stuck with Julie all day. He held out his hand, "Come over here."

When she took his hand, he gave a little tug and pulled her onto his lap. She wrapped her arms around his neck, which made him think it wouldn't be too hard to convince her to do other things. "So what do you want to do today?"

"Well," her brow wrinkled, as though she were deep in thought. Then she dipped her head and kissed his ear. He nearly jumped out of the chair. She giggled as his hands tightened around her waist.

"Where did you learn to do that?" he asked.

"Oh," she pressed her lips against his ear again. "You taught me. Last night."

He moved to kiss her, but she teasingly pulled back. He smiled and leaned back in the chair. He'd never suspected playing games with words could be so much fun. Or guessed she would be comfortable enough with him to do so. His hand wandered down from her waist to cup her rear end. "You want me to teach you something else?"

She smiled. A blush spread across her cheeks. "As a matter of fact, there is something I want you to teach me."

He grinned with satisfaction.

She took a deep breath then said, "I want you to teach me to play poker."

He blinked, surprised. "A card game?" Not exactly what he had in mind. She was a constant surprise. Charmed, he laughed, "Sure, honey." He lifted her from his lap to stand. "Let's see if we can find some cards." After all, there were all sorts of games of poker.

* * *

Boot heels ringing on the boardwalk, Wes walked down Broadway. The Monday morning sun shone brightly, and the clean, clear air smelled of earth and pine. The sun had finally struggled through the clouds yesterday around noon and dried out everything but the muddy streets. He took a deep breath and tried to wipe the silly smile off his face as he thought of yesterday. He never felt like this before.

With a start he realized he was happy. Content. He'd thought he knew about sex, but with Julie it was more than physical. More than just sex. His smile faded. The time he and Julie spent out of bed had been just as enjoyable as the time they spent in his bed.

The last forty-eight hours with her had changed his life. Now what was he going to do? He crossed G Street, walking on a line of wooden planks thrown across the muddy road. Julie loved him. She'd said it and she'd demonstrated it several times. Again the silly smile grew on his face. Thank God there weren't many people out this morning to see him grinning like an idiot.

The train depot and telegraph office came into view. If he received the telegraph answer he expected from the Denver office regarding the boiler plate numbers, once he turned the evidence over, his job here was done and Dan Challenge would send him somewhere else. To be somebody else. And what of Julie? Even if he could stay in Durango, she was only visiting. How could they stay together? And why was he so concerned? Hell, it wasn't as if he…

Wes stopped dead on the boardwalk.

Holy hell!

He did love her.

A wave of dizziness swept over him. He loved Julie! Things he'd never even dared dream about flashed through his mind. A wife. A home. A place with a woman who waited for him. A woman who accepted him with no pretense, loved him just as he was. And like the sun coming out yesterday, loving her let him see the solution to the problem. He loved her, she loved him. So why not? They could get married.

He started walking again, anxious to get his business over and get back to Julie. As soon as this assignment was finished, he'd ask if Wells Fargo had a different job for him. He had money in the bank in San Francisco, as well as all that Wells Fargo stock that had been part of his pay over the years. He could afford a wife.

Wife. Julie.

With the silly smile back on his face, he walked into the telegraph office. Across the room the telegraph operator looked up.

"Morning," Wes said as he crossed to the counter. "Any messages for Westmoreland?"

"Just a moment, sir." The operator sorted through a pile of messages. "I think it's right here." He pulled a sheet from the stack, folded it in half and handed it across the counter to Wes.

"Thanks." Wes tipped the man and went back outside to the bright sunlight. Now he had the goods on Kennedy, he thought in anticipation. Unfolding the message, he read the neat, block printed words.

Re: your request on Philadelphia information. Arrest warrant for J. Lawson issued by Philly police. Apprehend J. Lawson, take into custody and hold for Pinkerton Agent presently on route to Durango. Boiler number to follow, today latest.

Best – Dan Challenge

The words didn't make sense to Wes at first. He stared harder at the message, noticing the damn thing trembled in his hand. What the hell was going on? Arrest Julie? He crushed the message in his fist and jammed it in his pocket.

He took a few halting steps. Julie wanted by the police? He ran a hand over his face, surprised to find it wet with perspiration. He couldn't feel the boardwalk beneath his feet.

He felt sick. She'd made a fool of him. How could he ever have believed that anyone could love him? One whispered profession of love and he'd fallen like an egg from a tall chicken. Only a damn fool makes the same mistake twice. This time he'd make sure no one suffered the consequences but himself.

All business now, he stalked back up the boardwalk, the paper in his pocket like a knife sticking in his gut.

* * *

Julie hummed as she picked up a plate to dry. In a few minutes, Wes would be returning from his errand. The sunshine streamed through the kitchen window, extra bright after the two days of rain. She smiled. Of course, the two days of rain could have been forty days for all she cared if it stranded them together. She sighed as she took off her apron. She should be worried about making love to Wes, but being with him seemed to be real, the rest of her life just imagined. Her love for him was a warm glow inside her.

She heard the front door open and boots in the hall. "Wes?" she called, wondering why he'd come in the front door when he usually came around to the kitchen. She turned in anticipation of seeing the man she loved. At the doorway, he stopped short. One look at him and her smile faded. He stood ramrod stiff, his green eyes like winter ice.

"What's wrong?" Her heart began to pound. For an instant, he didn't answer, but then the stiffness went out of his shoulders. He smiled, a poor copy of the one she'd come to love.

"Nothing." He entered the kitchen. "Get your hat, will you? I want to show you something."

A few minutes later she walked with him up Second Street. Though he'd assured her nothing was wrong, an uneasiness rested between her shoulder blades. She glanced at him out of the corner of her eye. His mouth wore a smile that wasn't reflected in his eyes.

Just as she decided to ask once more, he took her elbow and brought her to a halt. "Here we are." He opened a door with a large glass pane without releasing his hold on her.

Bewildered, she glanced at the gold lettering and symbol on the glass. "But, this is the sheriff s office."

Chapter Twenty-Two

Confused, Julie looked at the gold lettering on the window. *Sheriff's Office. Thomas A. Rickman.* She suppressed a shiver of apprehension. Although Uncle Frank had introduced her to the sheriff and she'd seen him around town, she'd done her best to avoid him as his authority made her nervous.

Wes didn't answer but guided her inside. Her heart began to pound. Steady. There was no way the sheriff could know about the valise and Philadelphia. She swallowed, trying to calm herself. She instinctively moved closer to Wes for comfort and protection.

As they entered, Sheriff Rickman stood from his position behind a desk. He nodded in their direction, "Miss Lawson." He looked as bewildered as she felt as Wes marched her across the office halting in front of the desk.

"What's going on, Westmoreland?" Sheriff Rickman gave Wes a hard look.

Sheriff? No, it couldn't be, she though in panic. Wes's grip on her elbow tightened. She tried to pull away and his hold tightened to painfulness. "Wes," she pleaded, looking at him for the first time since they'd entered the office.

Her heart sank. The man holding her was not the man who'd kissed her this morning, but the hard-edged man, who'd accompanied Landham Kennedy to Uncle Frank's office. A man described as little more than a gunslinger.

In disbelief she watched Wes reach into his pocket and pull out a rumpled yellow paper. With a look as cold and hard as granite, he thrust it at the sheriff. "There's a warrant out for her arrest."

No! It can't be! Nausea swept over her and she pressed a hand to her stomach. He couldn't. A loud buzzing filled her ears. But not loud enough to drown out the rest of the hard, cold words he spoke.

"I'm arresting her and placing her in your custody. The Philadelphia police have a lady Pinkerton agent already on route to pick her up tomorrow."

Closing her eyes against the verbal blow, she swayed. Oh, Cory, I'm so sorry.

"What?" Sheriff Rickman's bellow jerked her eyes open. "What authority do you have?" He looked Wes up and down with suspicion.

His jaw tightened as he reached into his pocket once more. This time he withdrew a brown leather folder. He flipped it open to reveal a shiny silver badge for the sheriff's inspection. "I'm a detective for Wells Fargo."

A detective? But he worked for Uncle Frank. Bewildered, she allowed Wes to propel her toward a cell as the sheriff stood dumbfounded. Her legs felt wooden. Had there been enough time for her sister and baby to be safe? "No, wait." She tried once more to free her elbow from his cruel grip.

Wes snorted. "Wait? What for? Or don't you think I have the authority either?" He cast a glance at the sheriff.

Sheriff Rickman regarded him with narrow eyed speculation. "Wells Fargo," the sheriff mused. "You've been in Durango for over a month. How come you're just now arresting her? And for a crime in Philadelphia?"

"Orders."

What orders? She struggled to gather her scattered thoughts. This couldn't be happening.

"So," the sheriff continued, "she wasn't what you came to Durango for, right?" He looked at the telegram Wes had thrust at him. "This just came today. You're here for another reason."

He didn't answer.

What did it matter why Wes came to Durango? She stared as the two men glared at each other.

After a moment, the sheriff reached down and pulled open a desk drawer. He extracted a large ring of keys and tossed them on the desk. "Lock her up, Detective. I'll be back later."

As the sheriff left the office, she found herself maneuvered into one of the cells. Wes released her elbow. She turned and grabbed the iron bars of the door, needing something to help steady her knees.

"Why are you doing this?" she pleaded.

He gave her a cold, unreadable stare, his knuckles white where he gripped the open cell door.

"Please." Her closed throat could hardly let the word escape. "What's going on?"

"You tell me what's going on." His voice, usually so mellow, sounded coarse, strained. "Why the hell do I get orders to arrest you? What went on in Philadelphia in that fire?"

"The fire? How did you?" Her stomach rolled, she felt lightheaded. "You found the valise." Her remaining strength washed away. Cory and the baby. She'd failed them both. And Wes, the man she loved, was the instrument of that failure.

"How could you?" she said feeling as if her soul was dying.

"How could I what? Do my job?" His anger was a palatable force. "Or did you mean the lie about who I am?" He gave a harsh laugh. "Lying is easy. You know that. Hell, you never asked why. You knew there was a warrant out for your arrest."

How could she have been so foolish? She had trusted him, this stranger who had destroyed everything. "I don't even know you," she whispered.

"You know me." He looked her up and down, making sure she realized he meant in the biblical sense.

The memory brought a hot flush to her cheeks. She looked away, grateful they were alone in the office. She dashed a hand across her face, brushing away tears she hadn't known she shed. Too weak to stand any longer, she turned and sat on the cot next to the wall.

After a moment, she heard him enter the cell. She stared blankly at the knees of his denim pants, refusing to raise her eyes. Failure to protect her sister and Wes's betrayal had left her too battered to feel.

She'd given him everything, her body, her soul, and her love. In return he had destroyed her life and all chances of happiness.

Cory and her baby's safety were a high price to pay for her hopes and dreams of a life with Wes. She stared blankly at the wood floor, unpinned her bonnet and dropped it on the course gray blanket covering the cot. Closing her eyes she leaned back against the brick wall.

Wes looked at the tear tracks on Julie's pale face, the dark smudges under her closed eyes, the defeated slump of her shoulders. He'd done this to her. He ought to be glad…glad he hurt her as much as she hurt him. But looking at her his anger drained away leaving only misery. He ran a hand over his face.

"Why," he asked, unaware he spoke until he heard his voice.

"Does it matter?" She looked up at him, her blue eyes blurry and confused. Then with a soul deep sadness she turned her back on him. "Go away."

Turning he left the cell. He pushed the door closed, the click loud and harsh in the silent office. He looked around, realizing Sheriff Rickman had left. Odd that he'd leave the two of them....

He swore under his breath. Think. Rickman wasn't dumb, he'd realized Wes was in Durango for something other than Julie. There was only one other aspect of Durango Wells Fargo would be interested in. The smelters, as Wells Fargo handled all the shipments.

With a curse, he remembered how close Rickman and Kennedy were. How they were always together in the Double Eagle.

He took a few hasty steps toward the door, but stopped short at Julie's quiet voice.

"Please." She'd come to the cell door. "Could you bring me the valise? I need what s in it."

He hesitated. Just the fact that he did made him angry. He should be going after the sheriff. That was his job. A job that had taken him out of the saloon and given him an identity. Given him everything that was good in his life. Honor and discipline said he should be going after the sheriff. What did he owe Julie?

More than you know, came the unwanted answer. He swallowed hard, knowing he abandoned ten years of principles. "I'll get it." For you, he thought. He slammed the office door as he left

The sheriff hadn't returned to the office when he returned with Julie's valise. He crossed the office. On the cot, Julie still sat slumped against the wall, eyes closed.

"Here's your bag."

She didn't even open her eyes. "Thank you," she said in a weak, polite voice.

And that was that.

* * *

Wes hurried down Main Street. The only thing he'd ever had was the job. Hell, now he'd be lucky if he still had that. Where had the sheriff gone? The Double Eagle was just down the block. Maybe Kate knew something. He entered the saloon. A quick glance showed no sheriff, but Kate stood talking to Jake the bartender.

"Kate," he said. "You seen the sheriff recently?"

She nodded. "He and Landham left not five minutes ago for Landham's place."

"Thanks."

Kate called after him but Wes was already out the batwing doors.

A gust of wind tugged at his Stetson as he ducked down the alley behind Kennedy's place. The mansion stood three stories high. He remembered Kate telling him Kennedy wanted everyone to know how much money he'd spent on the place.

Several horses stomped and neighed as he came up to Kennedy's stables. The sounds had a distressed quality to them that caught his attention. Another gust of wind brought the smell of smoke to his nostrils. Fire!

At a half run, he rounded the corner of the stables. A quick glance through the open stable door showed nothing wrong. He turned toward the house. Smoke curled from the edges of the closed door.

Fire! He was half way across the yard when a sheet of flames engulfed the curtains at a back window of the house. He raced to the back door and wrenched it open. A wall of heat and flames drove him back. Covering his face with his arm, he swore as he retreated. Smoke and flames billowed from the door. Glass shattered as an upstairs window exploded. Sparks flew.

Shouts of fire echoed as a handful of neighbors joined him in the yard. A tall man grabbed a bucket while a gray-haired man worked the yard pump handle.

"Too late," Wes yelled. He grabbed the tall man's arm. "Get the horses out of the stables." He pointed to where the stable roof smoldered under a rain of sparks.

"My God," the gray-haired man stared. "The wind's carrying the flames." He dropped the pump handle and grabbed the arm of a gray-haired woman. "Hurry. Our house is too close."

Leaving the rescue of the horses to the tall man, Wes raced around to the front of Kennedy's house. He ran up the wide porch steps. No flames here, but the smell of smoke was strong. Black shadows roiled behind curtained windows. With a boot heel, he kicked the door open. Hot, dark smoke billowed out. Bent double, he cautiously entered the burning house.

Immediately, he began to cough. He swore. Vision was less than an arm's length. He took a step, two. Then tripped and fell to his knees. He reached out and touched corduroy wrapped around something heavy, something that moaned. Grabbing two handfuls of cloth, he pulled. Coughing, he scrambled back out the door.

Once on the porch, other hands helped him and his burden on to the lawn. He wiped his tearing eyes. He'd pulled the sheriff from Kennedy's.

"Wes, you all right?" a familiar voice shouted over the fire's roar.

He looked up to see Frank Lawson. The wind ruffled his fair hair and his tie was crooked. "Where'd you come from?" Wes gasped.

"I jumped off the train as soon as we came over the bridge. You can see the smoke for a mile." He pulled Wes to his feet.

"Let one of them take care of Rickman. We have to get this under control or the whole north end of town will go up."

Wes's chest hurt as they ran back around to the stables. The backyard was deserted. The stable doors hung open, the roof ablaze.

Frank in the lead, they crossed the alley and ran out on the next street. Up and down the block women loaded children and household goods into buggies and wagons while men formed bucket brigades from every yard pump.

One house was already afire, and several roofs smoked ominously. Frank looked over his shoulder. "Thank God it's not heading for our house." He went to help a woman load her crying children into a wagon.

Fear gripped Wes's heart. Whipping his head around, he saw the fire headed for the sheriff's office. He took off at a dead run.

Every breath hurt as his lungs fought to cough up smoke. He couldn't move fast enough. His feet were lead, every step took an hour. He burst through the sheriff's door. The smell of smoke was faint. Julie sat in the same position as when he'd left.

"Thank God," he wheezed. He grabbed the keys from the desk. "Julie! Come on!" he croaked as he unlocked the door. "We've got to get out of here!"

She straightened up and blinked. "What's wrong?" He grabbed her hand and dragged her toward the door.

"Fire!" He had her half way across the office before she pulled against him.

"The valise!" She looked back to where the bag sat by the cell door.

Swearing, he again crossed the office, grabbed the hated valise and pulled her unceremoniously out the door. He hustled her south down Main street. After a few blocks they were well out of the way of the fire and caught up in the milling crowd. It seemed as though every Durango citizen swarmed the streets. He tugged her to the edge of the chaos as people and wagons surged around them.

"Here," he shoved the valise into her startled hands. "Go back to the house and stay out of danger."

Julie tried to catch her breath. She looked blankly at Wes. "You're letting me go?"

"Where the hell are you going to go?" he shouted over the crowd noise. "The whole damn town may go up!"

She blinked. Dark, dirty smoke streaked the sky. People yelled and ran. Someone shoved past them, bumping her shoulder. He was right. The whole town was in danger.

"Frank was on the morning train," he said. "He'll want to know you're safe."

"Uncle Frank?" Thank goodness. Relief flooded her. Just knowing Uncle Frank was close gave her comfort. Maybe somehow he could help her, help Cory. She took a step back in the direction they'd come from. "I have to find him."

Chapter Twenty-Three

"Oh, no, you don't." Wes said. He grabbed Julie's arm as she tried to go past him.

Angry, she wrenched her arm free. "Will you quit grabbing me?" The anger felt good, deflating the despair that had swamped her in the cell. She raised her chin high. "I must find Uncle Frank and explain."

"Frank's a little busy right now. I'll tell him you're safe. Go home and stay there."

How dare he? She gave him an imperious look. "Mr. Westmoreland, I suggest you cease giving me orders."

"You're still in custody, just not in jail. And I will keep you safe," he said through clenched teeth, "if I have to tie you to a tree somewhere."

She glared at him. "Then, sir, you had better find a tree."

Before he could reply, a wild clanging heralded the approach of one of the volunteer fire companies. The people milling in the street dashed for the boardwalk. Wes yanked her to his side as a team of horses pulling the fire equipment galloped toward the blaze. As soon as they passed, the crowd began to follow.

Again, he stepped in front of her. "Go home."

And without another word, he turned and hurried after the fire engine.

She watched Wes run down the street after the fire engine. Smoke billowed over the area, an errant breeze bringing a flurry of ashes. Her anger died as fast as it had flared. He was right. Obviously she couldn't look for Uncle Frank in this confusion. Even if she found him, then what? Her shoulders slumped and she wished the anger that had sustained her through her last encounter with him would return.

When she'll see Uncle Frank she'd have to explain about the stolen books and ledgers in the valise. How she'd tried to protect Cory, the baby. There was nothing more to do but return to Philadelphia and face the consequences of her actions. And pray that she'd accomplished her task by delaying long enough for the baby to be safely born. She straightened her shoulders and turned toward home.

A buggy raced down the street and a female voice called, "Julie, Julie!"

Julie looked up and saw Clare waving and shouting. Lieutenant Sullivan pulled the buggy to a halt. Clare jumped out. Julie hugged the trembling girl as she babbled questions.

"My goodness, what's going on?" Clare asked. "What caused the fire? And after that terrible storm. My lands, I thought that thunder would deafen me. I just couldn't let Ryan bring me home during the storm. And then of course, the ford flooded and we couldn't get home until this morning. We could see the smoke on the way in. This is just terrible."

As the words poured out of Clare, Julie looked up to where Lieutenant Sullivan sat in the buggy. "Don't worry," she reassured the army man, "I'll take care of Clare. Our house is out of the path of the fire."

"Thank you," Lieutenant Sullivan said. "I'll get some troops in here to help keep order." He looked at the street still milling with people. Some fleeing the blaze, some heading toward the fire, buckets in hand. Children cried. Men swore. The lieutenant snapped the reins and headed in the direction of the fire.

"Oh, Julie, let's go home," Clare pleaded.

She looked around. If she went home, she'd just brood and worry. She spied Mrs. Peterson, the matronly newspaper editor, her notepad in her hand as she hurried toward the fire. "Here," She pushed the valise into Clare's hands. "You take this and go home. I want to talk to Mrs. Peterson."

She gave Clare a gentle push toward the Lawson house, and turned and hurried after Mrs. Peterson.

* * *

Between the arrival of a troop of cavalry and Mrs. Peterson's commanding ways, the town organized to fight the fire that continued to consume block after block of Durango. The troops helped evacuate the remaining families. Many had fled east and south, but others had gathered in the large open area across from the Stratler Hotel where Julie now stood.

She looked around. Just a few weeks ago on the Fourth of July people had danced here. Now the area contained a hodgepodge of carriages, buggies and wagons loaded with household goods. Young boys played tagged around and through the wheels. The Methodist minister's wife in a borrowed rocking chair read a story to a group of young children gathered around her feet. Women stood in small groups, looking anxiously north toward the billowing smoke. Speculation on the cause of the fire ran rife. The only known fact seemed to be that it started at Landham Kennedy's and no one had seen him since early morning.

Julie dragged a weary hand across her face. Her nose wrinkled in disgust at the grime on her hand. The long shadows of late afternoon stretched over the temporary tables where the hotel management, thanks to the bullying of Mrs. Peterson, supplied sandwiches, coffee and water to feed the men fighting the fire.

Ignoring the breeze which blew another gust of ash over everything, she moved down the line of men seated at the makeshift table, pouring water from the pitcher. Along with others whose homes weren't in danger, she had spent the long afternoon helping comfort and care for the unfortunate citizens who watched their town fight for its life, as their homes and business went up in smoke.

Throughout the afternoon, the men fighting the fire had come to the area for rest and food before returning. Once Uncle Frank had appeared, his fair hair dark with ashes. "Julie!" he'd called and enveloped her in a hug. Without privacy and time to talk, she had simply hugged him back, accepting the warmth and unqualified love of family that gave and received support. The unquestioning support she'd expected from Wes. She pushed thoughts of the man she'd trusted away.

She refilled her pitcher and started down the other side of the table.

"Thanks, ma'am," the man she recognized as the grocery clerk said. The clerk turned to address the bald man next to him. "So, Jake, 'pears you're about the last person to see Kennedy."

The bald man nodded and opened his mouth to reply. A horrendous boom of an explosion drowned out his words. All heads turned north as a pillar of smoke and flames shot skyward. Children cried and ran for their mothers who smothered their own screams and questions.

"Don't panic," one of the fire fighters yelled. "They're trying dynamite to stop the fire."

She turned to the grocery clerk and Jake. "Isn't that dangerous?"

"Only for the man settin' charges in the burnin' buildings," the clerk replied with what sounded like admiration.

"Yeah," Jake said. "That Westmoreland's not afraid of much."

Her heart thumped. "Westmoreland?" she asked in a weak voice.

"Sure," Jake replied. "You know, the guy who works for your uncle. Frank and Wes are pretty much running the firefighting effort. The mayor's too old and fat, the sheriff's hurt. Anyways, Frank suggested dynamite and Westmoreland's settin' the charges."

Her knees felt weak. She looked back north. Smoke still streaked the sky. She found herself praying for the safety of a man she no longer loved.

The clerk and Jake stood. "Thanks for the water, Miss Lawson," the clerk said.

"Don't you worry none, missy, this fire may be bad, but we ain't lost any folks," added Jake. "Your uncle's is doing a fine job up there."

But what about Wes? Was he fine? Neither man seemed worried about the dynamite blast.

"Time we was getting back," added Jake. "Hope that dynamite worked," he said to the clerk as they headed back to take up their firefighting duties.

She sank down on one of the vacated seats. Her whole world was in chaos. How could she still be worried about the safety of the man who betrayed her? She flinched as another dynamite blast split the air. Tired and dirty, she sat slumped in the chair, suddenly too exhausted to do anything but pray. For Cory. For Uncle Frank. And for Wes. She blinked back tears that threatened.

She had no idea how long she sat. But it was almost dark when Mrs. Peterson touched her shoulder.

"Julie, dear. You look all in. Why don't you go home and get some rest? Your shift here is over. The dynamite blasts are slowing the fire so now they think they'll have it out soon."

Glancing north, it seemed to Julie that the smoke was less dense than before. Durango, apparently, would survive.

"Thanks, Mrs. Peterson." She rose and slowly made her way toward the Lawson house.

After a block or so, she picked up her pace and straightened her shoulders. If Durango could survive and rebuild, then she would survive, too. She'd return to Philadelphia and go on. She had to believe that Cory and the baby would be fine. That they would be able to convince the authorities of their innocence, of the guilt of those really responsible. Eventually things would be straightened out.

She would be fine too. After all, she wouldn't be the first person to survive a broken heart. And maybe in Philadelphia, surrounded by her family, the memory of Wes would fade from the sharp pain of betrayal to the dull ache of love lost.

Chapter Twenty-Four

In the hour before dawn, the high, full moon bathed the devastated part of Durango in a silvery light. Smelling of smoke and tasting ashes, Wes walked toward the Double Eagle. His head ached, his eyes were gritty and his ribs hurt. But at least the fire was out. A cavalry patrol watched for flare-ups as all townsmen wearily made their way home, if they still had one.

Tired beyond belief, he stumbled over an uneven plank in the boardwalk. "That's what you get for sleeping one night in the past four," he muttered. Had to be lack of sleep making him feel so ill. Not anything else. He tried to forget feeling as though all his guts had been ripped out since he'd received Dan Challenge's telegram.

As he neared the saloon, he saw a faint light from the window. He wouldn't have to wake Kate up to let him in. All his gear was at the Lawson's but he'd be damned if he'd go back there.

Tomorrow morning, with a clear head, he'd have to talk to Frank and Julie, arrange for her to meet the Pinkerton Agent. Right now he needed to lie down before he fell down. A minute later he let himself into the small back room Kate had given him before he'd been hurt and moved to Lawson's. Stopping only to pull off his boots, he fell onto the cot, closer to passing out than going to sleep.

* * *

A wall of flames pushed him back. On the other side, Julie sat in a jail cell, her head down, oblivious to the danger. Shouting a warning, he rushed to the blaze again. The strangely cold flames wrapped themselves around his legs, holding him in place. He shouted another warning. Julie turned and looked blankly in his direction. The fire started to lick at her skirts. He struggled to wrench himself free.

"Julie," he shouted.

She sat, calm and unmoving.

"No!" he yelled. The inferno flared, her image wavered. A high-pitched scream beat against his ears.

"Julie!" he screamed in despair as she dissolved and disappeared.

Wes bolted awake, the sound of his own voice and a second high-pitched scream ringing in his ears. A heartbeat later, the screams of his dream became a train whistle fading into the distance as he came fully awake. And aware of Frank Lawson standing across the room, his hand still on the door knob.

The anger on Frank's face faded to a softer expression. Had he really shouted Julie's name out loud. And how much desperation, he wondered sourly, had Frank heard in that cry?

"So," Frank closed the door behind him. "What the hell is going on around here? Julie just got on the train to Philadelphia with a lady Pinkerton. What's your story?"

Wes muttered a curse as he swung his legs off the bed and rubbed his hands over his face. He glanced at Frank as he leaned against the door with his arms folded across his chest. His suit was clean and pressed, his shirt snow white, his fair hair neatly combed. Looking at him made Wes feel dirtier and lower than a snake's belly. He'd grown up in a saloon and here he was, still living in a back room. Why had he ever considered he had a chance at happiness?

Wes took a deep breath. "I'm an agent for Wells Fargo."

"I know."

Stunned, he watched Frank peel himself off the door and sit down on the cot next to him.

"I knew right away things didn't add up," Frank said. "You're too smart, too sharp just to be a drifter. That's why I went to Denver. To check you out." He reached into his pocket and handed Wes a piece of paper. "Here's the information the Denver Wells Fargo office sent on the boiler plate numbers you asked about."

Dumbfounded, Wes stared at the paper. He cleared his throat. "You check out all your employees this way?"

Frank gave a ghost of a smile. "Only the one my niece looks at all starry-eyed.'

The mention of Julie made his chest tighten. Just taking a breath to talk hurt. "The train's already gone, hasn't it? I meant to be over early this morning to talk with you." Not only had he lost Julie, but now he was fairly sure he was going to lose the friendship of a man he'd come to admire.

"I've heard Julie's side of the story. Now tell me why you arrested her."

"Just doing my job." God, how pitiful that sounded. "Look," he ran his hand over his face. "I didn't want to arrest her."

Frank looked skeptical. "That's not the impression she gave me."

The memory of his actions made him wince. But then he remembered her response. "She never denied there was a warrant, but she didn't tell me what it was for. Did she tell you?" She sure hadn't offered him any explanation.

"She did it to protect Cory."

"Her sister? Protect her how?" Then he remembered a conversation he and Julie had had. "Isn't Cory, ah, expecting?"

Frank gave him another speculative look, as though wondering how familiar he and Julie had become for her to have included this information. For Julie's sake he only hoped Frank didn't figure out how familiar.

"Then you probably know that Julie and Cory worked at the Bradley Center."

He nodded.

"Julie forgot something one day. When she went back to the office, she overheard the director and a councilman talking in the next room. Since they were talking about the fire that had killed several of the Center's clients, Julie listened. She realized that the two of them had bribed a city fire inspector. They'd arranged, through papers Cory had signed as Assistant Director to make it look as though Cory was behind the bribes. Turned out the director and councilman, through the Bradley center, were the owners of the factory that burned down.

"But..."

"Of course, Julie should have told the authorities. But she didn't even want Cory questioned," Frank said.

He wondered Frank would explain further. Not that he deserved any consideration from the Lawsons.

But after a pause, Frank went on. "Cory had lost two babies. Her husband, Mark, had already sent her to the country to avoid anything that could upset her and cause her to lose this one. Julie thought if she could steal the evidence, she could delay the investigation long enough for Cory to safely have the baby."

"And when Julie took the papers, she caused the investigation to focus on her," he guessed.

Frank sighed. "Silly girl. Her intentions were good, but not the way she went about it." He shook his head. "She's always been rash. My mother used to warn her that her impulsiveness would get her into trouble one day."

Impulsive. That was Julie. Open, charming Julie. But she was more. Julie had become a fugitive from the law by taking someone else's crime upon herself.

"Why would she do something like that?" he wondered aloud. In the world he knew, nobody looked out for anyone but themselves.

"Why?" Frank said it like the answer was obvious. "Because we're family."

Family? He rubbed the back of his neck. Julie's world was so different than his own. He'd been a double fool for thinking he and Julie could have anything together.

The orders to arrest her had knocked him for such a loop, he selfishly hadn't thought beyond the consequences to himself. What will happen to her now? Great to be worried about her now when it was too late.

Frank stood and looked out the small window. "I've telegraphed Philadelphia. Our lawyer will be waiting at the station when Julie gets in. I've contacted a friend who has a friend at the Pinkerton agency. With any luck we'll have everything sorted out in a couple of weeks. Before my brother gets back from Europe."

Wes wondered if in a few weeks, he'd be able to think of yesterday without feeling the leaden despair knotting his belly. He looked up to see Frank looking at him with a strange expression.

"And I thought that you two might, er ..." Frank paused.

He tried not to wince, hoping his expression concealed his guilt.

But Frank continued, "I thought perhaps you might be considering courting Julie."

Stunned, he blinked. "You'd allow me to court Julie?' he asked incredulously.

"Guess I don't have to make that decision now, do I?" There was silence in the room for a moment.

"Guess not," he agreed. He'd ruined any chance he might have had. Now it was too late. Too late for him. Too late for her. Too late for them. God, had there ever been a bigger bastard than he'd been? He shifted uncomfortably and the paper in his hand crinkled. He looked down at the message Frank had given him.

"So," Frank prompted, the subject of Julie obviously over for now, "what's this information from Denver mean?"

He unfolded the paper. What he saw should have brought the satisfaction he got from solving a case. But not this time. He passed the paper to Frank. "I asked for information from the company Kennedy bought his boiler from. The boiler plate number on the bill of sale and the actual number on the boiler, the one that exploded, are different."

"How do you know?"

"I've seen the number plate on the boiler, and I've looked at Kennedy's books and at your books."

Frank frowned. "That right. You worked both smelters. You snooped all over his place. Then you came to work at the Rio d'Oro. To check me out." Frank's expression said he didn't know whether to be insulted or not.

He nodded. "The mining boom has bottomed out. Both smelters used to run full capacity. But not lately. In fact, some months there's barely enough work to keep you both in business. So, if one of you went out of business, the other would be in pretty good shape."

Reluctantly, Frank nodded in agreement.

Wes held up the paper. "Kennedy's been skimming operating funds. Paying on paper for new equipment, but buying used and pocketing the difference. Probably to pay for that mansion he built." The one that now was a pile of burned and blackened rubble.

"It never occurred to me that Landham..."

Wes pulled on his boots. "When the accidents began to happen at the Mineral King because of cheap equipment, it most likely gave Kennedy the idea of sabotage. If he caused a bad enough accident at the Rio d'Oro, he could put you out of business."

"And now, nobody has seen Landham since before the fire." Frank sighed.

"When I, ah," he paused. Making sure his voice held no emotion, he explained. "When I took Julie to the sheriff's I had to identify myself as a Wells Fargo agent. Rickman guessed I hadn't come to Durango just to execute an arrest warrant from Philadelphia. He left the office and went straight to find Kennedy. I followed him. That's why I was at Kennedy's place when you showed up." He stood and stretched. "I'd guess Rickman was the one doing the actual dirty work. After all, who would suspect the sheriff? He could turn up anywhere, anytime."

Frank looked puzzled for a moment then his expression cleared. "The sheriff did show up at the Rio d'Oro once in a while. Seems to me he was there the day before the stamp broke and you got hurt." Frank also stood. "I think we'd better go and see Rickman is well enough to talk."

"We?"

Frank gave Wes a piercing look. "We. It's my smelter and you're the one who could have got killed. Get cleaned up. We'll go see the sheriff. Then we have to see what we can do about the town."

While Frank waited out by the bar, Wes washed his face. He supposed his boss would expect him to help Frank. After all, Wells Fargo still shipped the output of the Durango smelters. He pulled on a clean shirt, but he still smelled like smoke and felt like ashes. After the fire and the loss of Julie, both he and Durango were burned out wrecks.

Chapter Twenty-Five

Philadelphia, three weeks later

Julie dragged the chair, wooden legs bumping across her bedroom floor toward the wardrobe. By standing on the chair she could just reach the strap of the leather suitcase stored on the top of the wardrobe. With a heave, she pulled the case. The best she could do was control the fall of the awkward case as it hit the floor with a thud.

Drat. Haste did make waste. Gran proved right once again. But she was in a hurry. She dragged the chair back to its place and then heaved the leather suitcase up on the bed when the door to her room opened.

"Julie, what was all that noise?" Cory asked.

Double drat. She would have to explain now instead of later. "Oh, sorry. Did I wake the baby?"

"No, she's still sleeping."

With a puzzled frown, Cory came to stand beside the foot of the brass bedstead. "What are you doing?"

"I'm packing." She squared her shoulders. "I'm going back to Durango."

Cory started to protest, but Julie forestalled her. "With the court case settled and those two scoundrels in jail, everything here is back to normal. There's nothing to keep me here any longer."

She turned and crossed to the wardrobe. Keeping her eyes on the camisoles and pantaloons she pulled from the drawer, she said, "I fell in love. In Durango."

She heard Cory's quick intake of breath. Julie placed the clothes in the suitcase before facing her sister. It hurt her to see the worried look on Cory's face and Julie did her best to explain.

"I love you. And Mark, and the baby and Papa. Every day I see the love you and Mark have, remember Mother and Father's love."

She took Cory's hand. "I love Wes. I'm going back to Durango to see if that love is still there." She wouldn't admit it to Cory, but she admitted to herself she had doubts and concerns. Not that she doubted her feelings for Wes. Her love for him was the foundation of her soul. And she knew she had to see Wes again, whatever the outcome.

"But you don't even know if Mr. Westmoreland is still in Durango," Cory protested.

She shrugged. "If he's not, Uncle Frank will probably know where he is."

"Now, Julie," Cory started.

To avoid the shouldn't-you-think-about-it lecture her sister was about to start, Julie hugged her. "No, I don't need to think about it. I've done nothing else for the last week. I've made my decision. And I'm going to Durango."

There was a hint of moisture in Cory s eyes when the sisters broke the embrace. "I suppose you'd like me to help you pack?" Cory asked.

"Thanks." Julie smiled. "You can always count on your family." And the sisters began to pull clothes from the drawers.

* * *

The morning sun in Philadelphia was cool but bright as Wes paid off the hackney cab. He turned to look at the two story brick house surrounded by a white picket fence.

Once he'd got to the hotel last night, he had the bellman bring him old newspapers. He'd been reassured to read that Frank's guess had been right and the legal mess Julie had gotten herself into had been corrected. The guilty had been sent to jail without either Julie or her sister brought to trial. But of course, the paper didn't say anything about the reason for Julie's actions, or about a baby.

Well, here you are. Julie should be inside. After three weeks of misery he had to see her. Even if she told him to go away. He had to see her at least this once. Maybe then he could sleep without nightmares. Maybe food would taste again.

He brushed his hands down his dark brown jacket, did a quick rub of his polished boots on the back of his trouser legs, resettled his Stetson. Unsteady fingers checked his string tie as he opened the gate and headed up the walk.

He swallowed his nervousness. But he couldn't swallow his hope. Since he'd acknowledged his need to see her and headed east, he had lived on hope. Hope that Julie could forgive him. Hope. Something he'd never had until he met her.

A large brass knocker invited him to knock. He did and heard the knock resound inside the house. The brief wait seemed longer than the train trip from Durango. He shifted his feet. Then he heard footsteps.

The door opened, revealing a dark-haired man about his own age with a professorial air.

"Yes?" the man said.

Before Wes could get his mouth in gear, a baby's cry sounded. The man looked over his shoulder. Relief so strong it made his knees weak flooded Wes. That infant's wail rang in his ears like world's greatest music for it meant Julie's plan had been successful. The leaden knot in his belly lightened. His hope for her forgiveness took a leap.

"Cory and the baby," he said out loud.

The man's head snapped back, his face now scowling. "What?" he asked as if he didn't believe his ears. He moved slightly, blocking the doorway.

Damn, he hadn't meant to blurt that out. This man was obviously Cory's husband and the baby's father. Mark, the doctor.

The doc stared back at him, his raking gaze taking in the Stetson, the western cut suit, the boots. Then his scowl faded a bit. "You're the detective," he stated.

Wes nodded, wondering what Julie had said about him. At least the man hadn't shut the door in his face. "Frank gave me the address," Wes said in way of explanation. "I've come to see Julie. May I speak to her?"

The doc looked at him, considering his request. Wes all but held his breath. Somewhere in the background a gentle voice crooned and the baby ceased crying. "Why don't you come in and wait in the parlor. I'll ask if Julie will see you."

"Thanks." Wes took off his hat and followed the doc through the door.

They crossed the polished floor of the entry and entered the parlor. "Wait here," the doc said.

Alone, Wes let out a sigh. He didn't know what he might have done if they'd refused to let him in. Something stupid probably. Still holding his hat, Wes looked around the room which was furnished similar to the Lawson home in Durango.

He paced, his stomach jumping as he wondered if Julie would see him. He heard light footsteps come down the stairs. He turned toward the doorway as the steps quickly crossed the hall. And there she was. Dressed in simple white shirtwaist and dark skirt she was the best thing he'd ever seen. Wes thought his heart would burst. He took a deep breath, hoping against hope.

"Julie, I'm so sorry," he started.

A radiant smile lit her face. Without thinking, he opened his arms and the next second she was wrapped in his embrace. "I'm so sorry," he murmured over and over, his face buried in her hair. She was saying something too, but the wonder of her in his arms, soft, warm, and forgiving, swamped his mind. His heart beat as hard as the stamps at the smelter and she seemed to be laughing and crying at the same time.

He held her tight against him, afraid he might be hurting her, but unable to ease his hold. He might have lost this woman. And the horror made him shiver. "I'm sorry," he said into her hair. "I should have trusted you. I was a fool."

Gradually he loosened his embrace, looking at her. She smiled while a tear ran down her cheek. "Don't cry, sweetheart," he said. With the back of his hand he wiped her tear away.

Julie's knees went weak as joy flooded her. He was here. His fingers gentle against her cheek, concern written on his face. He had come for her, held so tight she could scarcely breathe. Slight tremors still shook his body, signaling emotions he felt, but couldn't yet say.

But she was content, within his embrace, enjoying his warmth, his masculine scent, the strength of his arms. "It's all right now," she mumbled, her face buried against his chest. "You came." Just his presence vanquished all the doubts and fears.

After a moment he stepped back, taking both her hands in his. "Julie, I..." but his words didn't come.

She looked into his beloved face and she understood his confusion. She knew love and forgiveness from example. But love was so new to him, he didn't yet realize that he had indeed trusted. Trusted enough to come for her. And she acknowledged, he'd made the decision to come and acted on it before she had. She told him what he needed to hear.

"I love you, Wes." She saw the joy leap in his eyes. "I was upstairs packing just now." She took a deep breath. "I was going to Durango. To find you."

He looked stunned. He blinked, then a look so full of love came over his face, she thought she might cry.

"Hot damn," he whispered and gathered her in his arms once more. His lips were warm and soft as he kissed her with fierce tenderness. She wrapped her arms around his neck and kissed him back. He groaned as she opened for him. The kiss went on and on as if he couldn't get enough. She couldn't get enough. Of his taste, his scent, the feel of her body against his.

With a gasp for air he broke the kiss. "Here." He led her to the sofa. "If your knees are a shaky as mine, we'd better sit."

She sat beside him. The tension had left his body, but his eyes still held sadness.

"Let me explain?" he asked.

She nodded, her heart too full for words.

He took her hand, holding it lightly in his. He cleared his throat and with words he healed her wounded heart. "You're the best thing that ever happened to me. And I was too blind to see it. When I got that telegram...."

He shook his head and then gave her a half smile, ticking up the corner of his mustache in the way she loved. "I told you about how I grew up, the kind of life I've led. All I ever had to feel good about was my job. It was the only decent thing in my life." He sighed and absently rubbed a hand over his ribs before he continued. "I should have asked you to tell me your side right away. My only excuse is I've never trusted anybody."

He looked away but his grip on her hand tightened. "And a few years ago, I had a job go bad on me. My partner got wounded and it was my fault. We found out later the girl I was with was part of the gang and was paid to keep me out of the way that night." He paused, and then as though uncertain of her reaction, glanced at her.

"Oh, Wes," she said, her heart hurting for him. "No wonder you were so suspicious."

"Yeah, well," he shrugged and gave her hand a squeeze. Then he sighed again. "But, I should have trusted you. Especially when you said you..." he swallowed as if the next words were hard to say. "When you said you loved me."

"And you didn't believe me." She saw how hard it would have been for him to believe.

He looked embarrassed. "Well, not at first. But I'd come to believe you meant it. And began to think about us, began to think about some sort of future together."

She smiled, her wounded pride soothed by the fact that he had begun to believe.

"And then I got that telegram. The thought that you might have lied to me about who and what you were was more than I could deal with." He looked down to where her hand rested in his. "And I told myself if you'd really loved me, you would have told me you were in trouble. Asked for my help." He looked up at her and she saw the memory of the hurt in his eyes.

Now it was her turn. "Oh, Wes. I wanted to. But it was family trouble. How could I share with you problems that involved Cory, Mark? Trouble that you had nothing to do with. At least that's what I thought at the time."

"But—"

"But, if I loved you, I should have trusted you enough to tell you," she finished for him. "And in a sense you were right. If I'd told you about," she waved her hand, "all the trouble, you would have reacted to the telegram differently."

Wes nodded.

"I realized that several days ago," she confessed. "After I stopped being angry with you."

"Thank God," he breathed. He gave her a full smile this time as he tugged her closer with the hand he held.

Willingly, she snuggled against him. She lifted her face. He kissed her gently this time, melting her heart. In too short a time his mouth left hers. Her hand rested on his chest, feeling the heavy beat of his heart.

He looked at her, his expression grave. He covered her hand with his and with tenderness that brought a lump of emotion to her throat, lifted it to his lips.

"I love you, Julie," he said. Her heart stopped. He loved her.

Her heart started again, almost thumping its way out of her breast for joy. To hear him say the words was more wonderful than she had ever imagined.

A great peace filled her. She and Wes were together. That was all that mattered. "Oh, Wes, I love you, too," was the only reply she was capable of making as she went into his arms.

He heaved a big sigh. After a moment he said, "I was worried you might have the doc throw me out." He cuddled her next to him as he continued. "Because I never had a family like yours, it took me a while to see that your family is the most important thing for you. Your love for Cory is what drove you. I figured that out in the last few weeks."

His understanding warmed and comforted, like his arm around her shoulder. "Yes. But I've learned something in the last few weeks, too. I'd always thought that family was who you're related to. But now I know family is defined by who you love." She looked at Wes, the man she loved. "I love you, Wes." Putting her hand to his cheek, she said it again. "I love you."

His eyes closed and a tremor shook him. He turned his head and kissed the palm of her hand. His mustache tickled, and the feel of his lips sent shivers up her spine. The look of profound emotion on his face pierced her heart. He held his position, and she waited in anticipation of another embrace.

To her surprise when he did move Wes simply slid off the edge of the sofa, going down on one knee at her feet. Her heart thumped. He took her hand in both of his large, warm ones.

"Miss Lawson," he said formally, his face dead serious. "I love you. Will you please do me the honor of becoming my wife?"

Her free hand pressed against her heart. She swallowed. "Yes," she squeaked and blushed.

He smiled, teeth flashing under his mustache. In a second he was back beside her on the sofa. A happy contentment settled over her. This morning she'd been worried if she'd ever see him again. He'd proven his love by coming for her, and she acknowledged, he'd come looking for her before she decided to look for him. Amazing, she hadn't realized love could bridge time and trouble this way. They sat together, comfortable and content. They might have been sitting in the Lawson kitchen, as though they had never been apart, never been estranged.

She turned her head and kissed him just under his ear. He made a sound of contentment, so she kissed him again. His arm around her tightened and he said teasingly, "Stop that. You'll get yourself into trouble."

"Good." And as she hoped, he shifted her so that she lay draped over his lap. She lifted her mouth for the kiss he willingly bestowed. Then he kissed her again and again. She trembled at the remembered taste of him. And thought longingly of the wedding, and of the wedding night. Just as she started to feel the heat awakening deep within her, he pulled back.

Wes looked at Julie, the way she relaxed in arms, and couldn't believe he'd been so lucky. Kissing her was too tempting, and he had to call a stop.

"I can see," he said, "this is going to be a short engagement." He gave her another quick kiss, then reversed her position to sit beside him.

She gave him her dimpled smile, and smoothed her skirts. "How short?"

He laughed. Being married was going to be more fun than he'd ever imagined. "There are some details we have to work out first." He hadn't been able to think ahead until she said yes. Now that he wasn't kissing her, his brain was starting to ask questions. "Do you want to stay here in Philadelphia? With your family?"

She looked startled for a second, then frowned. "No, I don't necessarily want to stay here. Our legal problem is all settled."

He told her how he'd checked the old newspapers. She nodded. "Mark and Cory don't really need me. Nor does Papa since he's remarried. In fact, I'd really rather live out west." She sounded wistful. Then she turned serious. "Besides, your job is out west."

Before he could answer, she went on. "What happened in Durango? Uncle Frank has been rather vague on that, although he's given much detail of the rebuilding in his letter."

He resisted the urge to get up and pace. Thinking about that day still made him uneasy. But he sat still and told her about Kennedy's embezzling and scheme to ruin the Rio d'Oro. How Rickman had gone to alert Kennedy, just as he'd theorized.

"The sheriff was in on it?" she asked.

"That's right. That next morning, after you'd, ah, left, Frank and I went to see Rickman."

"I heard you pulled him from Kennedy's house. And that nobody had seen Kennedy."

"That's because Kennedy was dead." Because he'd made a mess of things by alerting the sheriff. "Rickman was pretty badly burned in the fire. But he told Frank and me that he and Kennedy were cousins. They'd grown up poor and Kennedy wasn't about to risk exposure when Rickman told him I was Wells Fargo. Rickman and Kennedy argued about what to do about me, they fought, turned over a table and lamp and started the fire." That was enough to explain what happened. No need for details, such as Kennedy had ordered Rickman to kill Wes. And that was the cause of the fight.

"All that damage out of greed." She shook her head, looking sad.

"Don't think of the past," he said, sorry he'd made her sad. "Durango is already rebuilding. Frank and some of the other citizens have formed a revitalization committee, as they call it. Hired men to clear off the burned buildings, put up new ones. Even hired a new sheriff, one with law enforcement experience they say. And the Rio d'Oro is doing a great business."

He took her hand in his again. "We can go live in Durango if you're willing."

She smiled. "That would be wonderful." Then she frowned. "But what about your job?"

He smiled. Everything was working out just fine. "I've quit my job with Wells Fargo."

"Oh, Wes."

He held up a hand to at her protest. "It was time. After twelve years I was tired of traveling. And part of my pay was always in Wells Fargo stock. I have enough to buy us a house. Right down the street from Frank if you want."

"Wonderful," she replied, and rested her head on his shoulder. "But any place will be fine as long as I'm with you."

He smiled to himself. He had everything he'd wanted right here beside him.

After a few moments, she lifted her head. "What will you do in Durango? Are you still working for Uncle Frank?"

He chuckled, anxious to see her expression when he told her the news. "No. After the fire and all, it turned out there was another job available." With a flourish he pulled back his coat, and there, pinned to his vest the shiny five-pointed star bearing the words: *Sheriff, Durango, Colorado.*

"You don't mind being married to the sheriff?"

Her smile beamed, showing him the dimple. "I don't mind. I don't mind at all."

"Good," he said, and kissed her.

AUTHOR'S NOTE

Writing fiction can be difficult for the historian. The fiction half of me says "what if" when the historian half of me says "but it happened this way." So I have compromised, bending history to fit my story, and hope these notes will be of interest to those readers who want to know the factual history.

Although the Pinkerton agency is more well known, the Wells Fargo Company did, in fact, have its own detective force. Among these notables were Fred Dodge and James Hume. Dodge once held down a job as a deputy in Tucson while working undercover for Wells Fargo. James Hume, the chief of detectives, was one of the pioneers in the field of scientific investigations, catching the notorious stagecoach bandit Black Bart, by tracing a laundry mark on the bandit's handkerchief. Wells Fargo also employed a corps of young boys to ride messages around San Francisco at twenty-five cents a message.

In the 1880s there were no laws restricting the conduct of a law enforcement officer. A detective of that era wasn't constricted by such concepts of forcible entry, illegal search and seizure or jurisdictions. Wes's activities in the pursuit of his job would have been considered legal and acceptable.

For the purpose of my story I have made some changes and additions to Durango's fire. The fire actually started on July 1st, but I have moved it to several weeks later. It's true that a stiff wind fanned the blaze which burned over seven blocks. Half a million dollars in business and residential property went up in smoke as the residents tried everything, including dynamite to stop the fire. The actual cause of the fire was never determined, so I have supplied one out of my "what if."

The two major smelters that operated in Durango eventually consolidated due to the business climate in the late 1890s. The way Wes showed Julie to refine gold using quicksilver was one of the standard small scale methods used at the time. Today, more is known about the hazards of mercury poisoning.

For the events in Philadelphia, those familiar with history will recognize that I have anticipated history by a few years, and have borrowed the concept of Hull House in Chicago, which opened in 1889 as a model for the Bradley Center. I similarly borrowed the idea of the Triangle Shirtwaist fire in 1910 for the scandal involving Julie's sister.

And last, condoms made from latex rubber have been available since the 1840s, and were called, appropriately enough, rubbers. The primary purpose was for prevention of sexually transmitted disease, with the side benefit of contraception.

AUTHOR BIO

Terry Irene Blain was lucky enough to grow up in a large Midwestern family with a rich oral tradition. As a child she heard stories of ancestors' adventures with Indians, wildlife, weather and frontier life in general, so she naturally gravitated to the study of history and completed a BA and MA then taught the subject at the college level. Married to a sailor, now retired, she's had the chance to live in various parts of the country as well as travel to foreign places such as Hong Kong, Australia, England and Scotland.

UNDISCOVERED

Socialite Juliette Lawson fled west from Philadelphia on a train and in disguise. In Colorado she'd be safe; she'd take work with her uncle at the Rio d'Oro, his smelting operation. Her actions back east had been wrong, but to protect her pregnant sister from scandal she would have done anything. Then she met a man as hungry for answers as she was for independence. A handsome, honorable man. For him, she wished the truth was hers to tell.

From the first, Wes Westmoreland knew he couldn't trust her. Having grown up in the saloons and brothels of San Francisco, he saw trust, like love, as a luxury an undercover lawman couldn't afford. Not on a job like this one, not with gold involved. This woman dressed as a widow was clearly hiding something; he'd felt it the moment they touched. But he'd felt other things too, stirrings in his heart, and for the first time ever, he saw riches worth the peril.

Did you enjoy this book? Drop us a line and say so! We love to hear from readers, and so do our authors. To connect, visit www.boroughspublishinggroup.com online, send comments directly to info@boroughspublishinggroup.com, or friend us on Facebook and Twitter. And be sure to check back regularly for contests and new releases in your favorite subgenres of romance!

Are you an aspiring writer? Check out www.boroughspublishinggroup.com/submit and see if we can help you make your dreams come true.